THE UNLIKELY PILGRIMAGE OF HAROLD FRY

Rachel Joyce

WINDSOR
PARAGON

First published 2012
by Doubleday
This Large Print edition published 2012
by AudioGO Ltd
by arrangement with
Transworld Publishers

Hardcover   ISBN: 978 1 4713 1567 1
Softcover   ISBN: 978 1 4713 1568 8

British Library Cataloguing in Publication Data available

Printed and bound in Great Britain by
MPG Books Group Limited

For Paul, who walks with me, and for my father,
Martin Joyce (1936–2005)

Who would true valour see,
Let him come hither;
One here will constant be
Come wind, come weather.
There's no discouragement
Shall make him once relent
His first avowed intent
To be a pilgrim.

John Bunyan, *The Pilgrim's Progress*

HAROLD AND THE LETTER

The letter that would change everything arrived on a Tuesday. It was an ordinary morning in mid-April that smelt of clean washing and grass cuttings. Harold Fry sat at the breakfast table, freshly shaved, in a clean shirt and tie, with a slice of toast that he wasn't eating. He gazed beyond the kitchen window at the clipped lawn, which was spiked in the middle by Maureen's telescopic washing line, and trapped on all three sides by the neighbours' closeboard fencing.

'Harold!' called Maureen above the vacuum cleaner. 'Post!'

He thought he might like to go out, but the only thing to do was mow the lawn and he had done that yesterday. The vacuum tumbled into silence, and his wife appeared, looking cross, with a letter. She sat opposite Harold.

Maureen was a slight woman with a cap of silver hair and a brisk walk. When they first met, nothing had pleased him more than to make her laugh. To watch her neat frame collapse into unruly happiness. 'It's for you,' she said. He didn't know what she meant until she slid an envelope across the table, and stopped it just short of Harold's elbow. They both looked at the letter as if they had never seen one before. It was pink. 'The postmark says Berwick-upon-Tweed.'

He didn't know anyone in Berwick. He didn't know many people anywhere. 'Maybe it's a mistake.'

'I think not. They don't get something like a postmark wrong.' She took toast from the rack. She liked it cold and crisp.

Harold studied the mysterious envelope. Its pink was not the colour of the bathroom suite, or the matching towels and fluffed cover for the toilet seat. That was a vivid shade that made Harold feel he shouldn't be there. But this was delicate. A Turkish Delight pink. His name and address were scribbled in biro, the clumsy letters collapsing into one another as if a child had dashed them off in a hurry: *Mr H. Fry, 13 Fossebridge Road, Kingsbridge, South Hams*. He didn't recognize the handwriting.

'Well?' said Maureen, passing a knife. He held it to the corner of the envelope and tugged it through the fold. 'Careful,' she warned.

He could feel her eyes on him as he eased out the letter, and prodded back his reading glasses. The page was typed, and addressed from a place he didn't know: St Bernadine's Hospice. *Dear Harold, This may come to you as some surprise*. His eyes ran to the bottom of the page.

'Well?' said Maureen again.

'Good lord. It's from Queenie Hennessy.'

Maureen speared a nugget of butter with her

2

knife and flattened it the length of her toast. 'Queenie who?'

'She worked at the brewery. Years ago. Don't you remember?'

Maureen shrugged. 'I don't see why I should. I don't know why I'd remember someone from years ago. Could you pass the jam?'

'She was in finances. She was very good.'

'That's the marmalade, Harold. Jam is red. If you look at things before you pick them up, you'll find it helps.'

Harold passed her what she needed and returned to his letter. Beautifully set out, of course; nothing like the muddled writing on the envelope. Then he smiled, remembering this was how it always was with Queenie; everything she did so precise you couldn't fault it. 'She remembers you. She sends her regards.'

Maureen's mouth pinched into a bead. 'A chap on the radio was saying the French want our bread. They can't get it sliced in France. They come over here and they buy it all up. The chap said there might be a shortage by summer.' She paused. 'Harold? Is something the matter?'

He said nothing. He drew himself up tall with his lips parted, his face bleached. His voice, when at last it came, was small and far away. 'It's— cancer. Queenie is writing to say goodbye.' He fumbled for more words but there weren't any. Tugging a handkerchief from his trouser pocket, Harold blew his nose. 'I . . . um. Gosh.' Tears crammed his eyes.

Moments passed; maybe minutes. Maureen gave a swallow that smacked the silence. 'I'm sorry,' she said.

3

He nodded. He ought to look up, but he couldn't.

'It's a nice morning,' she began again. 'Why don't you fetch out the patio chairs?' But he sat, not moving, not speaking, until she lifted the dirty plates. Moments later the vacuum cleaner took up from the hall.

*   *   *

Harold felt winded. If he moved so much as a limb, even a muscle, he was afraid it would trigger an abundance of feeling he was doing his best to contain. Why had he let twenty years pass without trying to find Queenie Hennessy? A picture came of the small, dark-haired woman with whom he had worked all that time ago, and it seemed inconceivable that she was—what? Sixty? And dying of cancer in Berwick. Of all the places, he thought; he'd never travelled so far north. He glanced out at the garden and saw a ribbon of plastic caught in the laurel bush, flapping up and down but never pulling free. He tucked Queenie's letter into his pocket, patted it twice for safekeeping, and rose to his feet.

*   *   *

Upstairs Maureen shut the door of David's room quietly and stood a moment, breathing him in. She pulled open his blue curtains that she closed every night, and checked there was no dust where the hem of the net drapes met the windowsill. She polished the silver frame of his Cambridge portrait, and the black and white baby photograph

4

beside it. She kept the room clean because she was waiting for David to come back, and she never knew when that would be. A part of her was always waiting. Men had no idea what it was like to be a mother. The ache of loving a child, even when he had moved on. She thought of Harold downstairs, with his pink letter, and wished she could talk to their son. Maureen left the room as softly as she had entered it, and went to strip the beds.

*   *   *

Harold Fry took several sheets of Basildon Bond from the dresser drawer and one of Maureen's rollerball pens. What did you say to a dying woman with cancer? He wanted her to know how sorry he felt, but it was wrong to put *In Sympathy* because that was what the cards in the shops said after, as it were, the event; and anyway it sounded formal, as if he didn't really care. He tried, *Dear Miss Hennessy, I sincerely hope your condition improves*, but when he put down the pen to inspect his message, it seemed both stiff and unlikely. He crumpled the paper into a ball and tried again. He had never been good at expressing himself. What he felt was so big it was difficult to find the words, and even if he could, it was hardly appropriate to write them to someone he had not contacted in twenty years. Had the shoe been on the other foot, Queenie would have known what to do.

'Harold?' Maureen's voice took him by surprise. He thought she was upstairs, polishing something, or speaking to David. She had her Marigolds on.

'I'm writing Queenie a note.'

'A note?' She often repeated what he said.

5

'Yes. Would you like to sign?'

'I think not. It would hardly be appropriate to sign a note to someone I don't know.'

It was time to stop worrying about expressing anything beautifully. He would simply have to set down the words in his head: *Dear Queenie, Thank you for your letter. I am very sorry.* ~~Yours~~ *Best wishes—Harold (Fry).* It was limp, but there it was. Sliding the letter into an envelope, he sealed it quickly, and copied the address of St Bernadine's Hospice on to the front. 'I'll nip to the post box.'

It was past eleven o'clock. He lifted his waterproof jacket from the peg where Maureen liked him to hang it. At the door, the smell of warmth and salt air rushed at his nose, but his wife was at his side before his left foot was over the threshold.

'Will you be long?'

'I'm only going to the end of the road.'

She kept on looking up at him, with her moss-green eyes and her fragile chin, and he wished he knew what to say but he didn't; at least not in a way that would make any difference. He longed to touch her like in the old days, to lower his head on her shoulder and rest there. 'Cheerio, Maureen.' He shut the front door between them, taking care not to let it slam.

*   *   *

Built on a hill above Kingsbridge, the houses of Fossebridge Road enjoyed what estate agents called an elevated position, with far-reaching views over the town and countryside. Their front gardens, however, sloped at a precarious angle

6

towards the pavement below, and plants wrapped themselves round bamboo stakes as if hanging on for dear life. Harold strode down the steep concrete path a little faster than he might have wished and noticed five new dandelions. Maybe this afternoon he would get out the Roundup. It would be something.

Spotting Harold, the next-door neighbour waved and steered his way towards the adjoining fence. Rex was a short man with tidy feet at the bottom, a small head at the top and a very round body in the middle, causing Harold to fear sometimes that if he fell there would be no stopping him. He would roll down the hill like a barrel. Rex had been widowed six months ago, at about the time of Harold's retirement. Since Elizabeth's death, he liked to talk about how hard life was. He liked to talk about it at great length. 'The least you can do is listen,' Maureen said, although Harold wasn't sure if she meant 'you' in the general sense or the particular.

'Off for a walk?' said Rex.

Harold attempted a jocular tone that would act, he hoped, as an intimation that now was not the time to stop. 'Need anything posting, old chap?'

'Nobody writes to me. Since Elizabeth passed away, I only get circulars.'

Rex gazed into the middle distance and Harold recognized at once the direction the conversation was heading. He threw a look upwards; puffs of cloud sat on a tissue-paper sky. 'Jolly nice day.'

'Jolly nice,' said Rex. There was a pause and Rex poured a sigh into it. 'Elizabeth liked the sun.' Another pause.

'Good day for mowing, Rex.'

7

'Very good, Harold. Do you compost your grass cuttings? Or do you mulch?'

'I find mulching leaves a mess that sticks to my feet. Maureen doesn't like it when I tread things into the house.' Harold glanced at his yachting shoes and wondered why people wore them when they had no intention of sailing. 'Well. Must get on. Catch the midday collection.' Wagging his envelope, Harold turned towards the pavement.

*   *   *

For the first time in his life, it was a disappointment to find that the post box cropped up sooner than expected. Harold tried to cross the road to avoid it, but there it was, waiting for him on the corner of Fossebridge Road. He lifted his letter for Queenie to the slot, and stopped. He looked back at the short distance his feet had travelled.

The detached houses were stuccoed and washed in shades of yellow, salmon and blue. Some still had their pointed fifties roofs with decorative beams in the shape of a half-sun; others had slate-clad loft extensions; one had been completely rebuilt in the style of a Swiss chalet. Harold and Maureen had moved here forty-five years ago, just after they were married. It took all his savings to pay the deposit; there had been nothing left for curtains or furniture. They had kept themselves apart from others, and over time neighbours had come and gone, while only Harold and Maureen remained. There had once been vegetable beds, and an ornamental pond. She made chutneys every summer, and David kept goldfish. Behind the house there had been a potting shed that smelt of fertilizer, with high hooks for hanging tools, and coils of twine and rope. But these things too were long since gone. Even their son's school, which had stood a stone's throw from his bedroom window, had been bulldozed now and replaced with fifty affordable homes in bright primary colours and street lighting in the style of Georgian gas lamps.

Harold thought of the words he had written to Queenie, and their inadequacy shamed him. He pictured himself returning home, and Maureen calling David, and life being exactly the same except for Queenie dying in Berwick, and he was overcome. The letter rested on the dark mouth of the post box. He couldn't let it go.

'After all,' he said out loud, though nobody was looking, 'it's a nice day.' He hadn't anything else to do. He might as well walk to the next one. He turned the corner of Fossebridge Road before he could change his mind.

It was not like Harold to make a snap decision. He saw that. Since his retirement, days went by and nothing changed; only his waist thickened, and he lost more hair. He slept poorly at night, and sometimes he did not sleep at all. Yet, arriving more promptly than he expected at a pillar box, he paused again. He had started something and he didn't know what it was, but now that he was doing it, he wasn't ready to finish. Beads of perspiration sprouted over his forehead; his blood throbbed with anticipation. If he took his letter to the post office on Fore Street, it would be guaranteed next-day delivery.

The sun pressed warm on the back of his head and shoulders as he strolled down the avenues of

9

new housing. Harold glanced in at people's windows, and sometimes they were empty, and sometimes people were staring right back at him and he felt obliged to rush on. Sometimes, though, there was an object that he didn't expect; a porcelain figure, or a vase, and even a tuba. The tender pieces of themselves that people staked as boundaries against the outside world. He tried to visualize what a passer-by would learn about himself and Maureen from the windows of 13 Fossebridge Road, before he realized it would be not very much, on account of the net curtains. He headed for the quayside, with the muscles twitching in his thighs.

The tide was out and dinghies lolled in a moonscape of black mud, needing paint. Harold hobbled to an empty bench, inched Queenie's letter from his pocket and unfolded it.

She remembered. After all these years. And yet he had lived out his ordinary life as if what she had done meant nothing. He hadn't tried to stop her. He hadn't followed. He hadn't even said goodbye. The sky and pavement blurred into one as fresh tears swelled his eyes. Then through them came the watery outline of a young mother and child. They seemed to be holding ice-cream cones, and bore them like torches. She lifted the boy and set him down on the other end of the bench.

'Lovely day,' said Harold, not wanting to sound like an old man who was crying. She didn't look up, or agree. Bending over her child's fist, she licked a smooth path to stop the ice cream from running. The boy watched his mother, so still and close it was as if his face was part of hers.

Harold wondered if he had ever sat by the quay

10

eating ice cream with David. He was sure he must have done, although searching in his mind for the memory, he found it wasn't readily available. He must get on. He must post his letter.

Office workers were laughing with lunchtime pints outside the Old Creek Inn, but Harold barely noticed. As he began the steep climb up Fore Street, he thought about the mother who was so absorbed in her son she saw no one else. It occurred to him it was Maureen who spoke to David and told him their news. It was Maureen who had always written Harold's name ('Dad') in the letters and cards. It was even Maureen who had found the nursing home for his father. And it begged the question—as he pushed the button at the pelican crossing—that if she was, in effect, Harold, 'Then who am I?'

He strode past the post office without even stopping.

2

HAROLD AND THE GARAGE GIRL AND A QUESTION OF FAITH

Harold was near the top of Fore Street. He had passed the closed-down Woolworths, the bad butcher ('He beats his wife,' Maureen said), the good butcher ('His wife left him'), the clock tower, the Shambles, as well as the offices of the South Hams Gazette, and now he was at the last of the shops. The muscles in his calves pulled with every step. Behind him, the estuary shone like a sheet of tin against the sun; boats were already tiny flecks of white. He paused at the travel agent, because he wanted to take a rest without anyone noticing, and pretended to read about bargain holidays in the window. Bali, Naples, Istanbul, Dubai. His mother used to talk so dreamily about escaping to countries where there were tropical trees, and women with flowers in their hair, that as a boy he had instinctively distrusted the world he did not know. It had not been very different once he was married to Maureen, and they had David. Every year they spent two weeks in the same holiday camp in Eastbourne. Taking several deep breaths to steady his chest, Harold continued north.

The shops turned into homes, some built in pinky-grey Devon stone, some painted, others fronted with slate tiles, followed by cul-de-sacs of new housing. Magnolias were coming into flower; frilled white stars against branches so bare they looked stripped. It was already one o'clock; he had missed the midday collection. He would buy a snack to tide him over and then he would find the next post box. After waiting for a gap in the traffic, Harold crossed towards a petrol station, where the houses stopped and the fields took over.

A young girl at the till yawned. She wore a red tabard over a T-shirt and trousers, with a badge that said HAPPY TO HELP. Her hair hung in oily strips either side of her head so that her ears poked through, and her skin was pockmarked and pale, as if she had been kept inside for a long time. She didn't know what he was talking about when he asked for light refreshments. She opened her mouth and it remained hanging ajar, so that he feared a change in the wind would leave her like that. 'A snack?' he said. 'Something to keep me going?'

Her eyes flickered. 'Oh, you mean a burger.' She trudged to the fridge and showed him how to heat a BBQ Cheese Beast with fries in the microwave.

'Good lord,' said Harold, as they watched it revolve in its box behind the window. 'I had no idea you could get a full meal from a garage.'

The girl fetched the burger from the microwave and offered sachets of ketchup and brown sauce. 'Are you paying for fuel?' she asked, slowly wiping her hands. They were small as a child's.

13

'No, no, I'm just passing. Walking actually.'

'Oh,' she said.

'I'm posting a letter to someone I knew once. I'm afraid she has cancer.' To his horror, he found that he paused before saying the word and lowered his voice. He also found he had made a small nugget shape with his fingers.

The girl nodded. 'My aunt had cancer,' she said. 'I mean, it's everywhere.' She cast her eyes up and down the shop shelves, suggesting it was even to be found tucked behind the AA road maps and Turtle Wax polish. 'You have to keep positive, though.'

Harold stopped eating his burger and mopped his mouth with a paper serviette. 'Positive?'

'You have to believe. That's what I think. It's not about medicine and all that stuff. You have to believe a person can get better. There is so much in the human mind we don't understand. But, you see, if you have faith, you can do anything.'

Harold gazed at the girl in awe. He didn't know how it had happened, but she seemed to be standing in a pool of light, as if the sun had moved, and her hair and skin shone with luminous clarity. Maybe he was staring too hard, because she gave a shrug and chewed her lower lip. 'Am I talking crap?'

'Gosh, no. Not at all. It's very interesting. I'm afraid religion is not something I ever quite got the hang of.'

'I don't mean, like, religious. I mean, trusting what you don't know and going for it. Believing you can make a difference.' She twined a strand of hair round her finger.

Harold felt he had never come across such simple certainty, and in such a young person; she

14

made it sound obvious. 'And she got better, did she? Your aunt? Because you believed she could?'

The strand of hair was twiddled so tightly round her finger he was now afraid it was stuck. 'She said it gave her hope when everything else had gone—'

'Does anyone work here?' shouted a man in a pinstripe suit from the counter. He rapped his car keys on the hard surface, beating out wasted time.

The girl threaded her way back to the till, where the pinstripe made a show of checking his watch. He held his wrist high in the air and pointed to the dial. 'I'm supposed to be in Exeter in thirty minutes.'

'Fuel?' said the girl, resuming her place, in front of cigarettes and lottery tickets. Harold tried to catch her eye but she wouldn't. She had returned to being dull and empty again, as if their conversation about her aunt had never happened.

Harold left his money for the burger on the counter and made his way to the door. Faith? Wasn't that the word she had used? Not one he usually heard, but it was strange. Even though he wasn't sure what she meant by faith, or what there was left that he believed in, the word rang in his head with an insistence that bewildered him. At sixty-five he had begun to anticipate difficulties. A stiffening of the joints; a dull ringing in his ears; eyes that watered with the slightest change in the wind; a dart of chest pain that presaged something more ominous. But what was this sudden surge of feeling that made his body shake with its sheer energy? He turned in the direction of the A381, and promised again that at the next post box he would stop.

He was leaving Kingsbridge. The road narrowed

15

into a single lane, until the pavement disappeared altogether. Above him, the branches joined like the roof of a tunnel, tangled with pointed new buds and clouds of blossom. More than once he had to crush himself into a hawthorn to avoid a passing car. There were single drivers, and he supposed they must be office workers because their faces appeared fixed as if the joy had been squeezed away, and then there were women driving children, and they looked tired too. Even the older couples like himself and Maureen had a rigidity about them. An impulse to wave came over Harold. He didn't, though. He was wheezing with the effort of walking and he didn't want to cause alarm.

The sea lay behind; before him stretched rolling hills and the blue outline of Dartmoor. And beyond that? The Blackdown Hills, the Mendips, the Malverns, the Pennines, the Yorkshire Dales, the Cheviots, and Berwick-upon-Tweed.

But here, directly across the road, stood a post box, and a little way beyond it a telephone booth. Harold's journey was over.

He dragged his feet. He had seen so many he'd lost count, as well as two Royal Mail vans and a courier on a motorbike. Harold thought of all the things in life he'd let go. The small smiles. The offers of a beer. The people he had passed over and over again, in the brewery car park, or on the street, without lifting his head. The neighbours whose forwarding addresses he had never kept. Worse; the son who didn't speak to him and the wife he had betrayed. He remembered his father in the nursing home, and his mother's suitcase by the door. And now here was a woman who twenty years ago had proved herself a friend. Was this how it went? That just at the moment when he wanted to do something, it was too late? That all the pieces of a life must eventually be surrendered, as if in truth they amounted to nothing? The knowledge of his helplessness pressed down on him so heavily he felt weak. It wasn't enough to send a letter. There must be a way to make a difference. Reaching for his mobile, Harold realized it was at home. He staggered into the road, his face thick with grief.

A van shrieked to a halt and then skirted past. 'You stupid fucker!' yelled the driver.

He barely heard. He barely saw the post box either. Queenie's letter was in his hands before the door of the telephone kiosk had closed behind him.

He found the address and telephone number, but his fingers shook so hard he could barely tap the buttons to enter his pin code. He waited for the ringing tone, and the air hung still and heavy. A trickle of sweat slid between his shoulder blades.

After ten rings there was at last a clunk, and a heavily accented voice: 'St Bernadine's Hospice. Good afternoon.'

'I'd like to speak to a patient, please. Her name is Queenie Hennessy.'

There was a pause.

He added, 'It's very urgent. I need to know that she's all right.'

The woman made a sound as if she was breathing out a long sigh. Harold's spine chilled. Queenie was dead; he was too late. He clamped his knuckle to his mouth.

The voice said, 'I'm afraid Miss Hennessy is asleep. Can I take a message?'

Small clouds sent shadows scurrying across the land. The light was smoky over the distant hills, not with the dusk but with the map of space that lay ahead. He pictured Queenie dozing at one end of England and himself in a phone box at the other, with things in between that he didn't know and could only imagine: roads, fields, rivers, woods, moors, peaks and valleys, and so many people. He would meet and pass them all. There was no deliberation, no reasoning. The decision came in the same moment as the idea. He was laughing at the simplicity of it.

'Tell her Harold Fry is on his way. All she has to do is wait. Because I am going to save her, you see. I will keep walking and she must keep living. Will you say that?'

The voice said she would. Was there anything else? Did he know visiting hours, for instance? Parking restrictions?

He insisted, 'I'm not in a car. I want her to live.'

'I'm sorry. Did you say something about your car?'

'I'm coming by foot. From South Devon all the way up to Berwick-upon-Tweed.'

The voice gave an exasperated sigh. 'It's a terrible line. What are you doing?'

'I'm walking,' he shouted.

'I see,' said the voice slowly, as if the woman had picked up a pen and was jotting this down. 'Walking. I'll tell her. Should I say anything else?'

'I'm setting off right now. As long as I walk, she must live. Please tell her this time I won't let her down.'

When Harold hung up and stepped out of the phone box, his heart was pounding so fast it felt

18

too big for his chest. With trembling fingers, he unpeeled the flap of his own envelope and pulled out the reply. Cramming it against the glass of the kiosk, he scribbled a PS: *Wait for me. H*. He posted the letter, without noticing its loss.

Harold stared at the ribbon of road that lay ahead, and the glowering wall that was Dartmoor, and then the yachting shoes that were on his feet. He asked himself what in heaven's name he'd just done.

Overhead a seagull cracked its wings and laughed.

3

MAUREEN AND THE TELEPHONE CALL

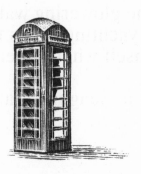

The useful thing about a sunny day was that it showed up the dust, and dried the laundry in almost less time than the tumble drier. Maureen had squirted, bleached, polished and annihilated every living organism on the worktops. She had washed and aired the sheets, pressed them, and remade the beds for both herself and Harold. It had been a relief to have him out of the way; in the six months of his retirement he had barely moved from the house. But now that she had nothing left to achieve, she was suddenly anxious and this in turn made her impatient. She rang Harold's mobile, only to hear a marimba tone coming from upstairs. She listened to his faltering message: 'You have reached the mobile phone of Harold Fry. I am very sorry but—he isn't here.' From the long pause he took in the middle, you'd think he was actually off looking for himself.

It was past five. He never did the unexpected. Even the usual noises, the ticking of the hall clock,

20

the hum of the fridge, were louder than they should be. Where was he?

Maureen tried to distract herself with the *Telegraph* crossword, only to discover he had filled in all the easy answers. A terrible thought rushed into her head. She pictured him lying in the road, with his mouth open. It happened. People had heart attacks and no one found them for days. Or maybe her secret fears were confirmed. Maybe he would end up with Alzheimer's like his father? The man was dead before sixty. Maureen ran to fetch the car keys and her driving shoes.

And then it occurred to her that he was probably with Rex. They were probably talking about lawn cutting, and the weather. Ridiculous man. She replaced her shoes by the front door, and the car keys on their hook.

Maureen crept into the room that had become known over the years as the 'best' one. She could never enter it without feeling she needed a cardigan. Once they had kept a mahogany dining table, and four upholstered chairs; they had eaten in here every evening with a glass of wine. But that was twenty years ago. These days the table was gone, and the bookshelves stored albums of photographs that no one opened.

'Where are you?' she said. The net curtains hung between herself and the outside world, robbing it of colour and texture, and she was glad of that. The sun was already beginning to sink. Soon the street lamps would be on.

*   *   *

When the phone rang, Maureen shot into the

21

hallway and plucked up the receiver. 'Harold?'

A thick pause. 'It's Rex, Maureen. From next door.'

She looked about her helplessly. In her rush to answer the phone, she had stubbed her foot on something angular that Harold must have left on the floor. 'Are you all right, Rex? Have you run out of milk again?'

'Is Harold home?'

'Harold?' Maureen felt her voice shoot upwards. If he wasn't with Rex, where was he? 'Yes. Of course he is here.' The tone she had adopted was not at all her usual one. She sounded both regal and squashed. Just like her mother.

'Only I was worried something had happened. I didn't see him come back from his walk. He was going to post a letter.'

Devastating images were already firing through her mind of ambulances and policemen, and herself holding Harold's inert hand, and she didn't know if she was being completely foolish, but it was as if her head was rehearsing the worst possible outcome in order to pre-empt the full shock of it. She repeated that Harold was at home, and then before he could ask anything else she hung up. She immediately felt terrible. Rex was seventy-four and lonely. All he wanted was to help. She was about to call back, when he beat her to it and the phone began ringing in her hand. Maureen reassembled her composed voice and said, 'Good evening, Rex.'

'It's me.'

Her composed voice rocketed sky high. 'Harold? Where are you?'

'I'm on the B3196. Just outside the pub at Loddiswell.' He actually sounded pleased.

Between the front door and Loddiswell there were almost five miles. So he hadn't had a heart attack and fallen into the road. He hadn't forgotten who he was. She felt more indignant than relieved. Then a new terrible thought dawned on her. 'You haven't been drinking?'

'I've had a lemonade but I feel brilliant. Better than I've felt in years. I met a nice chap who sells satellite dishes.' He paused as if he was about to deliver portentous news. 'I've made a promise to walk, Maureen. All the way to Berwick.'

She thought she must have misheard. 'Walk? To Berwick-upon-Tweed? You?'

He appeared to find this very funny. 'Yes! Yes!' he spluttered.

Maureen swallowed. She felt her legs and her voice failing her. She said, 'Let me get this clear. You're walking to see Queenie Hennessy?'

'I am going to walk and she's going to live. I'm going to save her.'

Her knees buckled. She threw her hand out to the wall to steady herself. 'I think not. You can't save people from cancer, Harold. Not unless you are a surgeon. And you can't even slice bread without making a mess. This is ridiculous.'

Again Harold laughed, as if this person they were talking about was a stranger and not himself. 'I was talking to a girl at the garage and she gave me the idea. She saved her aunt from cancer because she believed she could. She showed me how to heat a burger as well. It even had gherkins.'

He came across as so sure. It completely threw her. Maureen felt a spark of heat. 'Harold, you are sixty-five. You only ever walk to get to the car. And in case you haven't noticed, you left your mobile

23

phone.' He tried to reply, but she sailed straight through him. 'And where do you think you are going to sleep?'

'I don't know.' The laughter had stopped and his voice sounded stripped away. 'But it isn't enough to post a letter. Please. I need to do this, Maureen.'

The way he appealed to her, and added her name at the end, childlike, as if the choice was hers, when clearly he had already decided, was too much. The spark of heat ignited to a bolt. She said, 'Well, you head off to Berwick, Harold. If that's what you want. I'd like to see you get past Dartmoor—' The line was staccato'd with pips. She tightened her grip on the handset, as if it was a piece of him she was clinging to. 'Harold? Are you still in the pub?'

'No, a phone box outside. It's quite smelly. I think someone may have—' His voice cut off. He was gone.

*   *   *

Maureen groped her body into the hall chair. The silence was louder than if he had not phoned at all. It seemed to eat up everything else. There was no ticking from the hall clock, no humming from the fridge, no birdsong from the garden. The words Harold, Burger, Walk, rolled around her head, and in the midst of them came two more: Queenie Hennessy. After all these years. The memory of something long buried shivered deep inside her.

Maureen sat alone as the dark fell, while neon lights came on across the hills and bled pools of amber into the night.

4

HAROLD AND THE HOTEL GUESTS

Harold Fry was a tall man who moved through life with a stoop, as if expecting a low beam, or a screwed-up paper missile, to appear out of nowhere. The day he was born his mother had looked at the bundle in her arms, and felt appalled. She was young, with a peony-bud mouth and a husband who had seemed a good idea before the war and a bad one after it. A child was the last thing she wanted or needed. The boy learned quickly that the best way to get along in life was to keep a low profile; to appear absent even when present. He played with neighbours' children, or at least he watched them from the edges. At school he avoided attention to the point of appearing stupid. Leaving home when he was sixteen, he had set out on his own, until one night he caught Maureen's eye across a dance hall and fell wildly in love. It was the brewery that had brought the newly wed couple to Kingsbridge.

Harold had done the same job as a sales rep for

forty-five years. Keeping himself apart, he worked modestly and efficiently, without seeking either promotion or attention. Other chaps travelled and accepted jobs in senior management, but Harold had not wanted either. He made neither friends nor enemies. At his request, there was no farewell party for his retirement. And even though one of the girls in admin had organized a quick whip-round, few of the sales team knew much about him. Someone said they'd heard once that Harold had a story, but didn't know what it was. He finished work on a Friday, and returned home with no more to show for his lifetime's employment than a fully illustrated *Motorist's Guide to Great Britain* and a voucher for Threshers. The book had been placed in the best room, along with all the other things that no one looked at. The voucher remained in its envelope. Harold was teetotal.

*　　　*　　　*

Gnawing hunger woke him with a start. The mattress had both firmed up and moved overnight, and an unfamiliar rod of light fell across the carpet. What had Maureen done with the bedroom, that its windows were on the wrong side? What had she done with the walls, that they were lightly sprigged with flowers? It was then that he remembered; he was in a hotel just north of Loddiswell. He was walking to Berwick because Queenie Hennessy must not die.

Harold would have been the first to admit that there were elements to his plan that were not finely tuned. He had no walking boots or compass, let alone a map or change of clothes. The least planned part of the journey, however, was the journey itself. He hadn't known he was going to walk until he started. Never mind the finely tuned elements; there was no plan. He knew the Devon roads well enough, and after that he would simply head north.

Harold plumped his two pillows, and eased himself to a sitting position. His left shoulder was sore but otherwise he felt refreshed. He had enjoyed his best sleep in many years; there had been none of the pictures that regularly came to him in the dark. The quilt covering his body matched the floral fabric of the curtains and there was a stripped antique-pine wardrobe, below which were parked his yachting shoes. In the far corner stood a sink, beneath a mirror. His shirt, tie and trousers were folded small as an apology on a faded blue-velvet chair.

A picture surfaced of his mother's dresses scattered through his childhood home. He didn't know where it had come from. He glanced at the window, trying to have a thought that would smudge the memory. He asked himself if Queenie knew he was walking. Maybe she was thinking about that even now.

*   *   *

After the phone call to the hospice, he had followed the rising and turning of the B3196. Clear in his direction, he had passed fields, houses, trees, the bridge over the River Avon, and endless traffic had passed him. None of these made any real impression, except as one thing less between himself and Berwick. He had taken regular breaks

27

to calm his breathing. Several times he had to adjust his yachting shoes and mop his head. On reaching the Loddiswell Inn he had stopped to quench his thirst, and it was there that he spoke with the satellite-dish salesman. The chap had been so bowled over when Harold confided his intentions that he clapped Harold on the back and told everyone in the bar to listen up; and when Harold offered the briefest outline ('I'm going to head up England until I hit Berwick'), the satellite-dish chap roared, 'Good on you, mate.' It was with those words in mind that Harold had rushed out to telephone his wife.

He wished she could have said the same thing.

'I think not.' Sometimes her words sliced down on his before they had even reached his mouth.

After speaking to Maureen, his steps had grown heavier. You couldn't blame her for what she felt about him as a husband, and yet he wished it were otherwise. He had arrived at a small hotel, with palm trees growing at a lopsided angle as if cowering from the coastal wind, and enquired about a room. He was used to sleeping alone, of course, but it was a novelty to be in a hotel; when he worked for the brewery, he had always been home by nightfall. Closing his eyes, he had slipped into unconsciousness almost as soon as he was lying down.

Harold leaned against the soft upholstered headboard and crooked his left knee, clasping the ankle in his hands and drawing it up as far along his leg as he could, without losing balance and keeling over. He slipped on his reading glasses for a closer inspection. The toes were soft and pale. A little tender around the nails, and in the bulbous

28

joint at the middle, and there was a possible blister on the way at the top of his heel, but considering his years and his lack of fitness, Harold was quietly proud. He performed the same slow but thorough inspection of his right foot.

'Not bad,' he said.

A few plasters. A good breakfast. He'd be ready. He imagined the nurse telling Queenie that he was walking, and that all she had to do was keep living. He could see the features of her face as if she were sitting in front of him: her dark eyes, her neat mouth, her black hair in tight curls. The picture was so vivid he couldn't understand why he was still in bed. He must get to Berwick. He rolled his legs to the edge of the mattress and poked his heel towards the floor.

Cramp. The pain roared up his right calf, as if he had just stepped on an electric current. He tried to pull his leg back under the quilt but that made it even worse. What was it you were supposed to do? Point the toes away? Or flex them up? He hobbled out of bed and danced the length of the carpet, wincing and crying out. Maureen was right; he'd be lucky if he got as far as Dartmoor.

Clinging to the windowsill, Harold Fry peered at the road below. It was already rush hour and traffic was speeding in the direction of Kingsbridge. He thought of his wife making breakfast at 13 Fossebridge Road and wondered if he shouldn't go back. He could fetch his mobile, and pack a few things. He could look up the AA map on the internet, and order some walking essentials. Maybe the travel book he had been given for his retirement, and never looked at, would offer useful suggestions? But planning his route would involve both serious consideration and waiting, and there was no time for either of those things. Besides, Maureen would only give voice to the truth he was doing his best to avoid. The days when he might expect her help or her encouragement, or whatever it was he still wanted, were long since gone. Beyond the window, the sky was a fragile blue, almost breakable, flecked with wisps of cloud, and the treetops were bathed in warm golden light. Their branches swung in the breeze, beckoning him forward.

If he went home now, if he even consulted a map, he knew he would never go to Berwick. He washed quickly, dressed in his shirt and tie, and then he followed the smell of bacon.

*   *   *

Harold hovered outside the breakfast lounge, hoping it might be empty. He and Maureen could pass hours without saying a word, but her presence was like a wall that you expected to be there, even if you didn't often look at it. Harold took hold of the doorknob. It shamed him that after all those years at the brewery, he was still shy about a roomful of strangers.

He swung the door open and so many heads swivelled to shoot a look at him that he remained glued to the handle. There was a young family, dressed in holiday clothes, a pair of older ladies, both wearing grey, and a businessman with a newspaper. Of the two remaining free tables, one was in the centre of the room and the other was in the far corner, beside a potted fern on a stand. Harold gave a small cough.

'Top of the morning to you,' he said. He didn't know why; he hadn't a drop of Irish blood in him. It was the sort of thing his old boss, Mr Napier, might have said. He hadn't a drop of Irish blood in him either, but he liked laughing at people.

The hotel guests agreed that it was indeed a fine morning, and returned to their English breakfasts. Harold felt conspicuous standing up but thought it would be rude to sit when no one had invited him.

A woman in a black skirt and top rushed through a pair of swinging saloon doors with a laminated sign above them: KITCHEN. NO ENTRY. She had auburn hair that she had somehow or other puffed up, the way women could. Maureen had never been one for blow-drying. 'No time for beautification,' she'd say under her breath. The woman delivered poached eggs to the two grey ladies and said, 'Full breakfast, Mr Fry?'

With a stab of shame, Harold remembered. This was the same woman who had shown him to his room the night before. This was the woman whom, in a fit of exhaustion and elation, he had told he was walking to Berwick. He hoped she had forgotten. He tried to say, 'Yes, please,' but he couldn't even look at her now and the words came out as more of a tremble.

She pointed to the table in the centre of the room, which was the one he had been hoping to avoid, and as he moved he realized that the odd sour smell that had been dogging him all the way down the stairs was in fact himself. He wanted to rush up to his room and scrub himself all over, but that would look rude, especially since she had asked him to sit, and he was now doing so. 'Tea? Coffee?' she said.

31

'Yes, please.'

'Both?' said the waitress. She gave him a patient look. Now he had three things to worry about: that even if she couldn't smell him, or remember about the walking part, she still might think him senile.

'Tea would be very kind,' said Harold.

To his relief the waitress nodded and disappeared through her swing doors, and the room fell briefly silent. He adjusted his tie and placed his hands in his lap. If he sat very still perhaps the whole thing might go away.

The two grey ladies began saying something about the weather, but Harold didn't know if they were speaking to one another or the guests in general. He didn't want to appear rude, but neither did he want to appear to be eavesdropping, so he tried to appear busy. He studied the sign on his table, NO SMOKING, and then he read the one at the window: WOULD GUESTS KINDLY REFRAIN FROM USING MOBILE PHONES. He wondered what had happened in the past that the owners felt the need to prohibit so many things.

The waitress reappeared with a teapot and milk. He let her pour.

'At least you have a nice day for it,' she said.

So she did remember. He took a sip of tea but it scalded his mouth. The waitress was still hovering beside him.

'Do you do this sort of thing often?' she said.

He was aware of a tense stillness in the room that caused her voice to amplify. He glanced briefly up at the other guests, but none of them was moving. Even the potted fern seemed to hold its breath. Harold gave a small shake of his head. He wished the waitress would move on to someone else, but nobody seemed to be doing anything except looking at Harold. As a small boy he had been so afraid of attention, he crept like a shadow. He could watch his mother applying lipstick or staring at her travel magazine without her knowing he was there.

The waitress said, 'If we don't go mad once in a while, there's no hope.' She briefly patted his shoulder, and at last she retreated through the forbidden swing doors.

Harold felt that he had become the focus of attention without anyone wanting to say it. Even setting down his teacup was something he could see only from outside himself, and it made a clank that startled him as it hit the saucer. Meanwhile the smell was, if anything, getting worse. He berated himself for not thinking to rinse out his socks under the tap the night before; this was what Maureen would have done.

'I do hope you don't mind my asking,' piped up one of the old ladies, turning to catch his eye. 'My friend and I have been wondering what it is you are going to do.'

She was a tall, elegant woman, older than himself, and wearing a soft blouse with her white hair pinned away from her face into a pleat. He wondered if Queenie's hair had lost its colour. Whether she had grown it like this woman, or cut it short like Maureen. 'Is that frightfully rude?' she said.

Harold assured her it wasn't, but to his horror the room was silent again.

The second woman was altogether plumper, with a string of round pearls at her neck. 'We have a terrible habit of listening to other people's

33

conversations,' she said. She laughed.

'We really shouldn't,' they said to the guests in general. They spoke with the same cut-glass loud accent Maureen's mother had used. Harold found himself squinting in an effort to find the vowels.

'I think a hot-air balloon,' said one.

'I think a wild swim,' said the other.

Everyone looked expectantly at Harold. He took a deep breath. If he heard the sound of the words coming from his mouth enough times, maybe he would feel like the sort of person who could get up and do something about them.

'I am walking,' he said. 'I am walking to Berwick-upon-Tweed.'

'Berwick-*upon-Tweed*?' said the tall lady.

'That must be about five hundred miles,' said her companion.

Harold had no idea. He had not yet dared to work it out. 'Yes,' he agreed, 'although it's probably more if you are hoping to avoid the M5.' He reached for his teacup and failed to pick it up.

The family man in the corner glanced towards the businessman and his lips buckled into a grin. Harold wished he hadn't seen but he had; and they were right, of course. He was ridiculous. Old people should retire and sit at home.

'Have you been training for long?' said the tall lady.

The businessman folded over his newspaper, and leaned forward, waiting for the reply. Harold wondered if he could lie, but knew in his heart he wouldn't. He also felt that the women's kindness was somehow making him more pitiful, so that instead of feeling certain he felt only shame.

'I'm not a walker. It's more a spur of the

moment decision. A thing I must do for someone else. She has cancer.'

The younger hotel faces stared, as if he had broken into a foreign language.

'Do you mean a religious walk?' said the plump lady helpfully. 'A pilgrimage?'

She turned to her friend, who quietly began to sing 'He Who Would Valiant Be'. Her voice rose, pure and certain, while her slim face pinkened. Again, Harold wasn't sure if it was for the benefit of the room in general or her friend; but it seemed rude to interrupt. She fell silent and smiled. Harold smiled too, but this was because he had no idea what to say next.

'So she knows you're walking?' said the family man in the far corner. He wore a short-sleeved Hawaiian shirt and his arms and chest sprouted curls of dark hair. He leaned back expansively, rocking on the back legs of his chair, the way Maureen used to reprimand David for doing. You could feel his doubt all the way across the breakfast lounge.

'I left a telephone message. I also sent a letter.'

'That's all?'

'There wasn't much time for anything else.'

The businessman pinned Harold with his cynical expression. It was clear he also saw straight through him.

'There were two young men who set out from India,' said the plump woman. 'It was a peace march in 1968. They went to the four nuclear corners of the world. They took tea and asked the heads of state that if ever they were on the verge of pressing the red button, they should brew a pot first and reflect.' Her friend nodded her head

35

brightly.

The room seemed hot and closed in and Harold longed for air. He stroked the length of his tie, reassuring himself of his own presence, but he felt he was all the wrong shape. 'He's awfully tall,' his Aunty May had said of him once, as if this was something you could rectify, like a leaking tap. Harold wished he had not talked to the hotel guests about the walk. He wished no one had mentioned religion. He didn't object to other people believing in God, but it was like being in a place where everyone knew a set of rules and he didn't. After all he had tried it once, and found no relief. And now the two kind ladies were talking about Buddhists and world peace and he was nothing to do with those things. He was a retired man who had set out with a letter.

He said, 'A long time ago my friend and I worked together. It was my job to check the pubs were running smoothly. She was in the financial department. Sometimes we visited them together, and I gave her a lift.' His heart was pounding so fast that he felt unwell. 'She did something for me and now she is dying. I don't want her to die. I want her to keep living.'

The nudity of his words took him by surprise, as if it was Harold himself who was wearing no clothes. He looked down at his lap, and the room fell once more into silence. Now that he had conjured her into his mind, Harold wanted to linger with the image of Queenie, but he was too acutely aware of everyone in the room scrutinizing him and doubting what they saw, and so the memory of her slipped away, just as the real woman had done all those years ago. Briefly he

36

remembered the empty seat at her desk, and how he had stood beside it, waiting, not believing she had gone and wouldn't come back. He wasn't hungry any more. He was about to step out for fresh air when the waitress swooped out of the kitchen, bearing a full fried breakfast. Harold ate all that he could but it wasn't much. He chopped the bacon rasher and sausage into scraps and hid them in a tidy line beneath his knife and fork, like David used to; and then he retired.

*   *   *

Back in his room, Harold attempted to smooth the sheets and floral quilt over the bed the way Maureen would. He wanted to clear himself away. At the sink, he dampened his hair and patted it to one side, and picked at the bits in his teeth with his forefinger. Reflected in the mirror, he could see traces of his father. It wasn't just in the blue of his eyes but in the set of his mouth, slightly protruded, as if he were permanently storing something behind his lower lip, and in the expanse of his forehead where once there had been a fringe. He peered a little closer, trying to believe he could find his mother too but, apart from her height, she had left no trace of herself.

Harold was an old man. Not a walker, let alone a pilgrim. Who was he hoping to fool? He had spent his adult life sitting in confined spaces. His skin stretched like a million tessellations over tendons and bones. He thought of all the miles between himself and Queenie, and Maureen's reminder that the furthest he had ever walked was to the car. He thought too of the Hawaiian shirt laughing, and the businessman's scepticism. They were right. He didn't know the first thing about exercise, or Ordnance Survey maps, or even the open land. He should pay his bill and take the bus home. He closed the bedroom door without making any noise and it was like saying goodbye to something he hadn't even started. As Harold crept downstairs to the reception, his shoes on the carpet made no noise at all.

*   *   *

He was replacing his wallet in his back pocket when the door of the breakfast lounge burst open. The waitress emerged, followed by the two grey ladies and the businessman.

'We were worrying you'd left,' said the waitress, smoothing her red hair and slightly out of breath.

'We wanted to say bon voyage,' piped up the plump lady.

'I do hope you make it,' said her tall friend.

The businessman pressed his card into Harold's palm. 'If you make it as far as Hexham, you should look me up.'

They believed in him. They had looked at him in his yachting shoes, and listened to what he said, and they had made a decision in their hearts and minds to ignore the evidence and to imagine something bigger and something infinitely more beautiful than the obvious. Remembering his own doubt, Harold was humbled. 'That is so kind,' he said softly. He shook their hands and thanked them. The waitress nipped her face towards his and kissed the air above his ear.

It was possible that as Harold turned to leave,

the businessman snorted or even grimaced, and it was also possible that from the breakfast lounge came a shout of laughter, followed by a suppressed giggle. But Harold did not dwell on that; such was his gratitude, he heard and laughed with them. 'I'll see you in Hexham,' he promised, and threw a large wave as he strode towards the road.

The pewter sea lay behind, while ahead of him was all the land that led to Berwick, where once again there would be sea. He had started; and in doing so Harold could already see the end.

HAROLD AND THE BARMAN AND THE WOMAN WITH FOOD

It was a perfect spring day. The air was sweet and gentle and the sky stretched high, an intense blue. Harold was certain that the last time he had peered through the net drapes of Fossebridge Road, the trees and hedges were dark bones and spindles against the skyline; yet now that he was out, and on his feet, it was as if everywhere he looked, the fields, gardens, trees and hedgerows had exploded with growth. A canopy of sticky young leaves clung to the branches above him. There were startling yellow clouds of forsythia, trails of purple aubrietia; a young willow shook in a fountain of silver. The first of the potato shoots fingered through the soil and already tiny buds hung from the gooseberry and currant shrubs like the earrings Maureen used to wear. The abundance of new life was enough to make him giddy.

With the hotel behind him, and few cars on the road, it occurred to Harold how vulnerable he was, a single figure, without his mobile phone. If he fell, or if someone sprang out of the bushes, who would hear his cries? A cracking of branches sent him scurrying forward; only to look back, with his heart wildly beating, and discover a pigeon regaining its balance in a tree. As time passed and he found his rhythm, he began to feel more certain. England opened beneath his feet, and the feeling of freedom, of pushing into the unknown, was so exhilarating he had to smile. He was in the world by himself and nothing could get in the way or ask him to mow the lawn.

Beyond the hedgerows, the land fell away to his left and right. A small copse of trees had been shaped by the wind into a quiff. He thought of his own thick hair when he was a teenager, slicked to a peak every day with gel.

He would head north towards South Brent, where he would find modest accommodation for the night. From there, he would follow the A38 to Exeter. He couldn't recall the exact mileage, but in the old days he would allow a comfortable hour and twenty minutes for the drive. Harold walked the single-track lanes, and the walls of hedgerow were so dense and high, it was like journeying through a trench. It surprised Harold how fast and angry cars seemed when you were not in one. He took off his waterproof jacket and folded it over his arm.

He and Queenie must have driven this way countless times, and yet he had no memory of the scenery. He must have been so caught up in the day's agenda, and arriving punctually at their destination, that the land beyond the car had been no more than a wash of one green, and a backdrop of one hill. Life was very different when you walked through it. Between gaps in the banks, the land rolled up and down, carved into chequered fields, and lined with ridges of hedging and trees. He had to stop to look. There were so many shades of green Harold was humbled. Some were almost a deep velvety black, others so light they verged on yellow. Far away the sun caught a passing car, maybe a window, and the light trembled across the hills like a fallen star. How was it he had never noticed all this before? Pale flowers, the name of which he didn't know, pooled the foot of the hedgerows, along with primroses and violets. He wondered if, all those years ago, Queenie had looked out from her passenger window and seen these things.

'This car smells of sugar,' Maureen had said once, pulling at the air with her nostrils. 'Violet sweets.' He had taken care after that to drive home at night with the windows open.

When he arrived in Berwick, he would buy a bouquet. He pictured himself striding into the hospice, and Queenie sitting in a pleasant chair by a sunny window, waiting for his arrival. The nursing staff would stop whatever they were doing and watch him pass, and the patients would be cheering, maybe even clapping, because he had come such a long way, of course; and Queenie would be laughing in that quiet way of hers, as she took the flowers in her arms.

Maureen used to wear a sprig of blossom or an autumn leaf in the buttonhole of her dress. It must have been just after they were married. Sometimes, if there wasn't a button, she'd slide it over her ear, and the petals would fall into her

42

hair. It was almost funny. He hadn't thought of that in years.

A car slowed and drew to a halt. It was so close Harold had to crush his body into the nettles. The window lowered. There was loud music, but he couldn't see the faces. 'Off to see your girlfriend, Granddad?' Harold gave a thumbs-up, waiting for the stranger to pass. His skin fizzed where it had been stung.

On he went, one foot in front of the other. Now that he accepted the slowness of himself, he took pleasure in the distance he covered. Far ahead the horizon was no more than a blue brushstroke, pale as water, and unbroken by houses or trees, but sometimes it blurred as if the land and the sky had bled into one another and become matching halves of the same thing. He passed two vans, nose to nose, their drivers arguing over which of them should reverse to a passing point. His body ached for food. He thought of the breakfast he had not eaten and his stomach twisted.

At the California Cross junction, Harold stopped for an early pub lunch and chose two rounds of ready-made cheese sandwiches from a basket. Three men coated in plaster dust, like ghosts, were discussing a house they were renovating. A few other drinkers glanced up from their pints, but this had never been his patch, and thankfully he knew no one. Harold carried his lunch and lemonade to the door, blinking at the onslaught of light as he stepped out into the beer garden. Lifting the glass to his mouth, a swell of saliva pooled his tongue, and when he dug his teeth into the sandwiches, the nuttiness of the cheese and the sweetness of the bread exploded on

43

to his taste buds with such vigour it was as if he had never eaten before.

As a boy, he tried to chew without noise. His father didn't like to hear him masticate. Sometimes he said nothing, only held his ears and closed his eyes, as if the boy were a pain inside his head; other times he said Harold was a dirty beggar. 'Takes one to know one,' his mother would answer, screwing out a cigarette. It was nerves, he heard a neighbour say. The war had made people funny. And sometimes as a boy he had wanted to touch his father; to stand close beside him and know the feeling of an adult arm around his shoulder. He had wanted to ask what happened before he was born, and why his father's hands trembled when he reached for his glass.

'That boy's staring at me,' said his father sometimes. His mother would swipe his knuckles, not hard but as if she were brushing off a fly, and say, 'Leave off, sonny. Go and play outside.'

It surprised him that he was remembering all this. Maybe it was the walking. Maybe you saw even more than the land when you got out of the car and used your feet.

The sun poured like warm liquid on Harold's head and hands. He removed his shoes and socks under the table, where no one would see or smell them, and examined his feet. The toes were moist and an angry crimson. Where the shoe met his heel the skin had become inflamed; the blister was a tight pod. He paddled the arches of his feet in the soft grass and closed his eyes, feeling tired, but knowing that he mustn't sleep. It would be difficult to keep going if he stopped for too long.

'Enjoy it while it lasts.'

44

Harold turned, afraid of finding someone he knew. It was only the landlord, partially eclipsing the sun. He was as tall as Harold, but of wider build, dressed in a rugby shirt and long shorts, and those sandals that Maureen said looked like Cornish pasties. Harold returned his feet quickly to his yachting shoes.

'Don't let me disturb you,' said the landlord, rather loud, and without moving. In Harold's experience, publicans often behaved as if it was their responsibility to suggest there was a conversation happening, even in silence, and that it was hugely entertaining. 'The nice weather makes people want to do something. Take my wife. First sunny day, she cleans out the kitchen cupboards.'

Maureen seemed to clean all year round. Houses don't clean themselves, she'd mutter. Sometimes she cleaned the bits she had just cleaned. It wasn't like living in a house, but more a question of hovering over the surfaces. He didn't say that, however. He merely thought it.

'I haven't seen you before,' said the landlord. 'Are you visiting?'

Harold explained that he was passing through. He had retired six months ago, he said, from the brewery. He belonged to the old days, when the reps drove out every morning and there was less technology.

'So you must have known Napier?'

The question took him unawares. Harold cleared his throat and said Napier had been his boss until he was killed in the car crash five years back.

'I know you shouldn't speak ill of the dead,' said the landlord, 'but he was a vicious sod. I saw him half kill a man once. We had to pull him off.'

Harold felt a twisting in his gut. It would be better not to speak about Napier. Instead he explained how he had set off with the letter for Queenie, and realized it wasn't enough. Before the landlord could point it out, he admitted he had no phone, walking boots or map, and that he probably appeared ridiculous.

'It's not a name you hear much, Queenie,' said the landlord. 'It's old-fashioned.'

Harold agreed and said she had been an old-fashioned sort of person. Quiet, and always wearing a brown wool suit, even in the summer months.

The landlord folded his arms, resting them over the soft shelf of his belly, and widened his feet, as if he had something to tell and it might take a while. Harold hoped it wasn't concerning the distance between Devon and Berwick-upon-Tweed. 'There was this young lady I knew once. Lovely girl. Lived in Tunbridge Wells. She was the first girl I ever kissed, and she let me do a few things besides, if you get my drift. This young lady would have done anything for me. I just couldn't see it. Too busy trying to get on in the world. It was only years later, when I was invited to the wedding, that I saw what a lucky bastard the chap marrying her was.'

Harold felt he should say that he had never been in love with Queenie, not in that way, but it seemed rude to interrupt.

'I fell apart. Started drinking. Got myself in a right mess, if you know what I mean.'

Harold nodded.

'Spent six years in prison in the end. My wife laughs but these days I do craftwork. Table decorations. I get the baubles and the baskets off the internet. The truth is,' and here he wiggled his ear with his finger, 'we've all got a past. We've all got things we wish we'd done, or hadn't. Good luck to you. I hope you find the lady.' The landlord removed his finger from his ear and studied it with a frown. 'If you're lucky, you should get there this afternoon.'

There was no point in correcting him. You couldn't expect people to understand the nature of his walk, or even the exact whereabouts of Berwick-upon-Tweed. Harold thanked him and continued on his way. He remembered how Queenie kept a notebook in her handbag to tot up their mileage. It wasn't in her to tell a lie; at least not one that was intentional. A flicker of guilt propelled him forward.

*   *   *

During the afternoon, his blister became more painful. He found a way of shoving his toes towards the front end of the shoe, to avoid the leather biting into his ankle. He wasn't thinking of Queenie and he wasn't thinking of Maureen. He wasn't even seeing the hedgerows or the horizon or the passing cars. He was the words, You will not die, and they were also his feet. Only sometimes the words marched themselves in different orders, and he realized with a start that his head was chanting, Die you will not, or Not will you die, or even plain Not not not. The sky above him was the same sky that hung over Queenie Hennessy and he knew with increasing certainty that she had learned what he was doing and was waiting. He knew he was going to reach Berwick, and that all he had to do was to place one foot in front of the other. The simplicity of it was joyful. If he kept going forward, he would of course arrive.

The land lay still, interrupted only by the traffic that rustled the leaves as it rushed past. The sound could almost convince him he was back at the sea. Harold found himself halfway through a memory that he was not aware of conjuring into his mind.

When David was six they had gone to the beach at Bantham and he had started swimming out. Maureen had shouted, 'David! Come back! Come back right now!' Only the more insistently she called, the smaller the little boy's head became. Harold had followed her to the water's edge, and stopped to unlace his shoes. He was about to pull them off when a coastguard had sprinted past, tearing off his T-shirt and hurling it behind him as an afterthought. The chap had gone ploughing into the water until he was waist deep, and then he had plunged his whole body in, slicing through the waves until he reached the child. He had carried David back in his arms. The boy's ribs stuck out like fingers, and his mouth was blue. 'He was lucky,' the coastguard said. He addressed Maureen, not her husband; Harold withdrew a step or two. 'There's a strong current out there.' His white canvas shoes shone wet in the sun.

And Maureen had never said it, but Harold knew what she was thinking because he was thinking the same thing: why had he stopped for his laces when his only son was in danger of drowning?

Years later, he had said to David, 'Why did you keep swimming? That day on the beach? Couldn't

48

you hear us?'

David must have been a young teenager. He had gazed back at Harold, with his beautiful brown eyes that were half-boy, half-man, and he'd shrugged. 'I dunno. I was already in shit. It seemed easier to stay in it than come back.' Harold had said it was better not to swear, especially in his mother's hearing, and David had said something like, Bug off.

Harold wondered why he was remembering all this. His only child ploughing an escape into the sea, and telling him years later to bug off. The pictures had come to him whole, as if they were part of the same moment; points of light dropped on the sea like rain, while David gazed at Harold with an intensity that seemed to undo him. He had been afraid; that was the truth. He had untied his laces because he was terrified that when there were no more excuses, he would not be up to saving his son. And what was more, they all knew it; Harold, Maureen, the coastguard, even David. Harold pushed his feet forward.

He feared there would be more. The images and thoughts that crammed his head at night, keeping him awake. Years later Maureen had accused him of almost drowning their son. He fixed his attention on what was outside.

The road stretched between the dense corridors of hedgerow, and light sieved through the cracks and fissures. Fresh shoots speared the earth banks. Far away a clock chimed three. Time was passing. He drove his feet faster.

Harold became aware of a dry sensation in his mouth. He tried not to imagine a glass of water, but now that his head had produced the image, it also conjured the feel and taste of cold liquid in his mouth, and his body grew weak with the need for it. He walked very carefully, trying to stabilize the ground while it tipped beneath his feet. Several cars slowed, but he waved them on, not wanting their attention. Each breath seemed too angular to pass through the cavities of his chest. There was no choice but to stop at the first home he came to. He secured the iron gate and hoped there weren't dogs.

The bricks of the house were new and grey; the evergreen hedging shaved hard back like a wall. Tulips grew in pert rows in beds that were without weeds. To the side hung a line of washing: several large shirts, trousers, skirts and a woman's bra. He looked away, not wanting to see things he shouldn't. As a teenager, he had often gazed at his aunts' pegged-up corsets, brassieres, support knickers and stockings. It was the first time he had realized the female world held secrets he wanted to know. He rang the doorbell of the house, and leaned against the wall.

When a woman answered, her face dropped. He wanted to reassure her not to worry, but his insides felt stripped. He could barely move his tongue. She hurried to fetch him a drink, and as he took the glass his hands trembled. The iced water broke over his teeth, his gums, the roof of his mouth, and rushed to his throat. He could have cried at the rightness of it.

'Are you sure you're all right?' she said, after she had fetched him a second glass and he had emptied that too. She was a wide woman, wearing a creased dress; childbearing hips, Maureen would have said. Her face was so weathered the skin

50

looked slapped. 'Do you need to rest?'

Harold promised he was feeling better. He was eager to get back to the road, and didn't want to intrude on a stranger. Besides, he felt he had already broken an unspoken English rule in asking for help. To do more would be to align himself with something both transient and unknown. In between the words he sought quick rasping breaths. He assured her he was walking a long way but probably hadn't got the hang of it yet. He hoped it would raise a smile, but she didn't seem to see the funny side. It was a long time since he had made a woman laugh.

'Wait here,' she said. Again she disappeared into the stillness of the house, to return with two fold-up chairs. Harold helped her to open them and repeated that he should get going, but she sank her body down as if she too had made a journey, and urged him to join her. 'Just for a moment,' she said. 'It will do us both good.'

Harold lowered his limbs into the seat beside hers. A heavy stillness crept over him and, after resisting for a moment, he closed his eyes. The light glowed red against his eyelids, and the sounds of birdsong and passing cars merged into one, that was both inside him and far away.

When he woke, she had set a small table at his knees with a plate of bread and butter, and slices of apple. She gestured with the upturned palm of her hand towards the plate, as if she were showing him the way forward. 'Please. Help yourself.'

Even though he hadn't been aware of his hunger, now that he saw the apple, his stomach felt scooped out. Besides it would be rude not to accept, after she had taken the trouble. He ate greedily, apologizing, but unable to stop. The woman watched and smiled, and all the while she played with a quarter of apple, turning it between her fingers, as if it were something curious she had picked up from the ground. 'You'd think walking should be the simplest thing,' she said at last. 'Just a question of putting one foot in front of the other. But it never ceases to amaze me how difficult the things that are supposed to be instinctive really are.'

She wet her lower lip with her tongue, waiting for more words. 'Eating,' she said at last. 'That's another one. Some people have real difficulties with that. Talking too. Even loving. They can all be difficult.' She watched the garden, not Harold.

'Sleeping,' he said.

She turned. 'Don't you sleep?'

'Not always.' He reached for more apple.

There was another silence. Then she said, 'Children.'

'I beg your pardon?'

'There's another one.'

He glanced again at her washing line, and the perfect rows of flowers. He felt the resounding absence of young life.

'Did you have any yourself?' she said.

'Just one.'

Harold thought of David, but it was too much to explain. He saw the boy as a toddler and how his face darkened in sunshine like a ripe nut. He wanted to describe the soft dimples of flesh at his knees, and the way he walked in his first pair of shoes, staring down, as if unable to credit they were still attached to his feet. He thought of him lying in his cot, his fingers so appallingly small and

52

perfect over his wool blanket. You could look at them and fear they might dissolve beneath your touch.

Mothering had come so naturally to Maureen. It was as if another woman had been waiting inside her all along, ready to slip out. She knew how to swing her body so that a baby slept; how to soften her voice; how to curl her hand to support his head. She knew what temperature the water should be in his bath, and when he needed to nap, and how to knit him blue wool socks. He had no idea she knew these things and he had watched with awe, like a spectator from the shadows. It both deepened his love for her and lifted her apart, so that just at the moment when he thought their marriage would intensify, it seemed to lose its way, or at least set them in different places. He peered at his baby son, with his solemn eyes, and felt consumed with fear. What if he was hungry? What if he was unhappy? What if other boys hit him when he went to school? There was so much to protect him from, Harold was overwhelmed. He wondered if other men had found the new responsibility of parenting as terrifying, or whether it had been a fault that was only in himself. It was different these days. You saw men pushing buggies and feeding babies with no worries at all.

'I hope I haven't upset you?' said the woman beside him.

'No, no.' He stood and shook her hand.

'I'm glad you stopped,' she said. 'I'm glad you asked for water.' He returned to the road before she could see that he was crying.

*   *   *

53

The lower creases of Dartmoor loomed to his left. He could see now that what had appeared to be a vague blue mass on the shoulder of the horizon was a series of purple, green and yellow peaks, unbroken by fields, and topped at the highest points with boulders of stone. A bird of prey, maybe a buzzard, swung over the land, skimming the air; suspended.

Harold asked himself if years ago he shouldn't have pressed Maureen to have another baby. 'David is enough,' she had said. 'He is all we need.' But sometimes he was afraid that having one son was too much to bear. He wondered if the pain of loving became diluted, the more you had? A child's growing was a constant pushing away. When their son had finally rejected them for good, they dealt with it in different ways. There was anger for a while, and then there was something else, that was like silence but had an energy and violence of its own. In the end, Harold had come down with a cold, and Maureen had moved into the spare room. Somehow or other neither of them had mentioned it, and somehow or other she had never moved back.

Harold's heel stung and his back ached, and now the soles of his feet were beginning to burn. Even the smallest flint caused him pain; he had to keep stopping to remove a shoe and shake it empty. From time to time, he also found that his legs buckled for no apparent reason, as if they had been jellied, causing him to stumble. His fingers were throbbing but maybe that was because they were not used to being swung back and forth in a downward direction. And yet, despite all this, he felt intensely alive. A lawn mower started up in the distance and he laughed out loud.

Harold joined the A3121 towards Exeter, and after a mile of heavy traffic at his back, he took the B3372, following the grass verges. When a group of professional-looking walkers caught him up, Harold stood out of their way and waved them past. They exchanged pleasantries about the good weather and the landscape, but he didn't tell them about heading for Berwick. He preferred to keep that tucked in his head, like Queenie's letter in his pocket. As they moved ahead he observed with interest that they all had backpacks, that some of them had loose-fitting tracksuits, and that others were equipped with sun visors, binoculars and telescopic hiking sticks. None was wearing yachting shoes.

A few waved, and one or two laughed. Harold didn't know if they were doing it because they thought he was a hopeless case or because they were admiring him, but either way, he found, it didn't really matter. He was already different from the man who had set out from Kingsbridge, and even from the small hotel. He was not someone off to the post box. He was walking to Queenie Hennessy. He was beginning again.

*   *   *

When he had first heard the news about her joining the brewery, he was surprised. 'Apparently there's a woman starting in the finances department,' he had told Maureen and David. They were eating in the best room, back in the days when she loved to cook and it was used for family

55

meals. Now that he thought about this scene, he could see it was Christmas, because the conversation was reliving itself with the added detail of festive paper hats.

'Is that supposed to be interesting?' David had said. It must have been his A-level year at the grammar school. He was dressed head to foot in black and his hair almost tipped his shoulders. He was not wearing a paper hat. He had skewered it with his fork.

Maureen smiled. Harold didn't expect her to stand up for him because she loved her son, and that was right, of course. He only wished that sometimes he didn't feel so outside, as if what bonded them was their disassociation from him.

David said, 'A woman won't last at the brewery.'

'Apparently she is very well qualified.'

'Everyone knows about Napier. He's a thug. A capitalist with sado-masochistic tendencies.'

'Mr Napier is not so bad.'

David laughed out loud. 'Father,' he said, the way he did; suggesting the bond between them was a whim of irony, rather than blood. 'He had someone kneecapped. Everyone knows.'

'I'm sure he didn't.'

'For stealing from the petty-cash tin.'

Harold said nothing; he mopped a sprout in gravy. He too knew the rumours, but he didn't like to think about them.

'Well, let's hope the new woman isn't a feminist,' David continued. 'Or a lesbian. Or a socialist. Eh, Father?' He had evidently finished with Mr Napier, and was moving to subjects closer to home.

Briefly Harold met his son's challenging eyes. In those days they still had their sharpness; it was

56

uncomfortable to engage with them for long. 'I don't object to people being different,' he said, but his son merely sucked his teeth and glanced at his mother.

'You read the *Daily Telegraph*,' he said. And after that he pushed back his plate, and stood, his body so pale and hollow Harold could barely look.

'Eat, love,' Maureen called. But David shook his head and slunk out, as if his father was enough to put anyone off their Christmas lunch.

Harold had looked to Maureen but she was already on her feet, clearing away the plates.

'He's clever, you see,' she said.

And implicit in the remark was the conviction that cleverness was both an excuse for everything and out of their reach. 'I don't know about you, but I'm too full for sherry trifle.' She bent her head and slipped off her paper hat, like something she had outgrown, and then she went to do the washing-up.

*   *   *

Harold arrived at South Brent in the late hours of the afternoon. He trod paving stones again, and was struck both by their smallness and their regularity. He came to cream-coloured houses, and front gardens, and garages with central-locking systems; and he felt the triumph of someone returning to civilization after a long voyage.

In a small shop, Harold bought plasters, water, an aerosol can of deodorant, a comb, a toothbrush, plastic razors, shaving foam, washing powder and two packets of Rich Tea biscuits. He took a room with a single bed and framed prints of extinct parrots on the wall, where he carefully examined his feet before applying plasters to the weeping blister on his heel and the swellings on his toes. His body throbbed with a deep aching. He was exhausted. He had never walked so far in a day but he had covered eight and a half miles and he was hungry for more. He would eat, and call Maureen from a pay phone, and after that he would sleep.

The sun slipped over the edge of Dartmoor, and filled the sky with russet cloud. The hills were shaded an opaque blue and the cows grazing them glowed a soft apricot against the dying light. Harold couldn't help wishing that David knew he was walking. He wondered if Maureen would talk to him about it, and the words she would use. The stars began to prick the night sky, one after another, so that the growing darkness trembled. Even as he looked he found them.

For the second night in a row, Harold slept without dreaming.

MAUREEN AND THE LIE

At first Maureen was convinced Harold would come back. He would phone, and he would be cold and tired, and she would have to go and fetch him, and it would be the middle of the night, and she would have to put a coat on over her nightdress and find her driving shoes; and all this would be Harold's fault. She had slept fitfully with the lamp on and the phone beside the bed, but he had neither rung nor come home.

She kept going over all that had happened. The breakfast, and the pink letter, and Harold not speaking, only weeping in silence. The smallest detail lurked in her mind. The way he had folded his reply twice and slipped it in the envelope before she could see. Even when she tried to think about something else, or nothing at all, she couldn't stop the picture swimming into her head of Harold staring at Queenie's letter, as if something deep inside him was undoing. She wanted very much to speak to David, but she didn't know how she would say it. Harold's walk was still too confusing and humiliating, and she was afraid that if she spoke to David she would miss him, and it would be more hurt than she could bear.

So when Harold said he was walking to Berwick, did he mean that once he got there, he was staying?

Well, he could go if he wanted. She should have seen it coming. Like mother, like son; although she had not met Joan, and Harold never spoke of her. What kind of woman packs a suitcase and leaves, without even a note? Yes, Harold could go. There were times when she herself had been tempted to call it a day. It was David who kept her at home, not marital love. She could no longer recall the details of how she had first met Harold, or what she had seen in him; only that he had picked her up at some municipal dance, and that on meeting him, her mother had found him common.

'Your father and I had better things in mind,' she had said, in that clipped way of hers.

In those days Maureen had not been one to listen to other people. So what if he had no education. So what if he had no class. So what if he rented a basement room and did so many jobs he barely slept. She looked at him and her heart tipped sideways. She would be the love he'd never had. Wife, mother, friend. She would be everything.

Sometimes she looked back to the past and wondered where the reckless young woman was that she had been.

Maureen went through his papers, but there was nothing to explain why he was walking to Queenie.

60

There were no letters. No photographs. No half-scribbled directions. All she discovered in his bedside drawer was a picture of herself just after they were married, and another crumpled black and white one of David that Harold must have hidden there, because she clearly remembered sticking it in an album. The silence reminded her of the months after David had left, when the house itself seemed to hold its breath. She put on the television in the sitting room, and the radio in the kitchen, but still it was too empty and quiet.

Had he been waiting for Queenie for twenty years? Had Queenie Hennessy been waiting for him?

It would be rubbish day tomorrow. Rubbish was Harold's department. She went online and ordered brochures from several companies who ran summer cruises.

As dusk fell, Maureen saw she had no choice but to do the rubbish herself. She hauled the bag down the path and threw it against the garden gate, as if in being Harold's neglected duty the rubbish was also to blame for his departure. Rex must have spotted her from an upstairs window because he was at the fence as she came back.

'Everything all right, Maureen?'

She said briskly that it was. Of course it was.

'Why is Harold not doing the rubbish this evening?'

Maureen glanced up at the bedroom window. Its emptiness struck her so forcefully that an unexpected rush of pain tore at the muscles inside her face. Her throat tightened. 'He's in bed.' She forced a smile.

'Bed?' Rex's mouth dropped. 'Why? Is Harold

poorly?'

The man worried so easily. Elizabeth had once confided across washing lines that his mother's fussing had turned him into the most appalling hypochondriac. She said, 'It's nothing. He slipped. He twisted his ankle.'

Rex's eyes widened like buttons. 'Did this happen during his walk yesterday, Maureen?'

'It was only a loose paving stone. He will be fine, Rex. What he needs is rest.'

'That's shocking, Maureen. A loose paving stone? Dear oh dear.'

He shook his head mournfully. From inside the house the phone began to ring, and her heart leapt to her mouth. It was Harold. He was coming home. As she ran for the door, Rex was still at the fence, saying, 'You should make a complaint to the council about a loose paving stone.'

'Don't worry,' she called over her shoulder, 'I will.' Her pulse was beating so fast she didn't know if she was going to laugh or cry. She darted to the phone and lifted the receiver, but the answer machine clicked on and he rang off. She dialled 1471, but the caller's number was not available. She sat watching the phone, waiting for him to call again or return home, but he did neither.

That night was the worst; she couldn't understand how anyone slept. She shook the batteries out of the bedside clock, but there was nothing she could do to stop the barking of dogs, or the cars that screeched past towards the new housing at three in the morning, or even the shrieking of gulls that started up at first light. She lay very still, waiting for inertia, and sometimes a moment of unconsciousness stole over her but then she would wake and remember again. Harold was walking to Queenie Hennessy. And reacquainting herself with this knowledge, after the ignorance of sleep, was even more painful than first hearing it on the telephone. It was a double deceit. But that was how it went; she knew that. You had to keep crawling up, not believing it, only to be punched back down again, until the truth well and truly hit home.

She opened Harold's bedside drawer and stared again at the two photographs he had hidden there. There was David in his first pair of shoes, balancing on one leg, and clinging on to her hand while lifting up his other foot, as if to examine it. And the other was of herself, laughing so much her dark hair fell over her face in long sweeps. She was nursing a courgette that had grown to the size of a small child. It must have been taken just after they moved to Kingsbridge.

*　　　*　　　*

When three large envelopes from cruise companies arrived, Maureen dropped them straight in the recycling box.

7

HAROLD AND THE HIKING MAN AND THE WOMAN WHO LOVED JANE AUSTEN

It had come to Harold's attention that several of the chaps at the brewery, including Mr Napier, had developed a peculiar walk that caused them to shriek as if it were uncontrollably funny. 'Look at this,' he'd hear them bragging from the yard. And one man would stick out an elbow like a chicken wing, and lower his torso as if to widen the shape of his lower half, before waddling forward.

'That's it! Fuck, that's it!' the others would scream. Sometimes the whole gang would spit out their cigarettes and have a go.

It had dawned on him, after several days of watching from a window, that what they were up to was being the new woman in finances. They were being Queenie Hennessy and her handbag.

Remembering this, Harold woke with an intense need to be back outside. Bright daylight frilled the curtains, as if straining to get at him. To his relief, while his body was unyielding and his feet tender, he could move both, and the blister on his heel appeared less angry. His shirt, socks and underpants were strung on the radiator; he had rinsed them in hot water and washing powder the previous night. They were stiff and not quite dry, but they would do. He applied a tidy parade of plasters to both feet, and carefully repacked the contents of the plastic bag.

Harold was the only resident in the dining room, which was really a small front room with a three-piece suite pushed flat against a wall and a table for two positioned at the centre. It was lit by a lamp with an orange shade and smelt of damp. A glass-fronted cabinet exhibited a collection of Spanish dolls and dead bluebottles, dry as twists of tissue paper. The woman who owned the B&B said that the girl who helped was off. She spoke the word as if there were something unsavoury about the girl's absence, as if she were maybe a piece of food that had to be disposed of. She put his breakfast on the table and watched him from the doorway, her arms folded. Harold was glad not to have to explain. He ate greedily and impatiently, staring out at the road beyond the window, and calculating how long it would take a man who wasn't used to walking to cover the six miles to Buckfast Abbey, let alone the further four hundred and eighty plus to Berwick-upon-Tweed.

Harold read the words of Queenie's letter, although he knew them now without looking. *Dear Harold, This may come to you as some surprise. I know it is a long time since we last met, but recently I have been thinking about the past. Last year I had an operation—*

'I hate South Brent,' said a voice.

Surprised, Harold looked up. There was no one

except him and the owner, and it seemed unlikely she had spoken. She was still leaning against the doorframe, with her arms folded, and jiggling her leg, so that her slipper dangled from her foot, on the verge of escape. Harold returned to his letter and his coffee, when the voice came again.

'We get more rain in South Brent than anywhere else in Devon.'

Clearly it was the woman, although she still didn't look at him. Her face remained fixed towards the carpet, her lips an empty O, as if her mouth were speaking despite the rest of her. He wished he could say something helpful but he couldn't think what it might be. Maybe his silence or simply his hearing was enough, because she went on.

'Even when it's sunny I can't enjoy it. I think to myself, Oh yes, it's nice now, but it's not going to last. I'm either watching rain, or waiting for it.'

Harold refolded Queenie's letter and returned it to his pocket. Something was bothering him about the envelope, but he couldn't find in his mind what it was; besides, it seemed rude not to give the woman his full attention, since she was evidently talking to him.

She said, 'I won a holiday to Benidorm once. All I had to do was pack my suitcase. But I couldn't do it. They sent me the ticket in the post, and I never opened the envelope. Why is that? Why, when the chance to escape came, couldn't I take it?'

Harold frowned. He thought of all the years he hadn't spoken to Queenie. 'Maybe you were afraid,' he said. 'I had a friend once but it took me a long time to see that she was. It was actually rather funny because we first met in a stationery cupboard.' He laughed, remembering the scene, but the woman didn't. It was probably difficult to imagine.

She stopped the foot that had been swinging like a pendulum, and studied her slipper as if she had not noticed it before. 'One day I will leave,' she said. She looked across the drab room and caught Harold's eye, and then at last she smiled.

*   *   *

Contrary to David's predictions, Queenie Hennessy had not turned out to be a socialist, feminist or lesbian. She was a stout, plain-looking woman with no waist and a handbag tucked over her forearm. It was well known that Mr Napier considered women to be little more than ticking hormone bombs. He gave them jobs as barmaids and secretaries and expected in return the odd favour in the back of his Jaguar. So Queenie marked a new departure at the brewery, and one that Mr Napier would not have made, had anyone other than her applied for the job.

Her manner was quiet and unassuming. Harold overheard a young chap saying, 'You forget she's a woman really.' Within a matter of days there were reports that she had brought an unprecedented order to the financial department. But this did not seem to stop the impersonations and laughter that now filled the corridors. Harold hoped she didn't hear. He watched her sometimes in the canteen with her sandwiches wrapped in greaseproof paper. She had a way of sitting with the young secretaries and listening, as if she, or they, were not there at all.

67

It was when he picked up his briefcase to go home one evening that he heard a snuffling sound from behind a cupboard door. He tried to walk past, but the noise didn't stop. He turned back.

Edging the door open, to his relief he had found nothing at first, just boxes of paper. Then the sound had come again, more like a sob, and he had discovered a squat figure, pressed against the wall, with her back to him. Her jacket tugged at the seam that ran the length of her spine.

'I do beg your pardon,' he'd said. He had been on the point of closing the door again and rushing away, when she had started to weep.

'I'm sorry. I'm sorry.'

'It's I who should apologize.' Now he was standing half in the cupboard and half outside it, with a woman he didn't know crying into manila envelopes.

'I'm good at my job,' she said.

'Of course.' He glanced down the corridor, hoping one of the younger chaps would appear and talk to her. He had never been very good with emotion. 'Of course,' he said again, as if saying it repeatedly would be enough.

'I've got a degree. I'm not stupid.'

'I know,' he said, although, of course, this was not strictly true; he knew almost nothing about her.

'Then why is Mr Napier always watching? As if he's waiting for me to make a mistake? Why must they all laugh?'

Their boss was a mystery to Harold. He didn't know whether the rumours about the kneecapping were true, but he had seen the man reduce the toughest landlords to jelly. Only the previous week

68

Napier had fired a secretary for touching his desk. He said, 'I'm sure he thinks you are a very good accountant.' He simply wanted her to stop crying.

'I need this job. It's not as if the rent pays itself. But I'm going to resign. Some mornings I don't even want to get up. My father always said I was too sensitive.' It was more information than Harold knew what to do with.

Queenie dropped her head low, so that he could see the soft dark hairs at the nape of her neck. It reminded him of David, and he felt a rush of pity.

'Don't resign,' he said, stooping a little and softening his voice. He was speaking from the heart. 'I found it hard to begin with too. I felt out of place. But it will get better.' She said nothing, and he wondered for a moment if she had even heard him. 'Would you like to come out of the stationery cupboard now?'

To his surprise, he held out his palm for her and, again to his surprise, she took it. Her hand was soft and warm against his.

Outside the cupboard, she pulled it away quickly. Then she smoothed her skirt, as if Harold were a crease and she needed to brush him out.

'Thank you,' she said, a little coldly, although her nose was a violent red.

She walked away from the stationery cupboard with her back straight and her neck tall, leaving Harold feeling that he was the one who had behaved out of turn. He supposed she had stopped thinking about resigning after that, because he looked out for her at her desk every day and she was there, working alone and without fuss. They rarely spoke. In fact he began to notice that if he entered the canteen, she seemed to pack up her sandwiches and leave.

Morning sun spilled gold over the highest peaks of Dartmoor, but in the shadows the ground was still brushed with a thin frost. Shafts of light struck the land ahead like torches, marking his journey forward. It would be another good day.

Leaving South Brent, Harold met a man in his dressing gown who was leaving food on a saucer for the hedgehogs. He crossed the road to avoid dogs and further on he overtook a young tattooed woman bawling beneath an upstairs window: 'I know you're there! I know you can hear me!' She paced up and down, kicking at garden walls, her body brittle with fury, and every time she appeared on the point of giving up, she returned to the foot of the house and yelled again: 'You bastard, Arran! I know you're there!' Harold also passed an abandoned mattress, the entrails of a sabotaged fridge, several single shoes, many plastic bags and a hubcap, until once again the pavements stopped, and what had been a road narrowed itself to a lane. It surprised him how relieved he felt to be under the sky again, and hedged between trees, and the earth banks that were thick with ferns and brambles.

Harbourneford. Higher Dean. Lower Dean.

He opened the second packet of Rich Tea biscuits, dipping into the bag for them as he went, although some had an unfortunate grainy texture and a slightly sulphuric taste of washing powder.

Was he fast enough? Was Queenie still alive? He mustn't stop for meals, or sleep. He must press on.

*   *   *

70

By the afternoon, Harold was aware of an occasional shooting pain along the back of his right calf, and a locking of his hip joints as he hit the downward slant of the hills. Even their upward slopes he took slowly, with his palms cupping the small of his back, not so much because he was sore as because he felt the need of a helping hand. He stopped to check the plasters on his feet, and replaced the ones on his heel where the blister had bled.

The road turned and rose and fell again. There were times when he could see the hills and fields and others when he saw nothing. He lost all sense of where he was in remembering Queenie, and imagining what her life might have become in the last twenty years. He wondered if she'd married? Had children? And yet from the letter it was clear she'd kept her maiden name.

'I can sing "God Save The Queen" backwards,' she told him once. And she did, while also sucking a Polo mint. 'I can also do "You Don't Bring Me Flowers", and I have almost got "Jerusalem".'

Harold smiled. He wondered if he had done so at the time. A herd of cows, chewing grass, looked up briefly, their mouths paused. One or two moved towards him, slowly at first but building to a trot. Their bodies looked too big for stopping. He was glad to be on the road, even though it was hard on his feet. The plastic bag with his shopping thumped against his thighs and dug white ridges into his wrists. He tried lodging it over one shoulder, but it kept careering back towards his elbow.

Maybe it was because Harold was carrying something too heavy, but he could suddenly picture his young son standing against the wood

71

chip of the hallway, his new satchel dragging down his shoulders. He was wearing his grey uniform; it must have been the day he started primary school. Like his father, David loomed a good few inches over the other boys, giving the impression that he was older, or at least oversized. He had gazed up at Harold from his place against the wall and said, 'I don't want to do this.' There were no tears. No holding on to Harold and not letting go. David spoke with a simplicity and self-knowledge that was disarming. In answer, Harold said—what? What had he said? He had looked down at his son, for whom he wanted everything, and been struck dumb.

Yes, life is terrifying, he might have said. Or, Yes, but it gets better. Or even, Yes, but it is sometimes good and sometimes bad. Better still, in the absence of words, he might have taken David in his arms. But he had not. He'd done none of those things. He felt the boy's fear so keenly, he could see no way round it. The morning his son looked up at his father and asked for help, Harold gave nothing. He fled to his car and went to work.

Why must he remember?

He hunched his shoulders and drove his feet harder, as if he wasn't so much walking to Queenie as away from himself.

* * *

Harold arrived at Buckfast Abbey before the gift shop closed. The square limestone profile of the church stood grey against the soft peaks behind. He realized he had come here before, many years ago, as a surprise for Maureen's birthday. David

72

had refused to get out of the car, and Maureen had insisted she would like to sit with him, and they had gone straight home without setting foot out of the car park.

In the monastery shop, Harold chose postcards and a souvenir pen, and briefly contemplated buying a jar of the monks' honey but it was still a long way to Berwick-upon-Tweed and he wasn't sure it would fit in his plastic bag, or survive the journey without the washing powder getting at it. He bought it anyway and asked for extra bubble wrap. There were no monks, only tourist parties. And there were more people queuing for the newly refurbished Grange Restaurant than the abbey. He wondered if the monks noticed, or minded.

Harold chose a large portion of chicken curry, and carried his tray to a window by the terrace, overlooking the lavender garden. He was so hungry he couldn't scoop the food fast enough into his mouth. At the next table a couple in their late fifties seemed to be discussing something, maybe a map. They both wore khaki shorts, khaki sweatshirts, brown socks and proper hiking boots, so that sitting opposite each other at the table, they looked like male and female models of the same person. They even ate the same sandwiches and drank the same fruit drink. Harold tried but he couldn't imagine Maureen dressing like him. He began to write his cards:

Dear Queenie, I have come approximately 20 miles. You must keep waiting. Harold (Fry)

Dear Maureen, Have reached Buckfast

73

Abbey. Weather good. Shoes holding up, as are feet and legs. H.

Dear Girl in the Garage (Happy To Help), Thank you. From the man who said he was off for a walk.

'Could I possibly borrow your pen?' said the hiking man. Harold passed it and the man circled a point on his map several times over. His wife said nothing. Maybe she even frowned. Harold didn't like to look too closely.

'Are you here for the Dartmoor Trail?' asked the man, returning the pen.

Harold said that he wasn't. He was travelling to a friend by foot, with a very specific purpose. He shuffled his postcards into a neat pile.

'Of course my wife and I are walkers. We come here every year. Even when she broke her leg we came back. That's how much we love it.'

Harold replied that he and his wife also used to take the same holiday each year at a holiday camp in Eastbourne. There had been entertainment every evening, and competitions among the residents. 'One year my son won the *Daily Mail* Twist prize,' he said.

The man nodded impatiently as if he were hurrying Harold along. 'Of course it's what you wear on your feet that counts. What kind of boots do you have?'

'Yachting shoes.' Harold smiled, but the hiking man didn't.

'You should wear Scarpa. Scarpa is what the pros wear. We swear by Scarpa.'

His wife looked up. '*You* swear by Scarpa,' she

said. Her eyes were round, as if she had contact lenses that maybe hurt. For a confusing moment Harold was caught in the memory of a game David used to play, where he timed how long he could stare without blinking. His eyes would be streaming but he wouldn't close them. It was not the sort of competition they would run at the holiday camp in Eastbourne. This one had been painful to watch.

The hiking man said, 'What kind of socks do you wear?'

Harold glanced at his feet. 'Normal ones,' he was about to say, but the man didn't wait for an answer.

'You need specialist socks,' he said. 'Anything else and you can forget it.' He broke off. 'What socks do we wear?' Harold had no idea. It was only when the man's wife supplied the answer that he realized the hiking man was addressing her and not himself.

'Thorlo,' she said.

'Gore-Tex jacket?'

Harold opened his mouth and closed it.

'Walking is what makes our marriage. Which route are you doing?'

Harold explained that he was making it up as he went along, but that he was, in essence, heading north. He mentioned Exeter, Bath, and possibly Stroud. 'I'm sticking to the roads because I have driven all my adult life. It's what I know.'

The hiking man continued talking. It occurred to Harold that he was one of those people who didn't require other people in order to have a conversation. His wife studied her hands. 'Of course the Cotswold Trail is overrated. Give me

Dartmoor any day.'

'Personally I liked the Cotswolds,' said his wife. 'I know it's more flat but it's romantic.' She twiddled her wedding ring so hard it looked as if she might unscrew her finger.

'She loves Jane Austen,' laughed the hiking man. 'She's seen all her films. I'm more of a man's man, if you know what I mean.'

Harold found himself nodding, although he had no idea what the man meant. He had never been what Maureen called the macho type. He had always avoided the big lock-ins with Napier and the chaps at the brewery. Sometimes it struck him as strange that he had worked all those years with alcohol, when it had played such a terrible part in his life. Maybe people were drawn to what they feared.

'We like Dartmoor best,' said the hiking man.

'*You* like Dartmoor best,' corrected his wife.

They looked at one another, as though they were complete strangers. In the pause that followed, Harold returned to his postcards. He hoped there wouldn't be a row. He hoped they weren't one of those couples who said in public the dangerous things they could not voice at home.

He thought again about the holidays in Eastbourne. Maureen would pack sandwiches for the journey, and they would arrive so early the gates were closed. Harold had always thought affectionately of those summers until recently when Maureen told him David referred to life's low points as being as dull as bloody Eastbourne. These days of course Harold and Maureen preferred not to travel, but he was sure she was wrong about the holiday camp. They had laughed.

David had found a playmate or two. There was the night he won the dancing. He had been happy.

'Dull as *bloody* Eastbourne.' Maureen hit the word so hard it sounded like an invasion of her mouth.

He was interrupted by the couple at the next table. They had raised their voices. Harold wanted to get away, but there appeared to be no safe slice of silence in which he might stand and excuse himself.

The woman who loved Jane Austen said, 'Do you think it was funny cooped up here with a broken leg?' Her husband kept on looking at his map as if she had not spoken, and she continued to speak as if he was not ignoring her. 'I never want to come here again.'

Harold wished the woman would stop. He wished the man would smile or take hold of her hand. He thought of himself and Maureen, and the years of silence at 13 Fossebridge Road. Had Maureen ever felt the impulse to say, where everyone could hear, such truths about their marriage? The thought had never occurred to him before, and was so alarming he was already on his feet and heading for the door. The couple didn't seem to notice that Harold had gone.

*   *   *

Harold checked into a modest guesthouse that smelt of central heating, boiled giblets and air freshener. He was sore with tiredness, but once he had unpacked his few things and inspected his feet, he sat on the edge of the bed, wondering what to do next. He was too unsettled to sleep. From downstairs came the sound of the early-evening news. Maureen would be watching too, while she did the ironing. For a while he stayed, listening without hearing, comforted by the knowledge they were joined in this way at least. He thought again of the couple in the restaurant, and missed his wife so much he could think of nothing else. If he'd played it otherwise, could he have made a difference? If he'd pushed open the door to the spare room? Or even booked a holiday and taken her abroad? But she would never have agreed. She was too afraid of not talking to David, and missing the visit she was always waiting for.

Other things came too. The early years of their marriage, before David was born, when she had grown vegetables in the garden of Fossebridge Road, and waited for Harold every evening on the corner beyond the brewery. They would walk home, sometimes taking in the seafront, or stopping at the quay to watch the boats. She made curtains out of mattress ticking and, with the remnants, a shift dress for herself. She took to looking up new recipes from the library. There were casseroles, curries, pasta, pulses. Over dinner, she would ask about the chaps at the brewery, and their wives, although when it came to the Christmas party, they never went.

He remembered setting eyes on her in a red dress, with a little sprig of holly she had pinned to her collar. If he closed his eyes, he fancied he could smell the sweetness of her. They had drunk ginger beer in the garden, and watched the stars. 'Who needs other people?' one or other of them had said.

He saw her holding out the wrapped-up body of

78

their baby and offering him to Harold. He wouldn't break, she'd smiled: 'Why won't you hold him?' Harold had said the baby liked her best and maybe dug his hands in his pockets.

So how was it that a truth that could make her smile once, and rest her head on his shoulder, would years later become the source of such resentment and fury? 'You never held him!' she had howled when things reached their worst. 'All his childhood you never even touched him!' It hadn't been strictly true and he had said something along those lines; although she was right in essence. He had been too afraid to hold his own son. But how was it that once she had understood, and then years later she didn't?

He wondered if David might come to her, now that Harold was at a safe distance.

It was too much to stay inside, thinking these things, and regretting so many others. Harold reached for his jacket. Outside a curve of moon hung above flakes of cloud. Noticing him, a woman with violent pink hair stopped watering her hanging baskets and stared, as if he were strange.

From a public phone box he rang Maureen, but she had no news to report and their conversation was brief and halting. Only once she referred to his walk, when she asked if he had thought of looking at a map. Harold said he was intending to buy proper walking equipment once he had made it as far as Exeter. There would be more choice in a city, he told her. He gave a knowing reference to Gore-Tex.

She said, 'I see.' The sound was flat, suggesting he had trodden in something unpleasant that she had been expecting all along. In the silence that followed he could hear the click of her tongue against the roof of her mouth, and the rattle of her swallowing. Then she said, 'I suppose you have worked out how much this is all costing.'

'I thought I'd use my retirement fund. I'm sticking to a budget.'

'I see,' she said again.

'It's not as if we had plans.'

'No.'

'So is that OK?'

'OK?' she repeated, as if the word were not one she had come across before.

For one chaotic moment he wanted to say, Why don't you come with me, only he knew she would stamp on that with her I think not, so instead he said, 'Is it OK with you? That I'm doing this? That I'm walking?'

'It has to be,' said Maureen, and then she hung up.

Again Harold left the phone box wishing he could make Maureen understand. But for years they had been in a place where language had no significance. She only had to look at him and she was wrenched to the past. Small words were exchanged and they were safe. They hovered over the surface of what could never be said, because that was unfathomable and would never be bridged. Harold returned to his temporary room, and rinsed his clothes. He pictured their separate beds at 13 Fossebridge Road and wondered when exactly she had stopped opening her mouth as they kissed. Was it before, or after?

Harold woke at dawn, surprised and thankful that he could walk, but this time he was weary. The heating was too much and the night had seemed

80

long and confined. He couldn't help feeling that, even though Maureen had not said it, what she was implying about his retirement fund was correct. He should not be spending it solely on himself and without her approval.

Though, God knows, it was a long time since he had done anything to impress her.

* * *

From Buckfast Harold took the B3352 via Ashburton, stopping overnight at Heathfield. He passed other walkers, and they spoke briefly, acknowledging the beauty of the land and the coming of summer, before they wished one another a safe journey and went their separate ways. Harold turned bends, followed the contours of the hills, his path always the road ahead. Crows scattered from trees with a clatter of wings. A young deer shot out from the hedgerow. Cars roared up from nowhere, and disappeared. There were dogs behind gates, and several badgers, like furred weights against the gutter. A cherry tree stood in a dress of blossom, and as the wind took up it loosened a drift of petals like confetti. Harold was ready for surprise, whatever form it took. Such freedom was rare.

'I am Father,' he had told his mother when he was maybe six or seven. She had looked up, interested, and it shocked him that he had been so bold. He had no idea what he was going to do next. There was nothing for it but to put on his father's flat cap, and his dressing gown, and stare accusingly at an empty bottle. His mother's face set like a jelly; he feared at least a slap. Then, to his

81

shock and profound delight, she stretched back her soft neck and the air tinkled with her laughter. He could see her perfect teeth and the pink of her gums. He had never made his mother laugh like that before.

'What a clown,' she had said.

He had felt as tall as the house. Grown up. Despite himself, he had laughed too; first as a grin and then with a great bellyful that sent him doubling over. After that, he sought out ways to amuse her. He learned jokes. He pulled faces. Sometimes it worked. Sometimes it didn't. Sometimes he hit on things without even knowing how they were funny.

Harold walked the streets and lanes. The road narrowed and widened, and rose and curved. Sometimes he was almost flat against the hedgerows; others he walked the pavements freely. 'Don't walk in the cracks,' he heard himself call after his mother. 'If you walk in the cracks there are ghosts.' Only this time she had looked at him as if she had never seen him before, and then stepped on every one of them, so that he had been forced to run after her, holding out his arms and flapping wildly. It had been hard to keep up with a woman like Joan.

A new set of blisters began to bulge on both Harold's heels. By the afternoon, further blisters rose also on the pads of his toes. He had no idea that walking could hurt so much. All he could think of were plasters.

From Heathfield, he walked to Chudleigh Knighton along the B3344, and on again to Chudleigh. It was an effort to get that far, with such exhaustion deep inside him. He took a room for the night, disappointed he had barely managed five miles, although the following day he pushed himself hard and walked from dawn, covering another nine. The early sun shone through the trees in spokes of light, and by mid-morning the sky was pasted with small stubborn clouds that, the more he looked, resembled grey bowler hats. Midges shot through the air.

Six days after leaving Kingsbridge, and approximately forty-three miles from Fossebridge Road, the waistband of Harold's trousers drooped from his stomach and patches of sunburnt skin peeled from his forehead, nose and ears. Referring to his watch, he found he already knew the hour. Morning and evening, he studied the toes, heels and arches of his feet, applying plasters or cream where the skin was broken or chafing. He preferred to take his lemonade outside, and sheltered with the smokers when it rained. The first of the forget-me-nots shone in pale pools under the moon.

Harold promised himself he would buy serious walking equipment in Exeter, and a further souvenir for Queenie. As the sun sank behind the city walls and the air chilled, he remembered again that there was something not right about her letter, but couldn't put his finger on what it was.

8

HAROLD AND THE SILVER-HAIRED GENTLEMAN

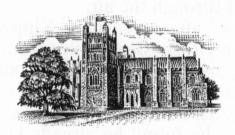

Dear Maureen, Writing this from a bench beside the cathedral. Two chaps are doing street theatre, though they seem to be in danger of setting themselves on fire. Have marked my position with an x. H.

Dear Queenie, Do not give up. Best wishes, Harold (Fry).

Dear Girl in the Garage (Happy to Help), I have been wondering whether you pray? I tried once but I was too late. I am afraid that did it for me. Kind regards, The man who was walking.
    PS. I am still doing it.

It was mid-morning. A crowd had gathered around two young men who were eating fire outside the cathedral to the accompaniment of a CD player, while an old man dressed in a blanket rooted through a bin. The flame-eaters wore dark, oily clothes and had tied their hair in ponytails; there was something shambolic about their act, as if it might go wrong at any time. They asked people to stand back, and then they started juggling flaming batons, while the crowd gave a nervous clap. The old man seemed to notice them for the first time. He pushed his way to the front of the crowd and stood between the two men, like a piggy in the middle. He was laughing. The two young men yelled at him to move away, but he began to dance to their music. His movements were jerky and unrefined; suddenly the flame-eaters seemed both slick and professional. They switched off their CD player and packed away their things, and the crowd diluted to a few passers-by, but the old man danced alone outside the cathedral, his arms outspread and his eyes closed, as if both the music and the people were still present.

Harold wanted to get on with his journey, but equally he felt that the old man was performing for the benefit of strangers and that, as the only one remaining, it would be discourteous to abandon him.

He remembered David jiving at the holiday camp in Eastbourne, the night he won the Twist prize. Embarrassed, the other contestants had peeled away, leaving only this eight-year-old child with his body jiggering so fast, it was impossible to tell whether he was happy or in pain. The compère began a slow clap, and made a joke that rang through the dance hall, so that everyone roared. Bewildered, Harold had smiled too; not knowing in that moment how to be anything so complicated as his son's father. He glanced at Maureen and found she was watching, her hands to her mouth. The smile dropped from his face and he felt nothing but a traitor.

There was more. There were David's school years. The hours in his bedroom, the top marks, the refusal to allow his parents' help. 'It doesn't matter he keeps to himself,' Maureen would say. 'He has other interests.' After all, they were loners themselves. One week David wanted a microscope. Another it was the collected works of Dostoyevsky. Then it was *German for Beginners*. A bonsai tree. In awe of the greed with which he learned new things, they bought them all. He was blessed with an intelligence and opportunities they had never had; whatever they did, they mustn't let him down.

'Father,' he would say, 'have you read William Blake?' Or, 'Do you know anything about drift velocity?'

'I beg your pardon?'

'I thought as much.'

Harold had spent his whole life bowing his head to avoid confrontation, and yet, spilled from his own flesh was someone determined to hold his eye and have it out with him. He wished he had not grinned the night his son jived.

The old man stopped dancing. He seemed to notice Harold for the first time. Throwing off his blanket, he gave a low bow, sweeping the ground with his hand. He was wearing some sort of suit, though it was so dirty it was hard to tell which was shirt and which jacket. He rose again, still gazing directly at Harold. Harold checked behind him in case the old man was looking at someone else, but other people were shooting past, avoiding connection. The person the old man wanted was undoubtedly him.

He moved towards the old man, slowly. Halfway he got so embarrassed he had to pretend he had something in his eye, but the old man waited. When they were maybe a yard apart the old man held out his arms, as if embracing the shoulders of an invisible partner. There was nothing for it but for Harold to lift his own arms and do the same. Slowly their feet fumbled a passage to the left and then to the right. They weren't touching but they danced together, and if there was a smell of urine and possibly vomit, it was also true that Harold had smelt worse. The only sound came from the traffic, and the crowds.

The old man drew to a halt and bowed a second time. Moved, Harold ducked his head. He thanked the old man for dancing, but the old man had already picked up his blanket and was limping away, as if music was the last thing on his mind.

In a gift shop close to the cathedral, Harold bought a set of embossed pencils that he hoped Maureen would like. For Queenie, he chose a small paperweight containing a model of the cathedral that covered itself in glitter when he tipped it upside down. It struck him as strange but true that tourists bought trinkets and souvenirs of religious places because they had no idea what else to do when they got there.

*   *   *

Exeter took Harold by surprise. He had developed a slow inner rhythm that the fury of the city now

87

threatened to overturn. He had felt comfortable in the security of open land and sky, where everything took its place. He had felt himself to be part of something bigger than simply Harold. In the city, where there was such short-range sight, he felt anything might happen, and that whatever it was he wouldn't be ready.

He looked for traces of the land beneath his feet and all he found was where it had been replaced with paving stones and tarmac. Everything alarmed him. The traffic. The buildings. The crowds pushed past, shouting into their mobile phones. He smiled at each face and it was exhausting, taking in so many strangers.

He lost a full day, simply wandering. Each time he resolved to leave, he saw something that distracted him, and another hour passed. He deliberated over purchases that he hadn't realized he required. Should he send Maureen a new pair of gardening gloves? An assistant fetched five different types, and modelled them on her hands, before Harold remembered his wife had long since abandoned her vegetable beds. He stopped to eat and was presented with such an array of sandwiches that he forgot he was hungry, and left with nothing. (Did he prefer cheese or ham or would he like the filling of the day, seafood cocktail? Or would he like something else altogether? Sushi? Peking duck wraps?) What had been so clear to him when he was alone, two feet on the ground, became lost in this abundance of choices and streets and glass-fronted shopping outlets. He longed to be back on the open land.

And now that he had the opportunity to buy walking equipment, he also faltered. After an hour with an enthusiastic young Australian man, who produced not only walking boots but also a rucksack, a small tent and a talking pedometer, Harold apologized profusely and bought a wind-up torch. He told himself that he had managed perfectly well with his yachting shoes and his plastic bag, and with a little ingenuity he could carry his toothbrush and shaving foam in one pocket, and his deodorant and washing powder in the other. Instead he went to a café close to the railway station.

Twenty years ago Queenie must have made her way to Exeter St David's. Had she gone straight from here to Berwick? Had she family there? Friends? She had never mentioned either. Once, a song had come on the car radio and she had wept. 'Mighty Like A Rose'. The male voice filled the air, steady and deep. It reminded her of her father, she said between gulps; he had died only recently.

'I'm sorry, I'm sorry,' she whispered.

'It's all right.'

'He was a good man.'

'I'm sure.'

'You'd have liked him, Mr Fry.'

She had told a story about her father; how he played a game when she was a child where he pretended she was invisible. 'I'm here! I'm here!' she'd be laughing; and all the time he'd look straight down at her, saying, as if she wasn't there, 'Come here this minute. Where are you, Queenie?'

'It was so funny,' she said, nipping the end of her nose with her handkerchief. 'I miss him very much.' Even her grief possessed a compact dignity.

The station café was busy. Harold watched the holidaymakers negotiating the small spaces

89

between the tables and chairs with their suitcases and backpacks, and he asked himself if maybe Queenie had sat in this same spot. He pictured her, alone and pale, in her old-fashioned suit; her neat face staring resolutely forward.

He should never have let her go like that.

'Excuse me,' a gentle voice above him said, 'is this seat free?'

He shook himself back to the present. A well-dressed man was standing to his left and pointing to the chair opposite. Harold wiped his eyes, surprised and ashamed to discover that once again he had been crying. He told the man that the seat was indeed free, and urged him to take it.

The man wore a smart suit and deep-blue shirt with small pearl cufflinks. His body was lean and graceful. His thick, silver hair was swept back from his face. Even as he sat he folded his legs so that the crease of his trousers fell in line with his knees. He lifted his hands to his lips, holding them there in an elegant steeple. He looked the sort of man Harold wished he had been; distinguished, as Maureen would say. Maybe he was staring too hard because after the waitress had delivered a pot of Ceylon tea (no milk) and a toasted teacake, the gentleman said with feeling, 'Goodbyes are always hard.' He poured tea and added lemon.

Harold explained that he was walking to a woman he had let down in the past. He hoped it was not a goodbye; he very much hoped his friend would live. He didn't look the man in the eye, but focused instead on the toasted teacake. It was the size of the plate. The butter had melted like golden syrup.

The man sliced one half into slim soldiers and

90

listened as he ate. The café was loud and busy; the windows so steamed they were opaque.

'Queenie was the sort of woman people don't appreciate. She wasn't a dolly bird, like the other women at the brewery. She maybe had a little hair on her face. Not a moustache or anything. But the other chaps laughed. They called her names. It caused her pain.' Harold wasn't even certain he could be heard. He marvelled at the neatness with which the gentleman posted the teacake between his teeth and mopped his fingers after each mouthful.

'Would you like some?' said the gentleman.

'I couldn't.' Harold raised both hands as if blocking the way.

'I only want half. It seems a shame to waste the other. Please. Share it.'

The silver-haired gentleman took his cut-up pieces and arranged them on a paper napkin. He slid the plate with the intact half towards Harold. 'Can I ask you a question?' he said. 'You seem a decent sort of man.'

Harold nodded because the teacake was already in his mouth and he couldn't exactly spit it out again. He tried to stop the butter from running by scooping it up with his fingers, but it shot down his wrist and oiled his sleeve.

'I come to Exeter every Thursday. I get the train in the morning, and I return in the early evening. I come to meet a young man. We do things. No one knows about this part of my life.'

The silver-haired gentleman paused to pour a fresh cup of tea. The teacake was lodged in Harold's throat. He could feel the man's eyes searching for his but he couldn't possibly look up.

91

'Can I go on?' said the gentleman.

Harold nodded. He gave a gulp that sent the teacake squeezing past his tonsils. It hurt all the way down.

'I like what we do, otherwise I would not come here, but I have also grown fond of him. He fetches me a glass of water afterwards and sometimes he talks. His English is not so good. I believe he had polio as a child, and sometimes it causes him to limp.'

For the first time the silver-haired gentleman faltered, as if he was fighting something inside. He lifted his tea but his fingers trembled when he steered the cup to his mouth, so that the liquid spilled over the rim and slopped on to his teacake. 'He moves me, this young man,' he said. 'He moves me beyond words.'

Harold looked away. He wondered if he could get up but realized he couldn't. He had eaten half the silver-haired gentleman's teacake, after all. And yet he felt it was an intrusion to witness the man's helplessness, when he had been so kind and appeared so elegant. He wished the man hadn't spilled his tea, and that he would mop it up, but he didn't, he just sat, bearing it, and not caring. His teacake would be ruined.

The gentleman continued with difficulty. The words were slow and spread apart. 'I lick his trainers. It's part of what we do. But I noticed only this morning that he has a small hole at the toe.' His voice quivered. 'I would like to buy him another pair but I don't want to offend him. And yet equally I can't bear the thought of him walking the streets with a hole in his trainers. His foot will get wet. What should I do?' His mouth folded over

92

itself, as if pressing back an avalanche of pain.

Harold sat in silence. The silver-haired gentleman was in truth nothing like the man Harold had first imagined him to be. He was a chap like himself, with a unique pain; and yet there would be no knowing that if you passed him in the street, or sat opposite him in a café and did not share his teacake. Harold pictured the gentleman on a station platform, smart in his suit, looking no different from anyone else. It must be the same all over England. People were buying milk, or filling their cars with petrol, or even posting letters. And what no one else knew was the appalling weight of the thing they were carrying inside. The superhuman effort it took sometimes to be normal, and a part of things that appeared both easy and everyday. The loneliness of that. Moved and humbled, he passed his paper napkin.

'I think I would buy him new trainers,' said Harold. He dared to lift his eyes to meet those of the silver-haired gentleman. The irises were a watery blue; the whites so pink they appeared sore. It tore at Harold's heart, but he didn't look away. Briefly the two men sat, not speaking, until a lightness filled Harold and caused him to offer a smile. He understood that in walking to atone for the mistakes he had made, it was also his journey to accept the strangeness of others. As a passer-by, he was in a place where everything, not only the land, was open. People would feel free to talk, and he was free to listen. To carry a little of them as he went. He had neglected so many things, that he owed this small piece of generosity to Queenie and the past.

The gentleman smiled too. 'Thank you.' He

wiped his mouth and his fingers, and then the rim of his cup. As he stood he said, 'I don't suppose our paths will cross again but I am glad we met. I am glad we talked.'

They shook hands and parted, and left the remains of the teacake behind.

9

MAUREEN AND DAVID

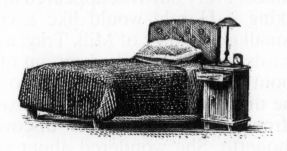

Maureen didn't know which was worse, the numbing shock that came with the first knowledge that Harold was walking to Queenie or the galvanizing fury that replaced it. She had received his postcards, one of Buckfast Abbey and another of the Dartmouth Railway (Hope you are well. H.), but neither of these offered any real comfort or explanation. He phoned her most evenings but he was so tired he made no sense. The money they had set aside for their retirement would be squandered in weeks. How dare he leave her, after she had put up with him for forty-seven years? How dare he humiliate her so painfully she could not even tell her son? A small number of household bills were arranged in a pile on the hall table, addressed to Mr H. Fry, and reminding her of his absence every time she rushed past.

She fetched out the hoover, searching out traces of Harold, a hair, a button, and sucking them into the nozzle. She shot his bedside table, his wardrobe, his bed, with disinfectant spray.

It wasn't simply anger that preoccupied Maureen. There was also the problem of what to say to her neighbour. She was beginning to regret the lie about Harold being in bed with a swollen ankle. Almost every day Rex appeared at the front door, asking if Harold would like a visitor and bearing small gifts: a box of Milk Tray, a packet of playing cards, an article he had cut out of the local paper about lawn feed. It had come to the point where she dreaded looking up at the frosted glass of the front door for fear of discovering his stout silhouette. She wondered about saying her husband had been rushed to A&E overnight, but it would cause Rex such anxiety she couldn't bear it. Besides, he would probably start offering her lifts to the hospital. She felt even more of a prisoner in her own home than she had done before Harold left.

Nearly a week after he had gone, Harold rang from a phone box to tell Maureen he was staying a second night in Exeter, and would head early the next morning towards Tiverton. He said, 'Sometimes I think I'm doing this for David . . . Did you hear me, Maureen?'

She had heard. But she couldn't speak.

He said, 'I think of him a lot. And I remember things. About him being a boy. I think it might help.'

Maureen drew in a breath so cold that her teeth felt stripped. She said at last, 'Are you telling me David wants you to walk to Queenie Hennessy?'

He said nothing and then he gave a sigh. 'No.' It was a dull sound, like something dropping.

She went on. 'Have you spoken to him?'

'No.'

'Seen him?'

Again, 'No.'

'Well then.'

Harold said nothing. Maureen stood and paced up and down the hall carpet, feeling the size of her victory with her feet. 'If you are going to this woman, if you are going to walk the length of England without a map and your mobile and without even telling me first, then at least have the goodness to own up to what you're doing. This is *your* choice, Harold. It's not mine and it certainly wouldn't be David's.'

Ending on such a blaze of righteousness, she had no alternative but to hang up. She instantly regretted it. She tried to ring him back, but the number wasn't available. Sometimes she said these things but she didn't mean them. They had become the fabric of the way she talked. She tried to find something to distract her, but the only thing left to wash was the net curtains and she couldn't face taking them down. Another evening came and went, and nothing happened.

Maureen slept fitfully. She dreamed she was at a social event, with a lot of people in black tie and evening dresses, whom she didn't know. She was sitting at a table to eat when she glanced down and found her liver in her lap. 'How lovely to meet you,' she said to the man beside her, smothering it with her hand before he could see. And all the time her liver was slithering between her fingers, squelching in at the gaps beneath her nails, until she was at a loss to know how she might contain it. The waiters began delivering plates covered with silver domes.

97

Yet she felt no physical pain. Not as such. What she felt was more like panic; the agony of panic. It came over her in a rush that left her skin prickling below her hairline. How was she going to get the liver back inside her body without anyone noticing, and when she couldn't feel any fleshy gap through which to post it? No matter how hard she flicked them below the table, her fingers were stuck all over with the thing. She tried to loosen it with her free hand, but in no time it clung to that too. She wanted to jump up and scream, but she knew she mustn't. She must remain very still and very quiet and no one must know she was nursing her entrails.

Maureen woke in a sweat at quarter past four, and reached for her bedside light. She thought of Harold in Exeter, and the pension fund dwindling to nothing, and Rex with his gifts. She thought of the silence that wouldn't be cleaned away. She couldn't take any more.

Some time after dawn, she spoke with David. She confessed the truth about his father walking to a woman from the past, and he listened. 'You and I didn't know Queenie Hennessy,' said Maureen. 'But she worked at the brewery. She had a job in accounts. I suspect she was the spinster type. Very lonely.' After that, she told David she loved him and wished he would visit. He promised it was the same for him. 'So what should I do about Harold, love? What would you do?' she said.

He told her exactly what the problem was with his father, and urged her to visit the doctor. He voiced the things she was too afraid to say.

'But I can't leave the house,' she argued. 'He might come back. He might come back and I

98

wouldn't be here.'

David laughed. A little harshly, she felt; but he had never been one to mince his words. She had a choice. She could stay at home, waiting. Or she could do something about it. She pictured David smiling and tears sprang to her eyes. And then he said something she didn't expect; he knew about Queenie Hennessy. She was a good woman.

Maureen gave a small gasp. 'But you never met her.'

He reminded her that while this was true, it was untrue that Maureen and Queenie had not met. She had come to Fossebridge Road with a message for Harold. Urgent, she'd said.

That settled it. As soon as the surgery was open, Maureen rang to book a doctor's appointment.

HAROLD AND THE SIGN

The morning sky was a single blue, combed through with cloud, while a slip of moon still loitered behind trees. Harold was relieved to be back on the road. He had left Exeter early, after purchasing a second-hand dictionary of wild flowers and a visitor's guide to Great Britain. These he kept in his plastic bag, along with the two presents for Queenie. He also carried replenished supplies of water, biscuits and, on the advice of a chemist, a tube of petroleum jelly for his feet. 'I could sell you a specialist cream but it would be a waste of your time and money,' the shopkeeper said. He also warned there was bad weather coming.

In the city, Harold's thoughts had stopped. Now that he was back on the open land, he was once again between places, and pictures ran freely through his mind. In walking, he unleashed the past that he had spent twenty years seeking to avoid, and now it chattered and played through his head with a wild energy that was its own. He no longer saw distance in terms of miles. He measured it with his remembering.

Passing allotments, he saw Maureen in the front garden of Fossebridge Road, wearing an old shirt of Harold's, her hair tied back against the wind and her face smutched with dirt, as she dug in French-bean plants. He saw a bird's broken egg and recalled with splintering tenderness the fragility of David's head when he was born. He heard the hollow cackle of a crow in the silence, and suddenly he was lying in his bed as a teenager, hearing that same cry, and overwhelmed with loneliness.

'Where are you going?' he had asked his mother. Already he loomed over his father, but he liked the fact he only reached her shoulders. She lifted her suitcase and arranged a long silk scarf round her neck. It hung down her back like hair.

'Nowhere,' she said, but she was opening the front door.

'I want to come.' He took hold of the scarf, just the tassels where she might not notice. The silk was soft between his fingertips. 'Can I come?'

'Don't be daft. You'll be fine. You're practically a man.'

'Shall I tell you a joke?'

'Not now, Harold.' She eased her scarf from his hold. 'You're making me silly,' she said, wiping her eyes. 'Am I smudged?'

'You're lovely.'

'Wish me luck.' She took a deep breath as if she were about to plunge into water, and stepped out.

The detail was so clear it was more real than the

earth beneath his feet. He could smell her musk scent. See the white powder on her skin and know, even without her being there, that if she had allowed him to kiss her cheek it would have tasted of marshmallows.

'I thought you might like these for a change,' said Queenie Hennessy once. She had prised the lid from a small tin and revealed squares of white confectionery, dusted in icing sugar. He had shaken his head and continued to drive. She didn't bring marshmallows again.

Sunlight broke through the trees so that the young leaves, rippling in the wind, shone like foil. At Brampford Speke, the roofs turned into thatch, and the brick was no longer the colour of flint but a warmer shade of red. Branches of spiraea bowed under sleeves of blossom and delphinium shoots nudged the soil. With the help of his guidebook, Harold identified old man's beard, hart's tongue, red campion, herb Robert, cuckoo pint, and discovered that the star-shaped flowers whose beauty he had marvelled at were wood anemones. Buoyed up by this, he covered the further two and a half miles to Thorverton with his head deep in his wild-plant dictionary. Despite the chemist's warning, it did not rain. He felt blessed.

The land fell away to the left and right, opening towards the faraway hills. Harold overtook two young women with buggies, a boy on a scooter with a multicoloured baseball cap, three dog walkers and a hiker. He spent the evening with a social worker who wanted to be a poet. The man offered to top up Harold's lemonade with beer but Harold declined. Alcohol had brought unhappiness in the past, he said; both to himself and those close to him. For many years he had chosen to avoid it. He talked a little about Queenie; how she liked to sing backwards, and tell a riddle, and had a sweet tooth. Her particular favourites were pear drops, sherbet lemons and liquorice. Sometimes her tongue would be a violent shade of red or purple, although he hadn't liked to tell her. 'I fetched her a glass of water and hoped that would do the trick.'

'You're a saint,' said the man, when Harold told him about walking to Berwick.

Harold crunched on a pork scratching and insisted that he wasn't. 'My wife would back me up on that.'

'You should see the people I have to deal with,' said the social worker. 'It's enough to make you give up. You really believe Queenie Hennessy is waiting?'

'I do,' said Harold.

'And that you can get to Berwick? In a pair of yachting shoes?'

'I do,' he repeated.

'Don't you ever get scared? All on your own?'

'At first I did. But I am used to it now. I know what to expect.'

The social worker's shoulders rose and dropped. He said, 'But what about other people? The sort I deal with? What will happen when you come across one of them?'

Harold thought of the people he had already met and passed. Their stories had surprised and moved him, and none had left him untouched. Already the world had more people in it for whom he cared. 'I'm an ordinary chap, passing by. I'm not the sort who stands out in a crowd. And I don't trouble anyone. When I tell people what I'm doing, they seem to understand. They look at their own lives and they want me to get there. They want Queenie to live, as much as I do.'

The social worker was listening so carefully, Harold felt a little hot. He reached for his tie and straightened it.

That night he dreamed for the first time. He got up before the images could settle, but the memory of blood sprouting from his knuckles was in his head and if he wasn't careful, worse would follow. He stood at the window, staring at the black scope of sky, and thought of his father glaring at the front door the day his mother left, as if persistence alone was enough to make it swing open and reveal her. He had set a chair there and two bottles. Hours he seemed to sit.

'She'll be back,' he had said, and Harold lay in his bed, his body so taut with listening he felt he was more silence than boy. In the morning, her frocks were strewn like empty mothers all over the small house. Some were even perched in the scrap of grass they called a front lawn.

'What's been going on?' said the lady from next door.

Harold had collected the clothes in his arms and screwed them into a ball. His mother's deep smell was so vividly present it was impossible to credit she wasn't coming back. He had had to shove his nails into his elbows in order not to make a noise. Playing the scene again, he watched the darkness loosen from the night sky. Once he was calm, he returned to bed.

A few hours later, he couldn't understand what had changed. He could hardly move. The blisters he could bear if he cushioned them with plasters, but every time he put any weight on his right foot it caused a spasmic pain to shoot from the back of his ankle into his calf. He did all his usual things; he showered, ate and repacked his plastic bag before paying his bill, but every time he tested it, the pain in his lower leg was still there. The sky was a cold cobalt blue, with the sun low over the horizon, so that vapour trails shone a luminous white. Harold followed Silver Street towards the A396, but failed to see what he passed. He had to stop every twenty minutes to roll down his sock and pinch at the muscle in his leg. To his relief there was no sign of damage.

He tried to distract himself with thinking about Queenie, or David, but none of these thoughts took shape. He would find a memory and lose it as quickly. He would recall his son saying, 'I bet you can't name all the countries in the continent of Africa'; but even as he tried to think of one, his leg would flash with pain and he would forget what it was he was trying to remember. After half a mile, it was as if his shin had been cut; he could barely put any weight on the leg. He had to use a heavy long step with his left foot, and only a skittish hop on his right. By mid-morning, the sky had filled with a dense blanket of cloud. No matter how he looked at it, he couldn't help feeling that walking north, walking up England, had become the same as climbing a hill. Even the flat stretches of road suddenly appeared to have an upward slant.

He couldn't lose the picture in his mind of his father slumped on a kitchen chair, waiting for his mother. The image had always been there, but he felt he was seeing it for the first time. His father had maybe been sick down his pyjamas. It was best

105

not to breathe through your nose.

'Go away,' he said. But his eyes swerved so fast from Harold to the walls, it was hard to tell which he found most offensive.

When they heard, neighbours consoled his father. Joan was her own person, they said. It's a blessing; at least you're young enough to start again. Suddenly there was an unprecedented abundance of female life in the house. Windows were thrown open, cupboards emptied, bedding aired. Casseroles, pies and jellied meat appeared, along with suet puddings, jams and fruitcake wrapped in brown paper. There had never been so much food; mealtimes were not of particular interest to his mother. Black and white photographs disappeared into handbags. Red lipsticks vanished from the bathroom, as did her bottles of scent. He saw her on street corners, and crossing roads. He even caught sight of her waiting for him after school, only to dash out and discover she was a lady he didn't know, wearing one of his mother's hats or skirts. Joan always liked the bright colours. His thirteenth birthday came and went, with no word from her. After six months, Harold couldn't even smell her in the bathroom cabinet. His father began to fill the spaces that had held his wife with distant relations.

'Say hello to your Aunty Muriel,' he'd say. He was out of his dressing gown. Instead he was wearing a suit that stuck out from his shoulders. He had even shaved.

'Goodness, he's big.' The woman was a wide face poking out of a fur coat, with fingers like sausages around a bag of macaroons. 'Would he like one?'

106

Harold's mouth drenched at the memory. He ate all the biscuits in his plastic bag, but they did not satisfy the craving for something that he thought was food, and he was not appeased by them. His spittle was thick and white as paste. Approaching passers-by, he hid his mouth behind his handkerchief, hoping not to cause alarm. He bought two pints of long-life milk and drank in gulps that spilled down his chin. He took it too fast but the need was so intense he couldn't reason with it; he tugged again and again at the carton with his mouth. The milk wouldn't flow swiftly enough. A few feet on, he had to stop to be sick. He couldn't stop thinking of the time his mother left.

In packing her suitcase, she had robbed him not only of her laughter but also of the only person taller than himself. You could never describe Joan as affectionate, but at least she stood between her son and the clouds. The aunts passed him sweets, or went to pinch his cheek, or even asked his opinion about the fit of a dress, but the world seemed suddenly to have no edges, and he shrank from their touch.

'I'm not saying he's odd,' his Aunty Muriel had said. 'He just doesn't look at you.'

Harold made it as far as Bickleigh, where according to his guidebook he should visit the small red-brick castle nestling on the banks of the River Exe. However, a long-faced man in olive trousers informed him that his guidebook was sadly out of date, unless Harold was interested in a luxury wedding or a murder mystery weekend. Instead he directed Harold to the craft and gift shop at Bickleigh Mill, where he might find something more to his taste and budget.

He looked at the glass trinkets and lavender bags and a selection of locally carved hanging bird feeders, but none of them struck him as desirable, or even necessary. This made him sad. He wanted to leave but since he was the only person in the shop, and the assistant was staring, he felt obliged to make a purchase. He came away with four tablemats for Queenie, offering laminated views of Devon. For his wife he chose a biro that shone a dull red when you pressed the nib, so that she could write in the dark, if she ever felt the inclination.

Harold no-mum, the boys called him at school. He began to take days off, weeks, until his classmates seemed such strangers he felt he was a different species. His Aunt Muriel wrote notes: *Harold had a headache, Harold looks pasty.* Sometimes she fetched out the dictionary and got more creative: *Harold had a spot of biliousness at about 6pm on Tuesday.* When he failed his exams he stopped going altogether.

'He's all right,' said his Aunt Vera, who took Muriel's side of the bed when she left. 'He's got some good jokes. He just mumbles the punchline.'

Weary and forlorn, Harold ordered a meal at the Fisherman's Cot, overlooking the river. He spoke with several strangers who informed him that the bridge crossing the troubled water was the inspiration for the song by Simon and Garfunkel, and all the time he felt that he was nodding and smiling, and trying to look like someone who was listening, while in reality his thoughts were preoccupied with his journey, the past, and what was happening in his leg. Was it serious? Would it

108

go away? He retired early, promising himself that sleep would heal. It didn't.

Deer son, read Joan's only letter. *New Zeeland is a wonderful plase. I had to go. Muthering was not me. Send my best regads to your dad*. It wasn't her leaving that was the worst part. It was the fact she couldn't even spell her explanation.

On Harold's tenth day, there was not an isolated moment in his walking, not one muscular flex, that did not fizz the length of his right calf and remind him he was in trouble. He remembered the urgency with which he had made his promise to the hospice nurse about walking to Queenie, and it seemed childishly inappropriate. Even his conversation with the social worker shamed him. It was as if something had happened overnight; as if the walk and his belief in it had broken into two separate pieces, and he was left only with the relentless slog. For ten days he had walked, and all his energy had been focused into the sheer act of putting one step in front of the other. But now that he had discovered his faith in his feet, the practical anxieties had been replaced by something far more insidious.

The three-and-a-half mile stretch along the A396 to Tiverton was his hardest yet. There were few spaces to hide from cars, and even though the hedges had been recently cut, offering silvery flashes of the River Exe, it gave them a barbaric appearance, and he preferred not to look. Drivers blared their horns and shouted at him to get off the road. He berated himself for managing so few miles; at this rate it would be Christmas before he reached Berwick. A child, he told himself, could have done better.

109

He remembered David dancing like a demon. He thought of the boy swimming out at Bantham. He saw again the occasion he had tried to tell his son a joke, and how David's face had creased. 'But I don't get it,' he'd said. He looked on the verge of tears. Harold had explained that the joke was funny. It was meant to make you laugh. He had told it a second time. 'I still don't understand,' the boy had said. Later Harold had heard him repeat the joke to Maureen in the bath. 'He said it was funny,' David had complained. 'He said it twice and it didn't make me laugh.' Even at that age he made the word sound dark.

And then Harold thought of his son as an eighteen-year-old; his hair flowing well below his shoulders; his arms and legs too long for clothes. He saw the young man lying on his bed with his feet on the pillow, staring so hard at nothing that Harold had briefly wondered if he saw things that Harold couldn't. His wrists were bone.

Harold heard himself saying, 'I hear from your mother you got into Cambridge.'

David had not looked at him. He kept staring at the nothing.

Harold had wanted to take him in his arms and hold on tight. He wanted to say, You beautiful boy of mine; how do you get to be so clever, when I am not? But he had looked at David's impenetrable face and said, 'Well, gosh. That's good. Golly.'

David scoffed as if he had just heard a joke that was all about his father. And Harold in turn shut the bedroom door and promised himself that one day, when his son was a full-grown man perhaps, things would be easier.

From Tiverton, Harold decided to continue with

the main roads. He reasoned that this route was the more direct. He would follow the Great Western Way and then cut across country lanes until he reached the A38. It should be twenty miles to Taunton.

A storm was coming. Clouds drew up like a hood over the earth, and threw an eerie luminous light over the Blackdown Hills. For the first time he missed his mobile phone; he felt unprepared for what lay ahead, and he wished he could speak to Maureen. The tops of the trees shone against the granite swell of the sky, and then shook as the first winds hit them. Leaves and twigs were tossed into the air. Birds cried out. In the distance, sails of rain came into view, and hung between Harold and the hills. He cowered into his jacket as the first drops hit.

There was no hiding. The rain shot at Harold's waterproof jacket and down his neck, and even up the elasticated rims of his sleeves. The drops hit like peppercorns. They swirled in pools and rivulets along the gutters, and with each passing car they sloshed over the rims of his yachting shoes. After an hour his feet were water, and his skin itched from the constant chafing of wet clothes. He didn't know if he was hungry and he couldn't remember if he had eaten. His right calf spangled with pain.

A car drew up next to him, and threw water the length of his trousers. It didn't matter. He could not get wetter. The passenger window steadily rolled downwards. There was a warm smell of new leather and heated air. Harold stooped his head.

The face on the other side was young and dry. 'Are you lost? Do you need directions?' it said.

'I know where I'm going.' The rain stung Harold's eyes. 'But thank you for stopping.'

'Nobody should be out in weather like this,' insisted the face.

'I made a promise,' said Harold, straightening up. 'But I am grateful to you for noticing me.'

For the next mile he asked himself whether he had been foolish not to ask for help. The longer he took to walk, the more unlikely it was that Queenie would keep living. And yet he was certain she was waiting. If he failed in his share of the bargain, albeit one without logic, he was afraid he would not see her again.

What should I do? Give me a sign, Queenie, he said, maybe out loud, maybe to himself. He wasn't sure any more where he officially stopped and the outside world began.

A large lorry thundered towards him, blaring a violent horn, and splattered him from head to foot with mud.

*   *   *

And yet something else happened, and it became one of those moments that he would walk into and realize, even as it was happening, that it was significant. Late in the afternoon, the rain stopped so abruptly it was hard to credit there had been any at all. To the east, the cloud tore open and a low belt of polished silver light broke through. Harold stood and watched as the mass of grey split again and again, revealing new colours: blue, burnt umber, peach, green and crimson. Then the cloud became suffused with a dulled pink, as if those vibrant colours had bled through, merging as they

112

met. He couldn't move. He wanted to witness every change. The light on the land was gold; even his skin was warm with it. At his feet the earth creaked and whispered. The air smelt green and full of beginnings. A soft mist rose, like wisps of smoke.

Harold was so tired he could barely lift his feet, and yet he felt such hope, he was giddy with it. If he kept looking at the things that were bigger than himself, he knew he would make it to Berwick.

11

MAUREEN AND THE LOCUM

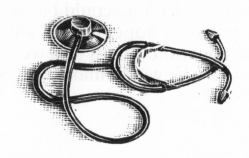

The receptionist apologized; due to the installation of an automated service, she was no longer able to check Maureen in for her doctor's appointment. 'But I am standing right here,' said Maureen. 'Why can't you do it?' The receptionist pointed to a screen set a few feet from the main desk, and assured Maureen that the new procedure was a simple one.

Maureen's fingers went clammy. The automated service asked if she was male or female, but she tapped the wrong button. It asked for her birth date, and she tapped the month before the day, and had to be helped by a young patient who sneezed all over her shoulder. By the time she had registered, there was a small queue behind her, groaning and creaking with illness. The screen flashed the words *Refer to main reception*. The small queue gave a uniform shake of its head.

Again the receptionist apologized. Maureen's regular GP had been called away unexpectedly, but she could take an appointment with a locum instead.

'Why couldn't you tell me this when I first arrived?' cried Maureen.

The receptionist offered her third round of apologies. It was the new system, she said; everyone had to check in electronically, 'Even OAPs.' She asked if Maureen would like to wait or come back the next morning, and Maureen shook her head. If she went home, she didn't trust she would have the will to return.

'Do you need a glass of water?' said the receptionist. 'You look pale.'

'I just need to sit a moment,' said Maureen.

Of course David had been right in reassuring her that she could leave the house, but he had no idea of the anxiety she would suffer in making her way to the surgery. It wasn't that she missed Harold, she told herself; but still it came as a fresh shock to find herself alone in the outside world. Everywhere around her people were doing ordinary things. They were driving cars and pushing buggies and walking dogs and coming home, as if life was exactly the same, when it wasn't. It was all new and wrong. She buttoned her coat to her neck, and pulled the tips of her collar against her ears, but the air felt too cold, and the sky too open, shapes and colours too forceful. She had rushed down Fossebridge Road before Rex could spot her, and fled to the centre of town. The petals of the daffodils along the quayside were a crumpled brown.

In the waiting room she tried to distract herself with magazines, but she looked at the words without connecting them into sentences. She was

115

aware of couples like herself and Harold, sitting side by side, keeping one another company. The late-afternoon light was sprinkled with dust motes, swirling in the thick air as if it had been stirred with a spoon.

When a young man opened the consulting-room door and mumbled a patient's name, Maureen sat waiting for someone to get up and wondering why they took so long, until she realized it was her own name and scrambled to her feet. The locum looked barely out of school, and his body didn't fill his dark suit. His shoes were polished like conkers; an image came to her from nowhere of David's school shoes, and she felt a twist of anguish. She wished she had not asked for her son's help. She wished she had stayed at home.

'What can I do for you?' murmured the locum, as he folded into his chair. Words seemed to slip out of his mouth without noise, and she had to crane her head closer in order to catch them. If she wasn't careful, he'd offer her a hearing test.

Maureen explained how her husband had set off to visit a woman he had not seen for twenty years, convinced he could save her from cancer. It was his eleventh day of walking, she said, rolling her handkerchief into a knot. 'He can't get to Berwick. He has no map. No proper shoes. When he left the house, he actually forgot his mobile.' Telling a stranger brought home the rawness of it, and she was afraid she would cry. She dared a glance at the locum's face. It was as if someone had stepped over to him while she wasn't looking and drawn in thick worry-lines with a black pen. Maybe she had said too much.

He spoke slowly, as if he were trying to

remember the right words. 'Your husband thinks he is going to save his former colleague?'

'Yes.'

'From cancer?'

'Yes.' She was beginning to feel impatient. She didn't want to have to explain; she wanted him instinctively to understand. She was not here to defend Harold.

'How does he think he will save her?'

'He seems to believe the walking will do it.'

He scowled, creating further deep lines towards his jaw. 'He thinks a walk will cure cancer?'

'A girl gave him the idea,' she said. 'A girl in a garage. She made him a burger as well. Harold never eats burgers at home.'

'A girl told him he could cure cancer?' If this appointment continued for much longer, the poor boy's face would be all over the place.

Maureen shook her head, trying to restore order. She was suddenly very tired. 'I am worried about Harold's health,' she said.

'Is he fit and well?'

'He is slightly long-sighted without his reading glasses. He has two crowns either side of his front teeth. But it's not that which worries me.'

'Yet he believes he can cure her by walking? I don't understand. Is he a religious man?'

'Harold? The only time he calls on God is when the throttle goes on the lawn mower.' She gave a smile, to help the locum realize she was being funny. The locum looked confused. 'Harold retired six months ago. Since then he has been very—' She broke off, hunting for the word. The locum shook his head, indicating he didn't have it. 'Still,' she said.

117

'Still?' he repeated.

'He spends every day in the same chair.'

At this the locum's eyes lit up and he gave a nod of relief. 'Ah. Depressed.' He lifted his pen and snapped off the lid.

'I wouldn't say he was depressed.' She felt her heart quickening. 'The thing is, Harold has Alzheimer's.' There. She had said it.

The locum's lips parted, and his jaw gave a disconcerting clunk. He returned the pen to his desk without reapplying the lid.

'He has Alzheimer's, and he's walking to Berwick?'

'Yes.'

'What medication is your husband on, Mrs Fry?' The silence was so solemn she shivered.

'I say Alzheimer's,' she said slowly, 'but it's not diagnosed as yet.'

The locum relaxed again. He almost laughed. 'Do you mean that he is forgetful? That he has senior moments? Just because we forget our mobile phone doesn't mean we all have Alzheimer's.'

Maureen gave a tight nod. She couldn't decide which irritated her most; the way he batted the term senior moments in her direction or the patronizing smile he was now showing her. 'It's in his family,' she said. 'I recognize the signs.'

From here, she gave a brief account of Harold's history; how his father had returned from the war an alcoholic, prone to depression. How his parents had not wanted a child, and his mother had packed her suitcase, never to return. She explained that his father had taken up with a succession of women until he showed Harold the door on his sixteenth

118

birthday. After that, the two men had remained estranged for many years. 'Then, out of the blue, a woman rang my husband and said she was his stepmother. You'd better fetch your father, she said; he's mad as a hatter.'

'This was the Alzheimer's?'

'I found him a nursing home but he was dead before he was sixty. We visited several times but his father shouted a lot, and threw things. He had no idea who Harold was. And now my husband is going the same way. It isn't just forgetting things. There are other symptoms.'

'Does he substitute words with inappropriate ones? Forget entire conversations? Does he leave things in strange places? Suffer rapid mood swings?'

'Yes, yes.' She gave an impatient flick of her hand.

'I see,' said the locum, chewing his lip.

Maureen smelt victory. She watched him carefully as she said, 'What I want to know is—if you, as a doctor, thought Harold was putting himself in danger by walking, could he be stopped?'

'Stopped?'

'Yes.' Her throat felt stripped. 'Could he be forced to return home?' The blood beat so hard through her head it hurt. 'He can't walk five hundred miles. He can't save Queenie Hennessy. He must be made to come back.'

Maureen's words rang through the silence. She placed her hands on her knees, palm against palm, and then she tidied her two feet one beside the other. She had said what she had set out to say, but she wasn't feeling what she had set out to feel, and needed to impose physical order on an uncomfortable emotion that was swelling inside her.

The locum grew still. From outside she heard a child crying, and wished to goodness someone would pick it up. He said, 'It sounds as if we have a strong case for getting the police involved. Has your husband ever been sectioned?'

*   *   *

Maureen rushed from the doctor's surgery, sick with shame. In explaining both Harold's past and his walk, she had been forced to see things for the first time from his point of view. The idea was insane and completely out of character, but it wasn't Alzheimer's. There was even a beauty in it, if only because Harold was doing something he believed in for once, and against all the odds. She had told the locum she needed time to think, and that she was worrying over nothing; Harold was just a little senior. He would be home soon. He might even be there already. She had ended up with a prescription for low-dosage sleeping tablets for herself.

As she walked towards the quay, the truth came as bright as a light snapping on through the dark. The reason she had stayed with Harold all these years was not David. It wasn't even because she felt sorry for her husband. She had stayed because, however lonely she was with Harold, the world without him would be even more desolate.

*   *   *

Maureen bought a single pork chop and a yellowing bunch of broccoli at the supermarket.

'Is that all?' said the girl at the check-out.

Maureen couldn't speak.

She turned into Fossebridge Road and thought of the silence of the house that lay waiting for her. The unpaid household bills, in their neat but no less intimidating pile. Her body grew heavy, her feet slow.

Rex was trimming the hedge with clippers as she reached the garden gate.

'How's the patient?' he said. 'Getting better?'

She nodded her head and went inside.

12

HAROLD AND THE CYCLING MOTHERS

Strangely, it was Mr Napier who had teamed Harold and Queenie together all those years ago. He had summoned Harold to his wood-panelled office and told him he required Queenie to check the pubs' account books on site. He didn't trust the landlords, and wanted to take them unawares. Since the lady didn't drive, however, someone was required to take her. He had thought carefully about the matter, he said, tugging on a cigarette; as one of the more senior reps, and also one of the few married ones, Harold was the obvious candidate. Mr Napier stood with his legs wide, as if by claiming more floor space he became bigger than everyone else, although actually he was a wily figure in a shiny suit, who barely reached Harold's shoulder.

Harold had no choice, of course, but to agree. Privately he was anxious. He had not spoken to Queenie since the embarrassing episode in the cupboard. And besides, he had seen his time in the car as his own. He didn't know if she would like Radio 2, for instance. He hoped she wouldn't want to talk. It was bad enough with the chaps. He was uncomfortable with female things.

'Glad that's sorted,' said Mr Napier. He held out his hand. It was disconcertingly slight and moist, like taking hold of a small reptile. 'How's the wife?'

Harold faltered. 'She's well. How's—?' He felt a cold panic. Mr Napier was on his third wife in six years; a young woman with high blonde hair, who had worked briefly as a barmaid. He didn't take it kindly when people forgot her name.

'Veronica is splendid. I hear your boy got into Cambridge.'

Mr Napier broke into a grin. His chain of thought shifted on a sixpence; Harold never knew what was coming next. 'All brain and no dick,' he said, spitting out a shot of smoke from the side of his mouth. He stood, watching and laughing, waiting for his employee to come back at him, and knowing that he wouldn't.

Harold lowered his head. On the desk stood Mr Napier's prized collection of Murano glass clowns, some with blue faces, some lounging on their backs, others playing instruments.

'Don't touch,' said Napier, and his forefinger shot out like a gun. 'They were my mother's.'

Everyone knew they were his prize possessions, but to Harold the figures looked misshapen and lurid, as if their limbs and faces had contorted like slime in the sun, and the colours congealed. He couldn't help feeling they were mocking him, even these glass clowns, and felt a wave of anger lick deep in his belly. Mr Napier twisted his cigarette in the ashtray, and moved to the door.

As Harold passed, he added, 'And keep an eye on Hennessy, will you? You know what those bitches are like.' He tapped his nose with that forefinger, as if it was now the pointer to a shared secret, and not a gun, except of course Harold had no idea what he was talking about.

He wondered if, despite her aptitude, Mr Napier was already trying to get rid of her. His boss never trusted the people who were better than himself.

The first drive came a few days later. Queenie appeared at his car, gripping her square handbag, as if she was off on a shopping trip instead of an inspection of a pub's account books. Harold knew the landlord of the pub; he was a slippery chap at the best of times. He couldn't help feeling afraid for her.

'I hear you're driving me, Mr Fry,' she said, slightly imperious.

They travelled in silence. She sat beside him, very neat, her hands tucked in a tight ball in her lap. Harold had never felt so conscious of how he took the corners, or pressed his foot into the clutch, or pulled at the handbrake when they arrived. He leapt out to open the passenger door, and waited as her leg slowly emerged and groped for the pavement. Maureen's ankles were so slim they made him weak with desire. Queenie's on the other hand were thick. Rather like himself, he had felt, she lacked physical definition.

When he glanced up he was mortified to find her staring straight back at him. 'Thank you, Mr Fry,' she said at last, clipping away, with the handbag wedged on her arm.

It therefore came as a surprise, when he was checking the beer levels, to find the landlord beetroot-faced and dripping sweat.

'Fuck me,' he said, 'that little woman's a demon. You can't get a thing past her.'

Harold felt a small rush of admiration, touched with pride.

On the journey back, she was silent and still again. He even wondered if she was asleep, but it seemed rude to look, in case she wasn't. He pulled into the yard at the brewery and she said suddenly, 'Thank you.'

He muttered something awkward about it being a pleasure.

'I mean, thank you for a few weeks ago,' she said. 'The time in the stationery cupboard.'

'Don't mention it,' said Harold, meaning exactly that.

'I was very upset. You were kind to me. I should have said thank you before but I was embarrassed. That was wrong.'

He couldn't meet her eye. He knew, without looking at her, that she was biting her lip.

'I was glad to help.' He reapplied the poppers on his driving gloves.

'You're a gentleman,' she said, spreading the word into two halves so that for the first time he saw it for what it meant: a gentle man. With that, she opened her door before he could do it for her, and stepped out of his car. He watched her pick her way across the yard, steady and neat, in her brown suit, and it broke his heart. The honest plainness of her. He had got into bed that night and silently promised that whatever Mr Napier had meant by his obscure remark, Harold would be

125

true to it. He would look out for Queenie.

Maureen's voice had sailed through the dark. 'I hope you're not going to snore.'

*   *   *

On the twelfth day, an endless bed of grey moved over the sky and land, bringing sheets of rain that smudged the colour and contours out of everything. Harold stared ahead, straining to find a sense of direction, or the break in the cloud that had so delighted him, but it was like looking at the world through net curtains again. Everything was the same. He stopped referring to his guidebooks because the gap between their sense of knowing and his own of not knowing was too unbearable. He felt he was fighting his body, and failing.

His clothes no longer dried. The leather of his shoes was so bloated with water, they lost their shape. Whitnage. Westleigh. Whiteball. So many places beginning with W. Trees. Hedgerows. Telegraph poles. Houses. Recycling bins. He left his razor and shaving foam in the shared bathroom of a guesthouse, and lacked the energy to replace them. Inspecting his feet, he was alarmed to discover that the burning in his calf had taken physical shape, and was a violent stain of crimson beneath the surface of the skin. For the first time, he was very frightened.

In Sampford Arundel, Harold phoned Maureen. He needed to hear her voice, and he wanted her to remind him why he was walking, even if she did it in anger. He didn't want her to suspect the doubt he was suffering, or the difficulty with his leg, so he asked how she was, and also the house; and she told him they were both well. She in turn asked if he was still walking, and he said that he had passed Exeter and Tiverton and was on his way to Bath, via Taunton. Was there anything he wanted sending on? His mobile, his toothbrush, his pyjamas or spare clothes? There was a kindness in her voice, but he was surely imagining it.

'I'm all right,' he said.

'So you must almost be in Somerset?'

'I'm not sure. I suppose I must.'

'How many miles today?'

'I don't know. Maybe seven.'

'Well, well,' she said.

The rain beat the roof of the phone box, and the dim light beyond the windows was like something fluid. He wanted to stay, talking to Maureen, but the silence and the distance, which they had nursed for twenty years, had grown to such a point that even clichés were empty and they hurt.

At last she said, 'Well, I must get going, Harold. Lots to do.'

'Yes. Me too. I just wanted to say hello and everything. Check you were all right.'

'Oh, I'm very well. Very busy. The days whizz by. I hardly notice you've gone. And you?'

'I'm very well too.'

'That's all right then.'

'Yes.'

Eventually there was nothing left. He only said, 'Well, goodbye Maureen,' because it was a sentence. He didn't want to hang up any more than he wanted to walk.

He looked out at the rain, waiting for it to break, and saw a crow with its head bowed, its feathers so wet they shone like tar. He wished the bird would move, but it sat sodden and alone. Maureen was so busy she had hardly noticed Harold had gone.

*   *   *

On Sunday it was almost lunchtime when he woke. The pain in his leg was no better, and the rain was still falling. He could hear the world outside, going about its business; the traffic, the people, all rushing to other things. No one knew who or where he was. He lay not moving, not wanting to face another day's walking, and yet knowing he couldn't go home. He remembered how Maureen used to lie at his side, and he pictured her nakedness; how perfect it was, and how small. He yearned for the softness of her fingers as they crept their passage over his skin.

When Harold reached for his yachting shoes, they were paper thin at the soles. He didn't shower or shave or inspect his feet, although putting them into his shoes felt like cramming them into cases. He dressed without thinking of anything because thinking would only lead to the obvious. The landlady insisted he could have a late breakfast, but he declined. If he accepted her kindness, if he so much as caught her eye, he was afraid he would cry.

Harold kept going from Sampford Arundel but hated every step. He screwed his face against the pain. It didn't matter what people thought; he was outside them anyway. He wouldn't stop, though his body cried out for rest. He was angry with himself for being so frail. The rain drove at him in slants. His shoes were so spent, he might as well not be

128

wearing them. He missed Maureen and could think of nothing else.

How was it that things had gone so wrong? They had been happy once. If David had caused a rift between them as he grew, it had been a complicit one. 'Where's David?' Maureen might ask, and Harold would simply reply that he had heard the front door shutting as he cleaned his teeth. 'Ah yes,' she would say, to show it wasn't a problem that their eighteen-year-old son had taken to wandering the streets at night. To voice Harold's private fears would only compound hers. And the fact was she still cooked in those days. She still shared Harold's bed.

But such unspoken tensions could not hide themselves for ever. It was just before Queenie's disappearance that things had finally ripped open and splintered apart. Maureen had railed. She had sobbed. She had beat his chest with her fists. 'Call yourself a man?' she had howled. And another time: 'It's your fault. All this. It would have been fine, if it hadn't been for you.'

It had been unbearable to hear those things, and even though she had wept in his arms afterwards, and apologized, they were in the air when he was alone, and there was no unsaying them. It all came from Harold.

And then it had stopped. The talking, the shouting, the catching his eye. This new silence was different from before. Whereas once they had wished to spare one another pain, now there was nothing left to salvage. She didn't even have to give voice to the words in her head. He knew simply by looking at her that there was not a word, not a gesture, he could say or do to make amends. She no longer blamed Harold. She no longer cried in front of him; she wouldn't allow him the comfort of holding her. She moved her clothes into the spare room and he lay in their marital bed, not going to her because she didn't want him, but tortured by her sobs. Morning would come. They would use the bathroom at different times. He would dress and eat breakfast while she paced from room to room, as if he was not there, as if never keeping still was the only way to contain a person's feelings. 'I'm off.' 'OK then.' 'See you later.' 'Yes. OK.'

The words meant nothing. They might as well have been Chinese. There was no bridging the gap that lies between two human beings. Just before his retirement, he had suggested they might for once go to the brewery Christmas party and she had stared back at him with her mouth gaping as if he was guilty of assault.

Harold stopped looking at the hills, the sky and the trees. He stopped looking for the road signs that would mark his journey north. He walked against the wind, with his head bowed, seeing only rain because that was all there was. The A38 was far worse than he had imagined. He stuck to the hard shoulder, and walked behind the barrier when he could, but traffic tore past at such speed he was drenched and constantly in danger. After several hours, he realized he had been so lost in remembering and mourning the past, he had wasted two miles heading in the wrong direction. There was nothing for it but to retrace his steps.

Walking the road already travelled was even harder. It was like not moving at all. It was worse; like eating into a part of himself. West of Bagley

Green, he gave up and stopped at a farmhouse advertising accommodation.

His host was a worried-looking man, who said he had one available room. The others were occupied by six female cyclists on the trail from Land's End to John o'Groats. 'They're all mothers,' he said. 'You get the impression they're letting their hair down.' He warned Harold it might be better to keep a low profile.

Harold slept poorly. He was dreaming again, and the mother-cyclists seemed to be having a party. Harold slipped between sleep and consciousness, afraid of the pain in his leg but desperate to forget it. The women's voices became those of the aunts who had replaced his mother. There was laughter, and a grunt as his father emptied himself. Harold lay with his eyes wide, and his leg throbbing, wishing the night was over and he was somewhere else.

In the morning the pain had worsened. The skin above his heel was streaked with purple, and so swollen it would barely fit inside the shoe. He had to ram it home, wincing at the pain. He caught his face in the mirror, and it was haggard and burnt, covered in sharp stubble like pinheads. He looked ill. All he could picture was his father in the nursing home, with his slippers on the wrong feet. 'Say hello to your son,' the carer had said. Catching sight of Harold, his father had begun to shake.

*   *   *

Harold hoped to finish his breakfast before the cycling mothers awoke but just as he was draining his coffee they descended on the farmhouse dining room in a burst of fluorescent Lycra and laughter.

'You know what,' said one, 'I don't know how I am going to get on that bike again.' The others laughed. Of the six women, she was the loudest and gave the impression of being the ringleader. Harold hoped that by remaining quiet he would go unnoticed, but she caught his eye and winked. 'I hope we didn't disturb you,' she said.

She was dark-skinned with a skeletal face and hair cropped so close her scalp looked fragile. He couldn't help wishing she had a hat. These girls were her life support, she told Harold; she didn't know where she'd be without them. She lived in a small flat with her daughter. 'I'm not the settling kind,' she said. 'I don't need a man.' She named all the things she could do without one. It seemed to Harold there were an awful lot, though she spoke at such speed he had to concentrate on her mouth in order to understand. It took effort to keep watching and listening, and taking her in, when within himself there was such pain. 'I'm free as a bird,' she said, and she stuck out her arms to show what she meant. Puffs of dark hair sprouted from her armpits.

There was a round of wolf whistles, and cries of 'Go, girl!' Harold felt the need to join in, but could only go so far as a light clapping of his hands. The woman laughed and smacked her palm against theirs, although there was something febrile about her independence that made him nervous on her behalf.

'I sleep with who I want. I had my daughter's piano teacher last week. I had a Buddhist on my yoga retreat, and he was sworn to celibacy.' Several of the mothers whooped.

The only woman with whom Harold had slept was Maureen. Even when she threw away her cookery books, and had her hair cut short, even when he heard her doorlock click at night, he had not looked for anyone else. He knew other chaps at the brewery had affairs. There had once been a bar lady who laughed at his jokes, even the poor ones, and nudged a glass of whisky across the bar so that their hands almost touched. But he hadn't the stomach for more. He could never imagine himself with anyone other than Maureen; they had shared so much. To live without her would be like scooping out the vital parts of himself, and he would be no more than a fragile envelope of skin.

He found himself congratulating the cycling mother, because he wasn't sure what else to do, and then he stood to make his excuses. A flash shot up his leg so that he stumbled and had to reach for the table. He pretended to be scratching his arm while it came and went, and came again.

'Bon voyage,' said the cycling mother. She rose to embrace him, bringing a thick smell of citrus and sweat that was half pleasant and half not so. She laughed as she pulled back and rested her arms on his shoulders. 'Free as a bird,' she told him; her face very full of it.

He felt a chill in his heart. Glancing beyond himself, he saw that her inner arm was lacerated with two deep scars that scissored the flesh between her wrist and elbow. In places, one still wore the beads of a scab. He nodded stiffly, and wished her luck.

*   *   *

Harold couldn't go for more than fifteen minutes without needing to stop and rest his right leg. His back, neck, arms and shoulders were so sore he thought of little else. The rain drove at him in thick pins that bounced off the roofs and tarmac. After only an hour, he was stumbling and desperate to stop. There were trees ahead and something red that was maybe a flag. People left the strangest things at the roadside.

The rain plashed on the leaves, making them shiver, and the air smelt of the soft leaf mould at his feet. As Harold grew closer to the flag, his shoulders hunched. The splash of red was not a flag. It was a Liverpool FC T-shirt, hanging from a wooden cross.

He had passed several roadside memorials but none of them disturbed him so much as this one. He told himself to walk on the other side and not look, but he couldn't. He was drawn to it, like something he shouldn't see. Evidently a relative or friend had decorated the cross with glittery Christmas baubles in the shape of pine trees, and a plastic wreath of holly. Harold examined the wilting flowers in cellophane, bled of colour, and a photograph in a plastic wallet. The man was maybe in his forties, thickset, with dark hair, and had a child's hand trailing his shoulder. He was grinning at the camera. *To the best dad in the world*, read the words on a sodden card.

What eulogy would you write for the worst one? 'Fuck you,' David had hissed, as his legs failed him and he seemed to be in danger of catapulting down the stairs. 'Fuck you.'

Harold wiped the rain from the photograph with a clean corner of his handkerchief, and flicked it

134

from the flowers. As he walked on, all he could think of was the cycling mother. He wondered when it was that she had felt so desolate she had cut her arm, and left it to bleed. He wondered who had found her, and what they had done. Had she wanted to be saved? Or had they dragged her back to life, just as she believed she was free of it? He wished he could have said something; something to make her never do it again. If he had comforted her, he could have let her go. As it was, he knew that in meeting her, and listening, he was carrying another weight in his heart and he wasn't sure how much more of that he could take. Despite the pain in his calf and the cold in his bones, despite the trouble in his mind, he drove himself harder.

Harold reached the outskirts of Taunton by late afternoon. The houses were packed together, and studded with satellite dishes. At the windows hung grey net drapes; some were boarded with metal shutters. The few gardens that were not concrete had been flattened by rain. The blossom of a cherry tree lay scattered like wet paper across the pavement. The traffic sped past so loud it hurt and the roads looked oiled.

A memory surged into his mind, one of those that Harold most feared. He was normally so good at repressing them. He tried to think about Queenie, but even that wouldn't work. He shot his elbows out sideways to go faster and drove his feet against the paving stones with such fury he hadn't the breathing to keep up. But nothing would hide him from the memory of an afternoon twenty years ago when it had all come to an end. He could see his hand reaching for the wooden door; feel the warmth of the sun on his shoulders; smell the mouldering, heated-up air; hear the stillness of a silence that was not what it should be.

'No,' he shouted, batting out at the rain.

Suddenly his calf exploded as if the skin-side of the muscle had been sliced open. The ground tipped at an angle, and seemed to swell. He reached out a hand to stop it, but in the same moment his knees buckled and his body lurched to the ground. He felt his hands and knees smart.

Forgive me. Forgive me. For letting you down.

The next thing he knew, someone was tugging at his arms, and shouting about an ambulance.

13

HAROLD AND THE DOCTOR

Harold's collapse caused cuts to his knees and hands, and bruising on both elbows. The woman who rescued him had spotted his fall from her bathroom window. She helped Harold to his feet and retrieved the contents of his plastic bag, and then she supported him across the road, waving at traffic. 'Doctor, doctor!' she shouted. Inside her house, she led him to an easy chair and loosened his tie. The room seemed sparse and cold; a television had been angled on top of a packing box. Close by, a dog was barking behind a closed door. Harold had never been comfortable with dogs.

'Did I break anything?' he said.

She said words he couldn't understand.

'There was a pot of honey,' he said, more panicky. 'Is it still in one piece?'

The woman nodded and reached for his pulse. She covered his wrist with her fingertips and stared into the middle distance, as if seeing shapes beyond the walls, while she counted under her breath. She was young, but her face had a scraped-back look, and her jogging trousers and sweatshirt hung from her body, suggesting they belonged to someone else. A man, perhaps.

'I don't need a doctor,' Harold said with a hoarse whisper. 'Please don't call an ambulance or a doctor.'

Harold didn't want to be in her house. He didn't want to take up her time or get close to another stranger, and he was afraid she would send him home. He wanted to speak to Maureen, but he was also afraid he wouldn't know what to say without troubling her. He wished he hadn't given in to his fall. It had been in him to keep going.

The young woman passed a mug of tea, offering the handle so that he wouldn't burn his fingers. She was saying something else but he couldn't make it out. He tried to smile as if he had understood but she kept looking at him, waiting for his reply, and then she said it again, with more volume and less speed: 'What the fuck were you doing out there in the rain?'

He realized now that she had a thick accent. Eastern European maybe. He and Maureen read about people like her in the news. They came over for the benefits, the papers said. Meanwhile, the dog was increasingly sounding not like a dog and more like a wild beast. It was hurling its full body weight against its temporary imprisonment, and sounded in danger of biting at least one of them when free. You read about dogs like that in the papers as well.

Harold reassured her that as soon as he had finished his tea, he would get going. He told his story, which she heard in silence. This was why he

138

couldn't stop or see a doctor; he had made a promise to Queenie and he must not fail her. He took a sip from his mug, and looked at the window. A large tree trunk stood right in front of it. Its roots were probably damaging the house and it needed cutting back. Beyond, the traffic came at fast intervals. The thought of returning outside filled him with dread, and yet he had no choice. When he looked back to the young woman she was still watching him, and still not smiling.

'But you're fucked.' She said it without emotion or judgement.

'Ah yes,' said Harold.

'Your shoes are fucked. So is your body. And your spectacles.' She held up the two halves of his reading glasses, one in each hand. 'Every way you look at it, you're fucked. How do you think you're going to make it to Berwick?'

It reminded him of the very deliberate way in which David swore; as if he had carefully considered all the options and, given what he felt for his father, the foulest expressions were the only ones suitable.

'I am—as you rightly point out—fucked.' Harold hung his head. His trousers were splattered with mud, and frayed at the knees. His shoes were sodden. He wished he had taken them off at the door. 'I admit it is an awfully long way to Berwick. I admit I am wearing the wrong clothes. And I also admit I have not the training, or the physique, for my walk. I can't explain why I think I can get there, when all the odds are against it. But I do. Even when a big part of me is saying I should give up, I can't. Even when I don't want to keep going, I still do it.' He faltered because what he was saying was

139

difficult and caused him anguish. 'I am terribly sorry but my shoes appear to have wet your carpet.'

To his surprise, when he stole a glance at the young woman, she was smiling for the first time. She offered him a room for the night.

*   *   *

At the bottom of the stairs, she kicked the door that housed the angry dog with the underside of her foot, and told Harold to follow. He was afraid of the dog and he didn't want her to worry about the amount of pain he was in, so he tried to keep up with her. The truth was that his knees and palms felt spiked after his fall, and he couldn't put any weight on his right leg. The woman told him that her name was Martina; she was from Slovakia. He would have to excuse this shithole, she said, and also the noise. 'We thought this fucking place was temporary.' Harold tried to make his face look like that of someone who was used to her sort of language. He didn't want to appear judgemental.

'I curse too much,' she said, as if reading his thoughts.

'It's your house, Martina. You must say what you like.'

The dog was still barking and clawing the paintwork behind the door below.

'Shut the fuck up,' she yelled. Harold could see the fillings at the back of her teeth.

'My son always wanted a dog,' he said.

'It's not mine. It's my partner's.' She threw open the door of an upstairs room and stood aside to let him enter.

The room smelt of emptiness and new paint. The walls were a stark white, with a purple bedspread that matched the curtains, and three sequined cushions over the pillows. It touched Harold that Martina, for all her bitterness, had taken such care over her soft furnishings. At the window, the upper branches and leaves of the tree crushed themselves against the glass. She said she hoped Harold would be comfortable, and he assured her that he would. Left alone, he eased his body on to the bed, and felt every muscle throbbing. He knew he should examine the cuts, and wash them, but he hadn't the will to move. He hadn't even the will to remove the shoes from his feet.

He didn't know how he was going to carry on like this. He was frightened, and he felt alone. It reminded him of his teens; of hiding in his room, while his father crashed into bottles or made love to the aunts. He wished he hadn't accepted Martina's offer to stay the night. Maybe she was already phoning a doctor? He could hear her voice downstairs, although listening hard he didn't recognize any of the words. Maybe it was her partner. Maybe her partner would insist on driving Harold home.

He pulled Queenie's letter from his pocket, but without his reading glasses the words spilled into one another.

Dear Harold, This may come to you as some surprise. I know it is a long time since we last met, but recently I have been thinking about the past. Last year I had an operation on a tumour, but the cancer has spread and there is nothing left to be done. I am at peace, and comfortable, but I would like to thank you for the friendship you showed me all those years ago. Please send my regards to your wife. I still think of David with fondness. With my best wishes.

He could hear her steady voice as clearly as if she were standing before him. But the shame. The shame of being the one who had let down a good woman, and never done anything about it.

'Harold. Harold.'

He must get there. He must get to Berwick. He must find her.

'Are you all right?'

He stirred himself. The voice wasn't that of Queenie. It was the woman whose room he was using. It was Martina. He was finding it hard to distinguish the past from the present.

'Can I come in?' she called.

Harold tried to stand, but the door opened before he made it to his feet, so that she caught him in an odd crouched position, half on the bed and half not. She stood at the threshold, holding a washing-up bowl, and two towels over one arm. In the other hand she held a plastic first-aid box. 'For your feet,' she said, nodding in the direction of his yachting shoes.

'You can't wash my feet.' Harold was standing now.

'I'm not here to wash them, but you're walking funny. I need to look.'

'They're fine. There is no problem.'

She frowned impatiently, and slouched with the

weight of the plastic bowl on her hip. 'So how do you take care of them?'

'I put on plasters.'

Martina laughed but not in a way that suggested she was amused. 'If you think you're going to get to fucking Berwick, we need to get you right, Harold.'

It was the first time anyone had referred to his walk as a shared responsibility. He could have wept with gratitude, but instead he nodded and sat back down.

Martina knelt and retied her ponytail, and then she carefully spread one of her towels on the carpet, smoothing out the folds. The only sound came from the traffic and the rain and the wind, jamming the branches of the tree with shrill cries at the glass. The light was dimming, but she did not put on a lamp. She held out her cupped hands, waiting.

Harold removed his socks and shoes, although it hurt to bend, and unpeeled the most recent set of plasters. He could sense her watching carefully. As he set his naked feet side by side, he couldn't help but see them through the eyes of a stranger and he was shocked, as if he were noticing them for the first time. They were an unhealthy white, verging on grey, the indent of his socks making ridges into the skin. Blisters swelled from his toes, heels and instep; some bleeding, others inflamed sacs of pus. The nail of his big toe was tough as a hoof, and a dark blueberry colour where it had rammed against the end of his shoe. A thickened layer of skin grew over his heel, cracked in places and also bleeding. He had to hold his breath against the smell.

'You don't want to see any more.'

143

'I do,' she said. 'Roll up your trouser leg.'

He winced as the fabric brushed over his right calf and scalded it. He had never let a stranger touch his bare skin before. He remembered how he had stood on his wedding night in the hotel bathroom in Holt, frowning at the reflection of his bare chest, and fearing Maureen would be disappointed.

Martina was still waiting. She said, 'It's OK. I know what I am doing. I'm trained.'

Harold's right foot shot of its own accord behind his left ankle, and hid there. 'You mean you're a nurse?'

She gave him a sardonic look. 'A doctor. Women are these days. I trained in a hospital in Slovakia. That's where I met my partner. He worked there too. Give me your foot, Harold. I won't send you home. I promise.'

He had no choice. Gently she lifted his ankle, and he felt the soft warmth of her palms. She touched the skin, working her path to the sole of his foot. Catching sight of the bruising above his right ankle, she winced and stopped, and craned her face closer. Her fingers crept over the damaged muscle, and sent a spasm fireworking deep inside his leg.

'Does that hurt?'

It did. Very much. He had to clench the insides of his buttocks, in order not to grimace. 'Not really.'

She lifted his leg and peered at the underside. 'The bruise goes all the way to the back of the knee.'

'It doesn't hurt,' he repeated.

'If you continue to walk on this leg, it will get

144

worse. And these blisters need treating. The bigger ones I will drain. Afterwards we'll bandage your feet. You need to learn how to do that.'

He watched as she punctured the first pocket of pus with a needle. He didn't flinch. She pressed out the fluid, careful to leave the flap of skin intact. Harold allowed her to guide his left foot towards the bucket of soft, warm water. It was an intensely private act; almost between the woman and his foot, and not the rest of him. He looked at the ceiling so as not to look in the wrong place. It was such an English thing to do, but he did it anyway.

He had always been too English; by which he supposed he meant that he was ordinary. He lacked colour. Other people knew interesting stories, or had things to ask. He didn't like to ask, because he didn't like to offend. He wore a tie every day but sometimes he wondered if he was hanging on to an order or a set of rules that had never really existed. Maybe it would have been different if he'd had a proper education. Finished school. Gone to university. As it was, his father had presented him with an overcoat on his sixteenth birthday and shown him the door. The coat wasn't new; it smelt of mothballs, and there was a bus ticket in the inside pocket.

'It seems sad to see him go,' said his Aunty Sheila, though she didn't cry. Of all the aunts she had been his favourite. She bent towards him to offer a kiss, bringing such waves of scent he had to walk away in order not to be silly and hug her.

It had come as a relief to leave his childhood behind. And even though he had done what his father never had—he had found work, supported a wife and son, and loved them, if only from the

145

sidelines—it sometimes occurred to Harold that the silence of his early years had followed him into his marital home, and lodged itself behind the carpet and curtains and wallpaper. The past was the past; there was no escaping your beginnings. Not even with a tie.

Wasn't David the proof of that?

Martina lifted his foot to her lap and dried it in a soft towel, taking care not to rub. She squirted antibiotic cream on to her finger and applied it in small strokes. A deep blush mottled the soft dip below her throat. Her face was knotted with concentration. 'You should be wearing two pairs of socks. Not one. And why haven't you got walking boots?' She didn't look up.

'I intended to buy them when I got to Exeter. But then, after so much time on the road, I changed my mind. I looked at the shoes on my feet and they seemed perfectly all right. I couldn't see why I needed new ones.'

Martina caught his eye and smiled. He felt he had said something that pleased her, and which forged a connection between them. She told him her partner liked walking. They were planning a summer holiday in the Fells. 'Maybe you could borrow his old boots? He bought a new pair. They're still in their box in my wardrobe.' Harold insisted he was happy with yachting shoes. He felt a sort of loyalty to them, he said.

'If my partner's blisters are really bad, he binds them with duct tape to keep going.' She wiped her hands with a paper towel. The movement was slick and reassuring.

'I think you must be a good doctor,' said Harold.

She rolled her eyes. 'I only get cleaning work in

England. You think your feet are bad. You should see the fucking lavatories I have to scrub at.' They both laughed, and then, 'Did your son ever get his dog?' she said.

A sharp pain bolted through him. Her fingers stopped suddenly and she looked up, afraid she had found another bruise. He held his body taut and calmed his breathing, until he was able to form words. 'No. I wish he had, but he didn't. I am afraid I failed my son very badly twenty years ago.'

Martina leaned back, as if she needed a new perspective. 'Your son and Queenie? You failed them both?'

She was the first person to ask about David in a long time. Harold wanted to say something else, but he had no idea where to begin. Sitting in a house he didn't know, with his trousers rolled up to his knees, he missed his son very much. 'It isn't good enough. It never will be.' Tears stung his eyes. He blinked to hold them back.

Martina broke off a ball of cotton wool to wash the cuts on his palms. The antiseptic stung the broken skin, but he didn't move. He offered his hands and let her clean them.

*   *   *

Martina lent him her phone, but when Harold rang Maureen the line was bad. He tried to explain where he was, but she didn't seem to understand. 'You're staying with whom?' she kept saying. Not wanting to mention his leg, or his fall, he told her that his walk was going well. Time was flying.

Martina gave him a mild painkiller but he slept badly. The traffic kept waking him, and the rain

147

thrashing at the tree by the window. Periodically he checked his calf, hoping the leg was better, flexing it softly but not daring to put weight on it. He pictured David's room, with the blue curtains, and his own with the wardrobe that held only his suits and shirts, and then the spare room that smelt of Maureen, until slowly he fell asleep.

The following morning Harold stretched first his left side and then his right, pulling each joint one by one, yawning until his eyes watered. He could hear no rain. The light from the window passed through the leaves of the tree outside, sending shadows that rippled like water on the whitened wall. He stretched again and immediately fell back to sleep, not waking again until it was past eleven.

After examining his leg, Martina said it looked a little better, but she would not advise him to walk. She changed the bandages on his feet, and asked if he would spend one more day resting; her partner's dog would like the company while she worked. The animal was too much alone.

'An aunt of mine had a dog,' he said. 'It used to bite me when no one was looking.' Martina laughed, and so did Harold; although it had been a source of great loneliness and not inconsiderable pain at the time. 'My mother left home just before my thirteenth birthday. She and my father were very unhappy. He drank and she wanted to travel. That's all I remember. After she went, he got worse for a while, and then the neighbours found out. They loved mothering him. My father suddenly blossomed. He brought home many aunts. He became a bit of a Casanova.' Harold had never spoken so openly about his past. He hoped he didn't sound pitiful.

148

Martina gave a smile that wriggled on her lips. 'Aunts? Were they real ones?'

'Metaphorical ones. He met them in pubs. They would stay for a while and then they would go. Every month the house smelt of new scent. There was always different underwear on the washing line. I used to lie on the grass, looking up. I had never seen anything so beautiful.'

Her smile tipped into another laugh. He noticed how Martina's face softened when she was happy, and how the colour suited her cheeks. A strand of hair escaped from the tight ponytail. He was glad she didn't scrape it back.

For a moment all he could see in his mind's eye was Maureen's young face; gazing up at his, opened up, almost stripped, her soft mouth parted, waiting for what he might say next. The recalled thrill of landing her attention was so powerful Harold wished he could think of something else to amuse Martina; but he couldn't.

She said, 'Did you never see your mother again?'

'No.'

'You never looked for her?'

'Sometimes I wish I had. I would have liked to tell her I was all right, in case she was worrying. But she wasn't cut out to be a mother. Maureen was the opposite. She seemed to know how to love David right from the start.'

He fell silent, and so did Martina. He felt safe with what he had confided. It had been the same with Queenie. You could say things in the car and know she had tucked them somewhere safe among her thoughts, and that she would not judge him for them, or hold it against him in years to come. He

149

supposed that was what friendship was, and regretted all the years he had spent without it.

* * *

In the afternoon, while Martina did her cleaning job, Harold fixed his reading glasses with plasters and then he wedged open the back door, in order to clear the small garden. The dog sat watching him with interest, but it didn't bark. Harold found her partner's tools and tidied the edges of the lawn, and pruned back the branches of the hedge. His leg was very stiff, and since he couldn't remember what he had done with his shoes, he walked with bare feet. The warm dust worked on his heels like velvet, and melted the tension. He wondered if he had time to tackle the tree that obscured the bedroom window, but it was too high and there was no ladder.

When she returned from work, Martina presented him with a brown paper bag inside which he found his yachting shoes, resoled and polished. She had even given them fresh laces.

'You don't get service like that on the NHS,' she said, moving away before he could thank her.

* * *

That night they ate together, and Harold reminded her she must let him pay for the room. She said they would see one another again in the morning, but Harold shook his head. He would be gone with the first light; he needed to make up for lost time. The dog sat at his feet, its head resting on Harold's lap. 'I'm sorry I didn't get to meet your partner,' he said.

Martina frowned. 'He isn't coming back.'

The shock hit him like a blow. He was suddenly having to reconfigure his idea of Martina and her life, and the abruptness of that seemed brutal. 'I don't understand,' he said. 'Where is he?'

'I don't know.' Martina's face buckled. She pushed aside her plate, although she had not finished.

'How can you not know?'

'I bet you think I'm fucking crazy.'

Harold thought of the people he had already met on his journey. All of them were different, but none struck him as strange. He considered his own life and how ordinary it might look from the outside, when really it held such darkness and trouble. 'I don't think you're crazy,' he said. He offered his hand, and she studied it a moment as if a hand was something she had not considered holding before. Her fingers touched his.

'We came to England so that he could get better work. We'd only been here a few months. Then one Saturday a woman turns up with two suitcases and a baby. He has a kid, she says.' Martina gripped harder and crushed his wedding ring against his fingers. 'I didn't know about the other woman. I didn't know about the kid. He came back and I thought he was going to boot them out. I knew how much he loved me. But he didn't. He picked up his baby and it was like seeing a man I didn't know. I said I was going for a walk. When I got back, they had gone.' Martina's skin was so pale he could see the veins on her eyelids. 'He left all his things. His dog. His gardening tools. Even the new boots. He loves walking. Every day I wake

151

up and I think, Today is the one he will come back. And every day, he doesn't.'

For a while there was only the silence that carried her words. It struck Harold afresh how life could change in an instant. You could be doing something so everyday—walking your partner's dog, putting on your shoes—and not knowing that everything you wanted you were about to lose.

'He might come back.'

'It was a year ago.'

'You never know.'

'I do.'

She gave a sniff as if she had a cold coming, although she wasn't fooling either of them. 'And yet here you are, walking to Berwick-upon-Tweed.' He was afraid she was going to point out again that he couldn't make it, but she said, 'If only I had a shred of your faith.'

'But you do.'

'No,' she said. 'I'm waiting for something that will never happen.'

She sat, not moving, and he knew she was thinking of the past. He knew too that his faith, such as it was, was a fragile thing.

Harold cleared their plates, and took them to the kitchen, where he ran hot water into the sink and rinsed the dirty pans. He gave the leftover scraps to the dog and thought of Martina waiting for a man who would not return. He thought of his wife, scrubbing away at stains he could not see. He felt in a strange way that he understood better, and wished he could tell Maureen that.

Later, as he packed his plastic bag in his room, a slight rustling from the hall, followed by a knock, took him to the door. Martina handed him two

152

pairs of walking socks, as well as a roll of blue duct tape. Then she hooked an empty rucksack over his wrist, and placed a brass compass in his palm. They had been her partner's things. He was about to insist he couldn't take anything more, but she nipped her face towards his, and planted a soft kiss on his cheek. 'Go well, Harold,' she said. 'And you owe me nothing for the room. You were my guest.' The compass was warm and heavy in his hand.

*   *   *

Harold left as he had said he would, with the first light. He propped a postcard against his pillow, in which he thanked Martina; and also the set of laminated place mats because her need for them might be greater than Queenie's. To the east the night had cracked open, revealing a pale band of light that began to climb and fill the sky. He patted her partner's dog at the foot of the stairs.

Harold closed the front door quietly, not wishing to wake Martina, but she was watching from her bathroom window, with her face pressed to the glass. He didn't look back. He didn't wave. He caught her profile at the window and then stepped as boldly as he could, wondering if she was worrying about his blisters, or his yachting shoes, and wishing he was not leaving her alone, with only a dog and some boots. It had been hard being her guest. It was hard to understand a little and then walk away.

14

MAUREEN AND REX

After her conversation with the locum, Maureen sank into a further decline. She thought with shame of the visit Queenie Hennessy had paid her twenty years ago, and wished she had been kinder.

Now, without Harold, the endless passage of days flowed one into the other and she watched them with apathy, not knowing how to fill them. She would decide to strip the beds only to realize there was no point, since there was no one to witness her slamming down the wash basket, or complaining that she could manage perfectly well without help, thank you. She opened the road map on the kitchen table, but every time she looked at it, trying to picture Harold's journey, she felt her loneliness more keenly. Inside her stretched such an emptiness, it was as if she were invisible.

Maureen heated a small tin of tomato soup. How had it happened that Harold was walking to Berwick while she sat at home, doing nothing? What were the steps she had missed? Unlike him, she had left school with decent qualifications. She had done a secretarial course, and when David was at primary school she had taught herself French with the Open University. She used to love gardening. There once wasn't an inch of the plot at Fossebridge Road that didn't bear fruit or flowers. She had cooked every day. She had read Elizabeth David and took pleasure in seeking out new ingredients. 'Today we are Italian,' she'd laugh, kicking open the door to the dining room and presenting David and Harold with an asparagus risotto. '*Buon appetito.*' The regrets about all she had let go flooded her. Where had all that enterprise gone? All that energy? Why had she never travelled? Or had more sex when she could? She had bleached and annihilated every waking moment of the last twenty years. Anything, rather than feel. Anything, rather than meet Harold's eye and say the unspeakable.

It was not a life, if lived without love. Maureen poured the soup down the sink, sat at the kitchen table and pressed her face in her hands.

*   *   *

It was David's idea that she should confess to Rex the truth about Harold's walk. He told her one morning that he had been thinking about her situation, and felt it would do her good to talk. She laughed and protested she hardly knew the man, but he pointed out that Rex was her neighbour; of course they knew each other.

'That doesn't mean we talk,' she said. 'They'd only been here six months when his wife died. Besides, I don't need to talk to other people. I

155

have you, love.'

David said that while of course this was true, it might do Rex some good if Maureen came clean. She couldn't keep hiding the truth for ever. She was about to say she missed him, when he told her she should do it right away.

'Will I see you soon?' she said. He promised she would.

Maureen found Rex in his garden, where he was trimming the borders of the grass with a blade in the shape of a half-moon. She stood at the fence that divided their gardens, slightly lopsided because of the slope, and asked in an airy way how he was getting along.

'Keeping busy. That's the best you can hope for. How's Harold?'

'He's good.' Her legs were trembling. Even her fingers felt light. She drew a new breath, like starting a fresh paragraph. 'The fact is, Rex, Harold isn't at home. I've been lying. I'm sorry.' She smothered her lips with her fingertips, forbidding further words. She couldn't look.

In the beating silence, she heard the lawn edger being laid on the grass. She felt Rex's presence as he drew close. There was a smell of mint toothpaste as he said softly, 'Did you think I didn't realize something was up?'

Rex held out his hand and placed it on her shoulder. It was the first time anyone had touched her in a very long time, and the relief was so intense that grief came shuddering up through her body, and tears slanted her cheeks. She had thrown away everything.

'Why don't you come over, and I'll put the kettle on?' he said.

Maureen had not stepped inside Rex's house since Elizabeth's funeral. In the intervening months, she had imagined there would be a felting of dust and a general level of mess, because these were not things men noticed; especially when mourning. But to her astonishment the surfaces shone. Potted cacti stood at intervals along the windowsill, so regular it was as if he had measured them with a ruler. There was no pile of unopened letters. No muddy steps on the mushroom carpet. It even looked as if Rex had bought himself a length of plastic protector and laid it down as a path from the front door, because she was certain it wasn't there when Elizabeth was alive. Maureen checked her face in the circular mirror, and blew her nose. She looked pale and tired, and her nose glowed like a warning light. She wondered what her son would say about her weeping in front of a neighbour. She tried so hard not to cry when she talked to David.

Rex called out from the kitchen that she should wait in the sitting room.

'Are you sure I can't do anything to help?' she said, but he insisted again that she should make herself comfortable.

The sitting room, like the hall, was so quiet and undisturbed Maureen felt her presence was an intrusion. She made her way to the mantelpiece and glanced at the framed photographs of Elizabeth. She had been a tall woman with a bovine jaw, a gravelly laugh and the distracted look of a guest at a cocktail party. Maureen had never said this to anyone except David, but she had always felt a little overpowered by Elizabeth. She wasn't even sure she liked her.

There was a rattling of cups and the door nudged open. She turned and found Rex at the doorway with a tray. He poured the tea without spilling and had even remembered a jug of milk.

Once she started, it surprised Maureen how much she had to say about Harold's walk. She told Rex about Queenie's letter, and his sudden decision to leave. She told him about the visit to the locum, and her shame. 'I'm frightened he won't come back,' she said at last.

'Of course he'll come back.' Rex's voice, slightly milky at the consonants, came with such simplicity she was immediately reassured. Of course Harold would come back. She felt a sudden lightness and wanted to laugh.

Rex passed her a cup. It was delicate china, set on a saucer that matched. She pictured Harold making coffee, the mug full to the brim so that you couldn't lift it without spilling it first and scalding your hand. Even that seemed funny.

She said, 'At first I thought it might be a mid-life crisis. Only, being Harold, he's doing it rather late.' Rex laughed; a little politely, she felt, but at least the ice was broken. He offered her a plate of party cream biscuits and a napkin. She took a biscuit. She hadn't realized how hungry she was.

'Are you sure Harold can do this walk?' he said.

'He's never done anything like it in his life. Last night he stayed in the house of a young Slovakian lady. He didn't even know her.'

'Good heavens.' Rex cupped his hand under his chin to catch the crumbs from a pink wafer. 'I hope

158

he's all right.'

'I'd say he seems very full of it.'

They smiled and fell into a silence that seemed to set them apart so that they gave another smile, politer this time.

'Maybe we should go after him,' said Rex, 'to check he's all right. I've got petrol in the Rover. I could make sandwiches and we might head straight off.'

'Maybe.' Maureen bit her lip, thinking this through. She missed Harold almost as much as she missed David. She wanted to see him very much. But when she imagined the next part, where she caught up with her husband, she floundered. How would she feel, if he didn't want her after all? If he really was leaving for good? She shook her head. 'The truth is, we don't talk. Not any more. Not properly. The morning he left, I was nagging him about white bread and the jam, Rex. The jam. It's no wonder he walked off.' She was sad again. She thought of their cold beds, in separate rooms, and the words they shared, which skimmed the surface and meant nothing. 'It hasn't been a marriage for twenty years.'

In the silence, Rex lifted his cup to his mouth, and Maureen did the same. And then he said, 'Did you like Queenie Hennessy?'

It wasn't the question she was expecting. She had to swallow her tea very quickly, and it washed a rogue crumb of ginger nut with it, causing her to cough. 'I only met her once. But that was a long time ago.' She patted her chest, easing the passage of the biscuit. 'Queenie disappeared very suddenly. That's all I remember. Harold went to work one day and when he came back he said there was someone new in accounts. A man, I think.'

'Why did Queenie disappear?'

'I don't know. There were rumours. But it was a difficult time for me and Harold. He never said, and I never asked. It's who we are, Rex. Everybody these days is spilling the beans about their darkest secrets. I look at those celebrity magazines at the doctor's and my head reels. But that's not how it was for us. We said a lot of things once. Things we shouldn't have said. When it came to Queenie disappearing, I didn't want to know.'

She hesitated, afraid she had confessed too much and unsure how best to continue. 'I heard she had done something she shouldn't have done at the brewery. Their boss was a deeply unpleasant man. He wasn't one to forgive and forget. It was probably best all round that she disappeared.' Maureen saw Queenie Hennessy as she had done all those years ago, on the doorstep of Fossebridge Road, her eyes swollen, and holding out a bunch of flowers. Rex's sitting room seemed suddenly very cold, and she hugged her arms around her waist.

'I don't know about you,' he said at last, 'but I could do with a small sherry.'

*   *   *

Rex drove Maureen to the Start Bay Inn at Slapton Sands. She could feel the passage of the alcohol, cold at first and then almost burning, as it slipped down her throat and loosened her muscles. She told Rex it was strange to set foot in a pub again; since Harold had become teetotal, she rarely drank. They agreed that neither of them was in the mood for cooking, and ordered an early bar meal

160

with a glass of wine. They made a toast to Harold's journey and she felt a lightness in her stomach that reminded her of being a young woman, and in love for the first time.

Since it was still light, they walked along the spit of land between the sea and the ley. After the two drinks, she felt warm inside, and slightly indistinct at the edges. A pack of gulls flew with the wind. You could find warblers here, he told her, and great crested grebes. 'Elizabeth was never very interested in wildlife. She said it all looked the same.' Sometimes Maureen listened and sometimes she didn't. She was thinking of Harold, and replaying in her mind the scene where they had met forty-seven years ago. Strange how she had mislaid the details of that night for so long.

She had noticed Harold straight away. She couldn't miss him. Jiving by himself in the middle of the dance floor, the flaps of his coat flying out like great dog-tooth-check wings. It was as if he were dancing something out that was locked inside himself. She'd never seen anything like it; the young men her mother introduced were all stiff partings and black tie. Maybe he had sensed her watching, even across that dark, throbbing hall, because he had stopped suddenly and caught her eye. He had danced some more, and she had continued watching. She was transfixed. It was the raw energy of him that moved her; the completeness of what he was. He had stopped again. Caught her eye again. Then he had threaded his way through the crowd, and halted so close she could smell the heat of his skin.

Now she had the moment in her mind, she saw it vividly: the way he stooped with his mouth towards

161

her ear, and parted a small lock of her hair so that he could speak into it. The boldness of the gesture had sent prickles of electricity shooting the length of her neck. Even now she felt a distant fluttering under her skin. What was it he had said next? It was very funny, whatever it was, and they had laughed so much it brought on an embarrassing bout of hiccups. She remembered how the coat had swung as he strode to the bar to fetch a glass of water, and how she had not moved, waiting for him. In those days, it was as if the world only put its lights on when Harold was near. Who were those two young people who had danced and laughed so completely?

She grew aware that Rex had stopped speaking. He was watching her.

'Penny for your thoughts, Maureen.'

She smiled and shook her head. 'It's nothing.'

They stood side by side, and looked out over the water. The sinking sun laid a red path from the horizon towards the shore. She wondered where Harold was sleeping, and wished she could say goodnight. Maureen stretched back her neck towards the sky, searching the dusk for the first sprinkle of stars.

15

HAROLD AND THE NEW BEGINNING

The end of the rain brought a period of wild new growth. Trees and flowers seemed to explode with colour and scent. The trembling branches of the horse chestnut balanced new candle spires of blossom. Umbrellas of white cow parsley grew thick at the roadside. Rambling roses shot up garden walls, and the first of the deep-red peonies opened like tissue-paper creations. The apple trees began to shake off their blossom, and bore beads of fruit; bluebells spread thick like water through the woodlands. The dandelions were already fluffheads of seed.

For five days, Harold walked without faltering, passing through Othery, the Polden Hills, Street, Glastonbury, Wells, Radstock, Peasedown St John, and arriving at Bath on a Monday morning. He averaged just over eight miles a day, and on Martina's advice he stocked up on sunblock, cotton wool, nail clippers, plasters, fresh bandages, antiseptic cream, Moleskin blister protection and a slab of Kendal Mint Cake for emergencies. He replenished his supplies of toiletries, as well as washing powder, and packed them neatly in her partner's rucksack, along with the roll of duct tape. Passing his reflection in shop windows, the man staring back at him was so upright and appeared so sure-footed, he had to look twice to check it was really himself. The compass pointed a steady north.

Harold believed his journey was truly beginning. He had thought it started the moment he decided to walk to Berwick, but he saw now that he had been naive. Beginnings could happen more than once, or in different ways. You could think you were starting something afresh, when actually what you were doing was carrying on as before. He had faced his shortcomings and overcome them, and so the real business of walking was happening only now.

Every morning the sun crept over the horizon, peaked and set every evening, as one day made way for another. He spent long moments watching the sky, and the way the land changed beneath it. Hilltops became gold against the sunrise, and windows reflecting its light were so orange you could think there was a fire blazing. The evening shadows lay long beneath the trees, like a separate forest that was made of darkness. He walked against an early-morning mist and smiled at the pylons poking their heads through the milk-white smoke. The hills softened and flattened, and opened before him, green and gentle. He passed through the flat stretches of the Somerset wetlands, where waterways flashed like silver

164

needles. Glastonbury Tor sat on the horizon, and beyond that the Mendip Hills.

Gradually, Harold's leg improved. The bruising turned from purple to green to a gentler shade of yellow, and he was no longer afraid. If anything, he was more sure. The stretch between Tiverton and Taunton had been full of anger and pain. He had wanted more than he could physically give, and so his walk had become a battle against himself, and he had failed. Now he followed a set of gentle stretching exercises each morning and evening, and rested every two hours. He treated the blisters before they became infected and carried fresh water. Taking out his wild-plant book again, he identified hedgerow flowers, and their uses; which bore fruit, culinary, poisonous or otherwise, and which had leaves with medicinal powers. Wild garlic filled the air with its sweet pungency. Once more, it surprised him how much was at his feet, if only he had known to look.

He continued to send postcards to Maureen and Queenie, informing them of his progress, and once in a while he also wrote to the garage girl. On the advice of his guide to Britain, Harold noted the shoe museum in Street and took a look at the shop in Clarks Village, although he still believed it would be wrong to give up on his yachting shoes, having come so far. In Wells, he bought Queenie a rose quartz to hang at her window, and a pencil for Maureen that had been carved from a twig. Urged by several pleasant members of the WI to purchase a Madeira cake, he chose instead a hand-knitted beret in a Queenie shade of brown. He visited the cathedral, and sat in its chilled light, pouring like water from above. He reminded himself that

165

centuries ago men had built churches, bridges and ships; all of them a leap of madness and faith, if you thought about it. When no one was looking, Harold slipped to his knees and asked for the safety of the people he had left behind, and those who were ahead. He asked for the will to keep going. He also apologized for not believing.

Harold passed office workers, dog walkers, shoppers, children going to school, mothers and buggies, and hikers like himself, as well as several tourist parties. He met a tax inspector who was a Druid and had not worn a pair of shoes for ten years. He talked with a young woman on the trail of her real father, with a priest who confessed to tweeting during mass, as well as several people in training for a marathon, and an Italian man with a singing parrot. He spent an afternoon with a white witch from Glastonbury, and a homeless man who had drunk away his house, as well as four bikers looking for the M5, and a mother of six who confided she had no idea life could be so solitary. Harold walked with these strangers and listened. He judged no one, although as the days wore on, and time and places began to melt, he couldn't remember if the tax inspector wore no shoes or had a parrot on his shoulder. It no longer mattered. He had learned that it was the smallness of people that filled him with wonder and tenderness, and the loneliness of that too. The world was made up of people putting one foot in front of the other; and a life might appear ordinary simply because the person living it had done so for a long time. Harold could no longer pass a stranger without acknowledging the truth that everyone was the same, and also unique; and that this was the dilemma of being human.

He walked so surely it was as if all his life he had been waiting to get up from his chair.

*   *   *

Maureen told him on the phone that she had moved out of the spare room and returned to the main bedroom. He had spent so many years sleeping alone, he was surprised at first, and then he was glad because it was the larger and more pleasant of the two and, being at the front of the house, enjoyed the wide view over Kingsbridge. But he assumed this also meant she had packed his things and carried them to the spare room.

He thought of the many times he had looked at the closed door, knowing she had exiled herself completely beyond his reach. Sometimes he had touched the handle, as if it were a sentient piece of her.

Maureen's voice crept under the silence: 'I've been thinking of when we first met.'

'I beg your pardon?'

'It was at a dance in Woolwich. You touched my neck. Then you said something funny. We laughed and laughed.'

He frowned with the effort of trying to picture it. He recalled a dance, but all he could see beyond that was how beautiful she had been, and how delicate. He remembered dancing like an idiot, and he remembered too her dark, long hair falling like velvet either side of her face. But it seemed unlikely he had been bold enough to walk across a crowded room and claim her. It seemed unlikely he had made her laugh and laugh. He wondered if

167

she was mistaking him for someone else.

She said, 'Well, I must let you get on. I know how busy you are.'

She was using the voice that she used for the doctor, when she wanted to show she wasn't going to be an inconvenience. And then she said, 'I wish I could think of what you said to me at the dance. It really was so funny.' She hung up.

For the rest of the day, his mind was full of remembering Maureen, and how it was in the beginning. He thought of the trips to the pictures, and Lyons Corner House, and how he had never seen anyone eat so discreetly, shredding her food into the smallest of scraps before lifting it to her mouth. Even in those days he had begun saving for their future. He had taken an early-morning job on the rubbish trucks, followed by a part-time afternoon job as a bus conductor. Twice a week he did an all-night shift at the hospital, and on Saturdays he worked at the library. Sometimes he was so exhausted he crawled under the bookshelves and fell asleep.

Maureen had taken to getting the bus from outside her house and staying for the full trip to the terminus. He would issue tickets and ring the bell for the driver, but all he was seeing was Maureen, in her blue coat, with her skin like porcelain and those vivid green eyes. She took to walking with him to the hospital so that he'd be scrubbing down the floors and all he could think of was where she was; what she was seeing as she hurried away. She took to nipping into the library and thumbing through cookery books, and he watched her from the main desk, his head reeling with desire and the need to sleep.

168

The wedding had been small, with guests he didn't know in hats and gloves. An invitation was sent to his father, but to Harold's relief he had not showed up.

Alone at last with his new wife, he had watched her across the hotel room as she unbuttoned her dress. He was desperate to touch her, and tremulous with fear. Removing both his tie and jacket, borrowed from another chap at the bus garage and slightly too short in the sleeve, he had looked up and found her sitting on the bed in her slip. She was so beautiful it was too much. He had to bolt to the bathroom.

'Harold, is it me?' she had called through the door, after half an hour.

It hurt to remember these things, when they were so far out of his reach. He had to blink several times, trying to lose the pictures, but they still swam back.

Harold walked the towns that were full of the sounds of other people, and the roads that travelled the land between, and he understood moments from his life as if they had only just occurred. Sometimes he believed he had become more memory than present. He replayed scenes from his life, like a spectator trapped on the outside. Seeing the mistakes, the inconsistencies, the choices that shouldn't be made, and yet unable to do anything about them.

He caught himself taking the phone call after Maureen's mother had died very suddenly, two months after her father. He had pinned her in his arms in order to break the news.

'There's only me and you,' she sobbed.

He had reached for the swell of her growing

belly and promised it would be all right. He would look after her, he'd said. And he'd meant it too. There was nothing Harold had wanted more than to make Maureen happy.

In those days she believed him. She believed Harold could be all she needed. He hadn't known it then; but he did now. It was fatherhood that had been the real test and his undoing. He wondered if he must spend the rest of his life in the spare room.

*   *   *

As Harold made his way north towards Gloucestershire, there were times when his steps were so sure they were effortless. He didn't have to think about lifting one foot and then the other. Walking was an extension of his certainty that he could make Queenie live, and his body was a part of that too. These days he could take the hills without thinking; he was becoming fit, he supposed.

Some days he was more engrossed in what he saw. He tried to find the right words to describe each shift; only sometimes, like the people he had met, they began to jumble. But there were days when he wasn't aware of himself, or his walking, or the land. He wasn't thinking about anything; at least not anything that was related to words. He simply was. He felt the sun on his shoulders, watched a kestrel on silent wings, and all the time the ball of his foot pushed his heel from the ground, and weight shifted from one leg to the other, and this was everything.

Only the nights troubled him. He continued to seek modest accommodation, but the inside world seemed to stand as a barrier between himself and his purpose. He felt a visceral need to leave some part of himself outside. Curtains, wallpaper, framed prints, matching hand and bath towels; these things had become superfluous and without meaning. He threw the windows open, so that he could continue to feel the presence of the sky and the air, but he slept badly. Increasingly he was kept awake by images from the past, or dreamed of his feet lifting and falling. Getting up in the early hours, he watched the moon at the window and felt trapped. It was barely light these days when he paid with his debit card and set off.

Walking into the dawn, he watched with wonder as the sky flamed with strong colour and then faded to a single blue. It was like being in an altogether different version of the day, one that held nothing ordinary. He wished he could describe it to Maureen.

*   *   *

The problem of when and how he would reach Berwick receded into the background, and Harold knew Queenie was waiting, as certainly as he saw his shadow. It gave him pleasure to imagine his arrival, and her place at the window in a sunny chair. There would be so much to talk about. So much from the past. He would remind her how she had once produced a Mars bar from her handbag for the homeward journey.

'You'll get me fat,' he'd said.

'You? There's nothing on you.' She'd laughed.

It had been a strange moment, not uncomfortable in an unpleasant way, but it marked

171

a shift in how they spoke to one another. It revealed she had noticed him, and that she cared. She carried a piece of confectionery for him every day after that and they called each other by their first names. They spoke easily when they were travelling. Once they had stopped at a Little Chef and, face to face across a laminated table, they found the words dried up.

'What do you call two robbers?' he heard her ask. This time they were back in the car.

'I beg your pardon?'

'It's a joke,' she'd said.

'Oh I see. Very good. I don't know. What do you call them?'

'A pair of knickers.' She had gripped her hand over her mouth but she was shaking so much that a violent snort shot between her fingertips, and turned her crimson. 'My father loved that one.'

In the end he had been forced to stop the car, they were laughing so much. He had repeated it that night to David and Maureen over spaghetti carbonara and they had both stared so blankly that the punchline, when he reached it, sounded not hilarious but vaguely smutty.

Harold and Queenie often talked about David. He wondered if she would remember that too? Having no children herself, and no nephews or nieces, she was very interested in his progress at Cambridge. How does David find the town? she'd say. Has he made lots of friends? Does he like punting? Harold assured her his son was having the time of his life, although in truth David rarely answered Maureen's letters and calls. There was no mention of friends, or studying. There was certainly no mention of punting.

172

Harold didn't tell Queenie about the empty vodka bottles he found stashed in his shed after the holidays. Nor did he mention the cannabis in a brown envelope. He told no one; not even his wife. He boxed them up and dumped them on his way to work.

'You and Maureen must be so proud, Harold,' Queenie would say.

He went over their shared time at the brewery, although neither of them had been part of the crowd. Would Queenie remember the Irish barmaid who claimed she was pregnant with Mr Napier's baby, and stopped working very suddenly? People said he had fixed for the girl to lose the child, and that there had been complications. There was another time when one of the new young reps got so drunk he was found tied to the gates of the brewery, stripped to his underpants. Mr Napier had talked about setting the dogs on him in the yard. It would be a crack, he said. The boy was screaming by the end. A trickle of brown liquid streaked his legs.

Living it again, Harold felt a nauseous stirring of shame. David had been right about Napier. It was Queenie who had shown the courage.

He saw her smiling the way she used to; slowly, as if even the happy things had a sadness.

He heard her saying, 'Something happened at the brewery. It was in the night.'

He saw her swaying. Or was it himself? He thought he might fall. He found her small hand gripping at his sleeve, and shaking it. She had not touched him since the stationery cupboard. Her face was white.

She said, 'Are you listening? Because this is

serious, Harold. It's very serious. Napier won't let it go.'

It was the last time he'd seen her. He knew she'd guessed the truth.

Harold wondered why she had taken the rap for him, and whether she understood how much he regretted what he had done. Again he asked why, all those years ago, she had not stopped to say goodbye. And thinking all this, he shook his head and kept walking north.

She had been fired on the spot. Napier's abuse was heard all over the brewery. There was even a rumour he hurled a small round object, an ashtray possibly but maybe a small paperweight, that narrowly missed Queenie's forehead. Mr Napier's secretary confirmed afterwards to a few of the reps that he had never liked the woman. She also confirmed that Queenie stood her ground. She couldn't hear Queenie's exact words because the door was closed, but from Mr Napier's screaming you could get the gist of what Queenie had said, and it was along the lines of 'I don't know what the fuss is about. I was only trying to help.' 'If she'd been a man,' someone told Harold, 'Mr Napier would have kicked the living shit out of her.' Harold had been sitting in a pub at the time. Feeling sick, he had reached for his double brandy and downed it in one.

Harold's shoulders hunched at the memory; he had been an unforgivable coward, but at least he was doing something about that now.

The city of Bath came into view, the crescents and streets cutting into the hillside like small teeth; the cream stone blazing against the morning sun. It was going to be a hot day.

174

'Dad! Dad!'

He looked round, startled, with the clear impression that someone was calling. The passing traffic rustled the trees, but there was no one.

16

HAROLD AND THE PHYSICIAN AND THE VERY FAMOUS ACTOR

Harold intended to keep his stay in Bath brief. He had learned from Exeter that a city diluted his purpose. He needed to get his shoes resoled but the cobbler was closed until midday, due to family affairs. While Harold waited, he would use the time to choose another souvenir for Queenie and Maureen. The sun fell in stark slabs of light in the abbey churchyard. It was so dazzling he had to shield his eyes with his hand.

'Could I ask you all to form a proper line?'

Glancing behind, Harold found himself included in a party of foreign tourists, wearing canvas sunhats and visiting the Roman Baths. Their guide was an English girl, barely out of her teens, with a fragile face and an upper-class trill to her voice. Harold was about to explain he was not one of the party, when she confessed this was her first tour as a professional. 'None of them has a clue what I'm talking about,' she whispered. She sounded so

176

startlingly like Maureen as a young woman that he couldn't move. Her mouth wobbled as if she were about to cry, and Harold was undone. He tried lingering at the back, and also attaching himself to a party who were almost finished; but each time he was on the verge of escape, he remembered his young wife in her blue coat and couldn't let the guide down. Two hours later, her tour ended in the gift shop where he bought postcards and mosaic key rings for both Maureen and Queenie. He had especially enjoyed her introduction to the Sacred Spring, he told her; they really were extremely clever, the Romans.

The young guide gave a slight wriggle of her nose, as if she had smelt something unpleasant, and asked if he had considered visiting the nearby Thermae Bath Spa, where he might enjoy picturesque views of the city, and a state-of-the-art cleansing experience?

Appalled, Harold rushed straight there. He had been careful to keep washing both his clothes and himself, but his shirt was frayed at the collar, and his fingernails were dirt ridges. It was only once he had paid for his entrance ticket and the hire of towels that it occurred to him he had no trunks. For these he had to leave and find a nearby sports shop, making the day his most expensive so far. The assistant fetched a choice of bathing costumes and goggles, although when Harold explained he was more of a walker than a swimmer she was keen to show him waterproof covers for his compass, and a selection of reduced-price, all-weather trousers.

By the time he left the shop with his swimming shorts in a small bag, a large crowd was packed on the pavement. Harold found himself squashed against a copper statue of a Victorian man in a top hat.

'We're waiting for that famous actor,' explained a woman beside him. Her face was red and filmy with the heat. 'He's signing his new book. If he catches my eye, I shall pass out.'

It was difficult to see the really famous actor, let alone catch his eye, because he seemed to be rather short, and surrounded by a wall of bookshop assistants in black uniforms. The crowd shouted out, and applauded. Photographers held up their cameras and the street was punctured with flashlight. Harold wondered what it must be like to have made such a success of your life.

The woman beside him was saying she had named her dog after the actor. The dog was a cocker spaniel, she said. She wished she could tell the actor. She had read all about him in magazines; she knew him like a friend. Harold tried to lean against the statue for a better look, but the statue gave him a sharp dig in the ribs. The bleached sky shone. Sweat broke out on Harold's neck and slid from his armpits, clamping his shirt to his skin.

By the time Harold made it back to the spa, a flock of young women on a hen party were playing in the water and he didn't want to alarm them or get in the way, so he took a quick steam and left in a hurry. At the Pump Room, he asked if he might take a sample of the health-giving water to a very good friend in Berwick-upon-Tweed. The waiter poured some into a bottle and charged five pounds because Harold had mislaid his ticket for the Roman Baths. It was already early afternoon, and he needed to get back on the road.

In the public lavatories, Harold found himself washing his hands next to the actor from the book signing. He was wearing a leather jacket and trousers, and cowboy boots with a small heel. The man stared at his face in the mirror, pulling at the skin, as if he were checking it for something missing. Close up, his hair was so dark it looked plastic. Harold didn't want to intrude on the actor. He dried his hands and pretended he was thinking of something else.

'Don't tell me you have a dog named after me as well,' said the actor. He was staring straight up at Harold. 'Today I am not in the mood.'

He told the actor he didn't have a dog. As a child, he added, he had been bitten many times by a Pekinese called Chinky. This was probably not politically correct; the aunt who owned him had not troubled herself with other people's feelings. 'But I have been walking and I have met some nice dogs recently.'

The actor returned to his reflection. He continued to talk about the dog-naming issue, as if Harold's interjections about his aunt had not been made. 'Every day, someone comes up to tell me about their dog and how they've given it my name. They say it as if I should be happy. They haven't the first idea.'

Harold agreed this was unfortunate, although secretly he thought it must be flattering. He couldn't imagine anyone calling their pet Harold, for instance.

'I spent years doing serious work. I did a whole

season at Pitlochry. Then I make one costume drama, and that's it. Everyone in the country thinks it's original to name a dog after me. Did you come to Bath for my book?'

Harold admitted he hadn't. He told the actor the barest details about Queenie. He didn't think he should mention the nurses he had imagined applauding as he arrived at the hospice. The actor appeared to be listening, although at the end of the story he asked again if Harold had a copy of the book, and if he would like the actor to sign it.

Harold agreed. He felt the book might be a perfect souvenir for Queenie; she had always liked reading. He was about to ask the actor if he wouldn't mind waiting while he nipped out to buy a copy, but the actor spoke instead.

'Actually, don't bother. It's rubbish. I haven't written a word of the thing. I haven't even read it. I'm a serial shagger, with a serious coke habit. I went down on a woman last week and discovered she had a cock. They don't put that sort of thing in the book.'

'No.' Harold glanced at the door.

'I'm on all the chat shows. I'm in all the magazines. Everyone thinks I'm this really nice guy. And yet no one knows the first thing about me. It's like being two people. You're probably about to tell me you're a journalist.' He laughed, but there was something both reckless and grim about the gesture that reminded Harold of David.

'I'm not a journalist. I think I would make a very poor one.'

'Tell me again why you're walking to Bradford.'

Harold said something quiet about Berwick, and atoning for the past. He was unnerved by the very

180

famous actor's confession and was still trying to find a place in himself in which to keep it.

'So how do you know this woman is waiting? Has she sent a message?'

'A message?' repeated Harold, although he hadn't misheard. It was more a stalling for time.

'Has she told you she's up for it?'

Harold opened his mouth, and reworked it several times, but he couldn't get the words to come.

'How does it work exactly?' said the actor.

Harold touched his tie with his fingertips. 'I send postcards. I know she is waiting.'

Harold smiled and the actor smiled too. He wanted the actor to be persuaded by what he had heard, because he wasn't sure there was any other way of putting it, and for a moment it appeared that the actor was; but then a scowl crept over his face as if he had just tasted something not right. 'If I were you, I'd get myself in a car.'

'I beg your pardon?'

'Bollocks to the walk.'

Harold's voice trembled. 'The walk is the idea. That's how she will live. John Lennon lay in a bed once. My son had a picture of him on his wall.'

'John Lennon had Yoko Ono and the world's press in the bed as well. You're on your own, slogging to Berwick-upon-Tweed. It's going to take weeks. And supposing she didn't get your message? They might have forgotten to tell her.' The actor's mouth arched in a frown, as if he were thinking through the implications of such a mistake. 'What does it matter if you walk or get a lift? It makes no difference how you get there. You've just got to see her. I'll lend you my car. My

181

driver. You could be there tonight.'

The door opened and a gentleman in shorts made his way to the urinal. Harold waited for him to finish. He needed the very famous actor to know that you could be ordinary and attempt something extraordinary, without being able to explain it in a logical way. But all he could picture was a car driving to Berwick. The actor was right. Harold had left a message, and sent postcards, but there was no proof she'd taken him seriously, or even heard about his call. He imagined sitting in the warmth of the car. If he said yes, he could be there in hours. He had to grip his hands to stop them from shaking.

'I haven't upset you, have I?' said the actor. His voice was suddenly tender. 'I told you I was an arse.' Harold shook his head, but kept it bowed. He hoped the gentleman in shorts wasn't looking.

'I have to keep walking,' he said quietly, although he knew he was no longer certain.

The newcomer placed himself between Harold and the actor in order to wash his hands. He began to laugh, as if remembering something private. Then he said, 'I've got to tell you. We have this dog—'

Harold made his way to the street.

*　　　*　　　*

The sky had filled with a dense layer of white cloud that pressed down on the city as if intending to squeeze the life out of it. Bars and cafés spilled on to the pavements. Drinkers and shoppers were stripped to vests, and skin that had not felt the sun for months was crimson. Harold carried his jacket over his arm, but he frequently had to mop his face with his shirtsleeve. Seedheads hung in the stiff air like fuzz. When Harold got to the cobbler, it was still closed. The straps of his rucksack were wet from his body, and dug into his shoulders. It was too hot to keep walking, and he hadn't the energy.

He thought he might take refuge in the abbey. He hoped it might be cool there, and inspire him again, remind him what it was to believe in something, but the abbey was closed to visitors for a music rehearsal. Harold sat in a pocket of shade and briefly watched the copper statue, until a small child burst into tears because it had waved and offered her a boiled sweet. He would wait in a small teashop where he reckoned he could afford a pot of tea for one.

The waitress scowled. 'We don't do drinks-only in the afternoon. You have to have the Regency Bath cream tea.' But he was already sitting down. Harold asked for the Regency Bath cream tea.

The tables were set too close together and the heat was so solid you could almost see it. Customers sat with their legs open and flapped the air with their laminated menus. When his order arrived, a small scoop of clotted cream swam in a pool of fat. The waitress said, 'Enjoy.'

Harold asked if she knew the quickest route towards Stroud but she shrugged. 'Do you mind sharing?' she said, only without making it sound like a question. She called out to a man at the door and pointed at the seat opposite Harold's. The man sat apologetically and pulled out a book. He had a neatly chiselled face, and closely cut light hair. His white shirt was open at the collar, revealing a perfect V-shape of toffee-coloured skin. Asking Harold to pass the menu, he also asked if he liked Bath. He was an American, he said, doing England. His girlfriend was currently enjoying the Jane Austen experience. Harold wasn't sure what this might be, but hoped for her sake that it didn't involve the very famous actor. He was relieved that they fell into silence. He didn't need another encounter like the one in Exeter, or even the one he had just had. Despite his obligation to other people, he wished at that moment he had walls.

Harold drank his tea, but couldn't face the scones. He felt dulled with such apathy it was like being at the brewery again in the years following Queenie's departure; like being an empty space inside a suit, that said words sometimes and heard them, that got in a car every day and returned home, but was no longer connected up to other people. The manager appointed after Napier suggested Harold should take a back seat until his retirement. Filing, he suggested. The odd piece of consultative advice. Harold was given a special desk with a computer and his name on a badge but no one had approached. He draped a serviette over his plate and caught the eye of the chiselled man opposite.

'Too hot for food,' said the man.

Harold agreed. He instantly regretted it. The chiselled man now seemed to feel obliged to make further conversation.

'Bath seems like a nice place,' he said. He closed his book. 'Are you on vacation?'

Reluctantly, Harold explained his story, but kept it brief. He left out, for instance, the detail about the garage girl and how she had saved her aunt.

184

Instead he added that after his son left Cambridge, he had gone on a walking trip to the Lake District, although he wasn't sure how much hiking he had done. David had returned home and not moved for weeks.

'Is your son joining you?' said the man.

Harold said he wasn't. He asked the American what he did for a living.

'I'm a physician.'

'I met a Slovakian lady who is a doctor. She can only get cleaning work. What sort of physician are you?'

'An oncologist.'

Harold felt his blood quicken, as if he had unintentionally broken into a run. 'Gosh,' he said. It was clear neither man knew what to say next. 'Goodness.'

The oncologist raised his shoulders and gave a regretful smile, as if he wished he could be something else. Harold glanced round for the waitress, but she was fetching water for another customer. His head was dizzy with the heat and he dabbed at his forehead.

The oncologist said, 'Do you know what sort of cancer your friend has?'

'I'm not sure. In her letter, she says there's nothing else they can do. She doesn't say any more than that.' He felt so exposed, the oncologist might as well have been probing at Harold's skin with his scalpel. He loosened his tie, and then his collar. He wished the waitress would hurry.

'Lung cancer?'

'I really don't know.'

'May I see her letter?'

He didn't want to show it, but the oncologist was

185

holding out his empty hand. Harold reached into his pocket and found the envelope. He adjusted the sticking plaster on his reading glasses, but his face was so slick with moisture he had to hold them in place. He wiped the table with his sleeve, and then again with his napkin, before unfolding the pink sheet of paper, and smoothing it flat. Time seemed to stop. Even as the oncologist reached for the letter and gently eased it closer, Harold's right fingers hovered over the page.

He read Queenie's words as the oncologist read them. He felt he had to protect the letter and that, by not letting it out of his sight, he could do that. His eye fell on the postscript: *No need to reply.* After that came an untidy squiggle, as if someone had made a mistake with their left hand.

The oncologist threw himself back in his chair, and blew out a sigh. 'What a moving letter.'

Harold nodded. He replaced his reading glasses in his shirt pocket. 'And beautifully typed,' he said. 'Queenie was always neat. You should have seen her desk.' At last he smiled. It was going to be all right.

The oncologist said, 'But I assume a care worker did it for her?'

'I'm sorry?' Harold's pulse stopped.

'She won't be well enough to sit in an office, typing letters. Someone at the hospice will have done it for her. It's nice she managed the address, though. You can see she really tried.' The oncologist gave a smile that was plainly intended to be reassuring, but it remained fixed on his face, looking like something forgotten or even misplaced.

Harold took up the envelope. The truth

186

dropped like a terrible weight straight through him and everything seemed to fall away. He didn't know any more if he was unbearably hot or freezing cold. Fumbling again with his reading glasses, he saw now what he had not been able to make sense of; the thing that had been wrong all along. How had he not realized it before? It was the childlike handwriting, with its downward slant and almost comical irregularity. It was the same as the messy squiggle at the bottom of the letter, which, now that he looked again, he found was a botched attempt at her name.

This was Queenie's handwriting. This was what she had become.

Harold replaced the letter in its envelope, although his fingers were trembling so hard he couldn't get the corner to fit. He had to take it out and fold it again, and give it another push.

After a long moment the oncologist said, 'How much do you know about cancer, Harold?'

Harold gave a yawn to stifle the emotion building up inside his face, while gently and slowly the oncologist told how a tumour is formed. He didn't rush. He didn't flinch. He explained how a cell may reproduce uncontrollably to form an abnormal mass of tissue. There were more than two hundred types of cancer, he said, each with different causes and symptoms. He described the difference between primary and secondary cancers, and how ascertaining the origin of the tumour dictated the type of treatment. He explained how, when a new tumour forms on a distant organ, it will behave like the original tumour. A breast cancer growing in the liver, for instance, would not be liver cancer; it would be primary breast cancer, with secondary breast cancer in the liver. But once other organs were involved, the symptoms could get worse. And once a cancer had begun to spread beyond its original site, it became more difficult to treat. If it had got into her lymphatic system, for instance, the end would be quick; although with the immunity so low, another infection might kill her first. 'Even a cold,' he said.

Harold listened without moving.

'I'm not saying cancer can't be cured. And when surgery fails, there are alternative treatments. But as a physician, I would never tell a patient there was nothing to be done, unless I was absolutely certain. Harold, you have a wife and son. If I may say so, you look tired. Is it really necessary to walk?'

Out of words, Harold stood. He reached for his jacket and slipped his arms into the sleeves but he kept missing one of them, and the oncologist had to stand to help. 'Good luck,' he said, holding out his hand. 'And please let me take the bill. It's the least I can do.'

*   *   *

For the rest of the afternoon, Harold continued to tread the streets but without knowing where he was going. He needed someone to share his faith in his walk so that he could believe in it too, but he barely had the energy to talk. He finally got his shoes resoled. He bought a new box of plasters to keep him going as far as Stroud. He stopped for a takeaway coffee and briefly mentioned Berwick, but nothing about how he was getting there, or why. No one said what he longed to hear. No one said, You are going to get there, and Queenie will live. No one said, There will be crowds applauding because this, Harold, is the best idea we have ever heard. You must definitely finish.

Harold tried to speak to Maureen, but worried he was taking up her time. He felt he had mislaid all the normal words and the everyday questions that would lead to an exchange of commonplaces, so that speaking caused further pain. He told her he was doing splendidly. He found the courage to hint that a few people had expressed doubt, hoping Maureen would laugh it away, but instead she said, 'Yes, I see.'

'I don't even know she's—' Again the words ran out.

'She's—what?'

'Still waiting.'

'I thought you did?'

'Not really.'

'Have you stayed with any more Slovakian ladies?'

'I met a physician, and a very famous actor.'

'Goodness,' said Maureen with a laugh. 'Wait till I tell Rex.'

A bald, thickset man wearing a patterned frock trudged past the kiosk. People were slowing to point him out, and laugh. The buttons on the dress strained at his belly, and his eye was a large closed-up bruise from a recent punch. Harold wished he hadn't seen, but he had, and he knew it would be unbearable for a while to keep thinking of the man, but that he would do it all the same.

'Are you sure you're all right?' said Maureen.

Along came another pause, and he was suddenly

afraid he was going to cry, so he told her someone else was waiting for the phone, and that he must get going. There was a red stretch in the western sky, and the sun was beginning to sink.

'Well, cheerio,' said Maureen.

For a long time, he sat on a bench close to the abbey, trying to work out where to go. It was as if Harold had taken off his jacket, followed by his shirt, and then several layers of skin and muscle. Even the most ordinary things seemed overwhelming. A shop assistant began to wind up the striped awning and it made such a rattle the noise cut into his head. He looked along the empty street, knowing no one, having nowhere to belong, when, emerging from the opposite end, he saw David.

Harold stood. His heartbeat came so fast he could feel it in his mouth. It couldn't be his son; he couldn't be in Bath. And yet, looking at the stooped figure striding towards him, tugging on a cigarette, and with his black coat billowing out like wings, Harold knew it was David, and that they were going to meet. He was shaking so much he had to reach for the bench.

Even from this distance, he could tell David had grown his hair again. Maureen would be so pleased. She had wept bitterly the day he shaved his head. His walk was still the same; toppling and long-paced, his eyes fixed to the ground, his head bowed, as if other people were to be avoided. Harold called out: 'David! David!' They were no more than fifty feet apart.

His son staggered as if he had lost his balance or tripped. He was maybe drunk, but that wouldn't matter. Harold would buy him a coffee. Or a drink, if he preferred that. They could eat. Or not eat. They could do whatever his son wanted.

'David!' he called. He started to edge towards him. Gently, to show he meant no harm. A few more paces; that was all.

He remembered the skeletal thinness of David after the Lake District; the way his head balanced on top of his neck, suggesting his body had rejected the rest of the world and was interested only in consuming itself.

'David!' he called again; a little louder to make him look up.

His son caught his eye, but failed to smile. He glanced at Harold as if his father wasn't there, or was part of the street but not something he recognized. Harold's insides turned. He hoped he wouldn't fall.

It wasn't David. It was someone else. Another man's son. He had allowed himself to believe for a few brief moments that David could appear at one end of a street, while Harold sat at the other. The young man took a sharp right and marched swiftly away, becoming smaller and less distinguishable, until with a snap he turned another corner. Harold kept watching, waiting in case the young man changed his mind and was David after all, but he didn't.

It was worse than not seeing his son for twenty years. It was like having him, and not having him, all over again. Harold returned to the bench outside the abbey, knowing he must find somewhere to sleep, and unable to move.

*   *   *

191

He ended up near the station, in a stuffy room overlooking the road. He wrenched up the sash window for air, but the traffic would not stop, and the trains shrieked in and out of the platforms. From beyond the wall came a voice in a foreign language, shouting into a telephone. Harold lay on a bed that was too soft, where so many people he didn't know had slept before him, listening to the voice he didn't understand, and he was afraid. He got up and paced the room, up and down, with the walls too close and the air too still, while the traffic and the trains went to wherever they were going.

The past could not be changed. Inoperable cancer could not be cured. He pictured the stranger dressed as a woman, with the blow to his head. He recalled the way David looked the day of his graduation, and in the months following, as if he were asleep with his eyes open. It was too much. It was too much to keep going.

As dawn broke, Harold was already on the road but he did not refer to his compass or his guidebooks. It took all his strength and will to keep putting one foot in front of the other. Only when three teenage girls on horseback asked him the way to Shepton Mallet did he realize he had lost a full day heading in the wrong direction.

He sat by the roadside, looking over a field ablaze with yellow flowers. He couldn't remember their name and he couldn't be bothered to take out his wild-plant guide. The truth was, he was spending far too much money. After three weeks of walking, Kingsbridge was still nearer than Berwick. The first of the swallows swooped and dived overhead, playing through the air like children.

Harold didn't know how he would ever get back on his feet.

17

MAUREEN AND THE GARDEN

'

'Yes, David,' Maureen told him, 'he's still walking. He rings most evenings. And Rex is being very kind. In a funny way, I'm almost proud. I wish I knew how to tell Harold that.'

Lying on the queen-sized bed she had once shared with Harold, she watched the block of bright morning light trapped behind the net curtains. So much had happened in one week, she sometimes had the feeling she had slipped into a different woman's skin. 'He sends postcards, and occasionally a present. He seems to favour pens.' She paused, afraid she had offended David because he wasn't replying. 'I love you,' she said. Her words trickled to nothing and still he did not speak. 'I should let you go,' she said at last.

It wasn't that it was a relief to stop, but for the first time she had begun to feel uncomfortable when she talked to her son. She had believed they would enjoy a greater intimacy now that Harold was gone. And yet, faced with hours, if she wished, to tell him how things were, she found she was too busy. Or she would speak, and it would dawn on her with creeping certainty that he wasn't listening. She found reasons not to tidy his bedroom. She even stopped thinking she might see him.

It was the trip to Slapton Sands that had marked her turning point. That night, she had fumbled her front-door key into the lock, calling her thank you to Rex across the dividing fence, and then she had climbed the stairs without taking off her shoes and walked straight into the master bedroom. Fully dressed, she had toppled on to the bed and closed her eyes. In the middle of the night she had realized where she was with a prickle of panic, followed by relief. It was over. She couldn't think what exactly it was, other than an unspecific weight of pain. She had pulled back the duvet and curled into Harold's pillow. It smelt of Pears soap and him. Waking later, she had felt the same lightness spreading through her like warm water.

After that, she had carried her clothes in armfuls from the spare room and hung them in the wardrobe, at the opposite end of the rail from Harold's. She had given herself a challenge: every day without him, she would attempt one new thing. She took the pile of unopened household bills to the kitchen table, along with the cheque book, and began to pay them. She rang the insurance company to make sure Harold's health care was up to date. She drove the car to the garage and had the air levels checked in the tyres. She even tied an old silk scarf round her hair, like in the old days. When Rex appeared unexpectedly at the garden fence, she had to shoot her hand up and tug the knot free.

'I look silly,' she said.

'Not at all, Maureen.'

He appeared to have something on his mind. They would be talking about the garden or Harold's whereabouts, and then a thought would occur to him, and he would go quiet. When she asked if he was all right, he merely nodded. 'Just wait,' he'd tell her. 'I have a plan up my sleeve.' She had a hunch it was something to do with herself.

Dusting behind the nets at the bedroom window the previous week, she couldn't help but notice the postman deliver something in a cardboard tube to Rex's front door. A day later, and from the same vantage point, she had spied Rex struggling up the path with a window-sized piece of board, which he was trying to hide under a tartan blanket from the Rover. Maureen was intrigued. She had waited for him in the garden; she even took out a basket of dried washing and pegged it again on the line, but he didn't come out all afternoon.

She knocked to ask if he had enough milk, and he mumbled through a crack in the door that he did, and that he was having an early night. And yet when she went out to check the back garden at eleven o'clock, the lights were still on in his kitchen, and she could see him pottering about.

The next day a rap at the letterbox had brought her rushing into the hallway, where she found a strange square shape against the bobbled glass, with what looked like a small head floating on top. Opening the door, she discovered Rex behind a large flat brown-paper package tied with loops of string. 'Do you mind if I come in?' he said. He could barely get the words out.

Maureen couldn't remember the last time someone had given her a gift when it wasn't Christmas or her birthday. She had ushered him inside, and into the sitting room, offering tea or coffee. He insisted there was no time for either; she must open her present. 'Tear the paper, Maureen,' he said.

She couldn't. It was too exciting. She had unpeeled one corner of brown paper and found a hard frame of wood, and then she unpeeled the other edge and found the same again. Rex sat with his hands clasped in his lap, and every time she peeled off a new strip his feet lifted as if he were jumping over an invisible rope, and he gasped.

'Hurry, hurry,' he said.

'Whatever is it?'

'Pull it out. Go on. Have a proper look, Maureen. I made it for you.'

It was a giant-sized map of England mounted on a pinboard. On the back he had attached two small mirror hooks, so that it could be hung from the wall. He pointed to Kingsbridge, and there she found a drawing pin, wound with blue thread, that stretched to Loddiswell. From there, the blue thread crept to South Brent, and on again to Buckfast Abbey. Harold's route to date was marked up with blue thread and drawing pins, ending at Bath. At the top of England, Berwick-upon-Tweed was marked with fluorescent-green highlighter pen, and a small homemade flag. There was even a separate box of drawing pins so that she could display Harold's postcards.

'I thought you could stick them on parts of the country he isn't visiting,' said Rex. 'Like Norfolk,

197

and South Wales. I am sure that would be OK.'

Rex put up nails in the kitchen for the map and they hung it above the table, so that Maureen could see where Harold was and fill in the rest of his journey. It was a little lopsided because he had difficulty with the drill, and the first Rawlplug was swallowed into the wall. But if she looked at the map with a slight tilt to her head, it was barely noticeable. Besides, as she told Rex, it didn't matter about things not being perfect.

This, too, was a new departure for Maureen.

After the map present, they had taken an outing every day. She accompanied him to the crematorium with roses for Elizabeth, and afterwards they stopped for tea at Hope Cove. They visited Salcombe and took a boat trip across the estuary, and another afternoon he drove her to Brixham to buy crab. They walked the coastal road towards Bigbury and ate fresh shellfish at the Oyster Shack. He said it was good for him to get out, and that he hoped he wasn't intruding, and she reassured him that it helped her too to stop thinking things over. They were sitting in front of the dunes at Bantham when she explained how she and Harold had first come to Kingsbridge forty-five years ago when they were newly married. They had so much hope in those days.

'We knew no one but it didn't matter. We only needed each other. Harold had a difficult childhood. I think he loved his mother very much. And his father must have had some sort of breakdown after the war. I wanted to be everything he'd never had. I wanted to give him a home and a family. I learned to cook. I made curtains. I found wooden crates and hammered them together to make a coffee table. Harold dug me vegetable plots at the front of the house, and I grew everything. Potatoes, beans, carrots.' She laughed. 'We were very happy.' It was such a pleasure to voice these things, she wished there were more words. 'Very happy,' she said again.

The tide was out so far the sand looked glazed under the sun. There was a clear stretch between the shore and Burgh Island. People had brought multicoloured windbreaks and small pop-up tents. Dogs were scampering across the sand, in chase of sticks and balls; children were running up and down with buckets and spades; and far out the sea glittered. She thought of how much David had wanted a dog. Maureen fumbled for her handkerchief and asked Rex to ignore her. Maybe it was coming to Bantham again after all these years. So many times she had blamed Harold for the day that David almost drowned.

'I say so many things that I don't mean. It's as if, even if I think something nice about Harold, by the time it's got to my mouth it's become not nice. He goes to tell me something and I'm saying, "I think not," before he's finished the sentence.'

'I always got cross with Elizabeth for leaving the top off the toothpaste. Now I throw it away as soon as I open a new tube. I find I don't want the lid.'

She smiled. His hand was near hers. She brought her own up and fingered the ridge of bone at her throat where the skin was still soft. 'When I was young, I looked at people our age and I assumed my life was sorted. It never occurred to me that when I got to sixty-three I'd be in the most appalling mess.'

There were so many things Maureen wished she

199

had done differently. Lying in bed in the morning light, she yawned and stretched, feeling the size of the mattress with her hands and feet; even the cold far corners. Then she moved her fingers to herself. She touched her cheeks. Her throat. The outline of her breasts. She imagined Harold's hands around her waist, his mouth on hers. Her skin was slack, and her fingertips no longer had the sensitivity of a young woman's, but all the same her heart beat wildly, and her blood throbbed. From outside came the click of Rex's front door closing. She sat up sharply. Moments later, his car started and she heard him driving away. She curled back into the duvet, pulling it close against her like a body.

The wardrobe door was partly open, revealing the sleeve of one of Harold's left-behind shirts, and she felt a stab of the old pain. She threw back the duvet, seeking distraction. The perfect job presented itself as she passed the wardrobe.

For many years it had been Maureen's system, just as it had been her mother's, to arrange clothing according to the season. Winter items would be placed at one end of the rail, along with thick pullovers, while summer clothing would be hung at the opposite end, beside lightweight jackets and cardigans. Somehow in her rush to put her own clothes in the wardrobe, she had failed to notice that Harold's clothes hung higgledy-piggledy, with no reference to weather or texture of fabric. She would go through each piece, throwing out those he no longer needed and hanging the rest properly.

There were his work suits, fraying at the lapels; these she lifted out and placed on the bed. There were a number of wool cardigans, all of them thin at the elbow; she would patch those. Skimming through a selection of shirts, some white, some checked, she came across the tweed jacket he had bought especially for David's graduation. She felt a beating against her chest, like something trapped inside. She hadn't cast her eyes on the jacket for years.

Maureen eased it off the hanger and held it high in front of her, at Harold level. Twenty years fell away, and she saw the two of them again, standing outside King's College Chapel, Cambridge, uncomfortable in their new outfits, in the exact spot where David had instructed them to wait. She saw herself wearing a satin dress with shoulder pads that, now she thought about it, was the colour of a boiled crustacean, and probably matched her cheeks. She saw Harold with his shoulders hunched, so that his arms shot out stiffly, as if the jacket sleeves were made of wood, not fabric.

It was his fault, she'd complained at the time; he should have checked the arrangements. It was nervousness that made her lash out. They had waited for over two hours, but it was the wrong place after all. They missed the whole ceremony. And even though David apologized when they bumped into him coming out of a pub (you could excuse him for that; it was a day of celebration), he also failed to meet them for the punting trip he had promised. The couple had made the long drive from Cambridge to Kingsbridge in silence.

'He said he's going on a walking holiday,' she said at last.

'That's good.'

'Just as a stopgap. Until he gets a job.'

'That's good,' he said again.

201

Tears of frustration had caught like a solid lump in her throat. 'At least he has a degree,' she fired. 'At least he can make something of his life.'

David returned home two weeks later, unexpectedly. He didn't explain why he was back so soon, but he carried a brown holdall that clunked as it hit the banisters and he often took his mother aside to ask her for money. 'University took it out of him,' she'd say, to excuse his failure to get up. Or she'd say, 'He just needs to find the right job.' He missed interviews; or he went to them, but forgot to wash and comb his hair. 'David is too clever,' she'd say. Harold would nod in that easy way of his, and she'd want to shout at him for appearing to believe her. The truth was, their son could barely stand up straight most of the time. There were moments when she stole a glance at him, and she wasn't even convinced he had graduated. With David, you could look back and there were so many inconsistencies that even the things you thought you knew began to unravel. And then she would feel guilty for doubting her son, and blame it instead on Harold. At least David has prospects, she'd say. At least he has his hair. Anything to throw Harold off balance. Money began to disappear from her purse. First coins. Then notes. She pretended they hadn't.

Over the years, she had asked David many times if she could have done more; but he had reassured her. After all, it was she who had underlined suitable vacancies in the jobs section of the newspaper. It was she who had fixed the doctor's appointment and driven him there. Maureen remembered how he dropped the prescription into her lap, as if it were nothing to do with him. There was Prothiaden for the depression and Diazepam to decrease anxiety, and then there was Temazepam if he still couldn't sleep at night.

'That's an awful lot,' she had said, scrambling to her feet. 'What did the doctor say to you? What does he think?'

He had shrugged and lit another cigarette.

But at least after that there had been an improvement. She listened out at night but it seemed he was sleeping. He no longer got up to eat breakfast at four in the morning. He no longer went for night walks in his dressing gown, or filled the house with the sick-sweet smell of his roll-ups. David was certain he would find a job.

She saw him again the day he decided to interview for the army, and took it upon himself to shave his scalp. There were curls of his long hair all over the bathroom. There were nicks in the skin where his hand had trembled and the razor slipped. The barbarity inflicted on that poor head, that poor head she loved to distraction, had made her want to scream.

Maureen lowered herself on to the bed, and dropped her face in her hands. What more could they have done?

'Oh Harold.' She fingered the coarse tweed of his English gentleman's jacket.

An urge came over her to do something completely different. It was like a shock of energy right through her, forcing her once more to her feet. She took out the shrimp garment she had worn for the graduation and hung it at the centre of the rail. Then she took Harold's jacket and arranged it on a hanger beside the dress. They looked lonely and too apart. She scooped up his sleeve, and draped it over the pink shoulder.

After that she paired each of her outfits with one of his. She tucked the cuff of her blouse in his blue suit pocket. A skirt hem she looped around a trouser leg. Another dress she wrapped in the embrace of his blue cardigan. It was as if lots of invisible Maureens and Harolds were loitering in her wardrobe, simply waiting for the opportunity to step out. It made her smile, and then it made her cry; but she didn't change them back.

She was interrupted by the sound of Rex's Rover drawing up outside. Soon afterwards, she was aware of a scraping sound from her front garden. Lifting the net curtains, she found he had marked rectangles of turf with string and posts, and that he was cutting into them with his spade.

He waved up at her. 'If we're lucky, we might be in time for runner beans.'

*   *   *

Wearing an old shirt of Harold's, Maureen planted twenty small shoots and tied them to bamboo stakes without damaging their soft green stems. She patted the soil at their roots, and watered them. At first she watched in fear, lest they were pecked by seagulls or killed by a May frost. But after only a day or so of constant watching, her worry subsided. In time, the plants thickened at the stems, and grew new leaves. She planted rows of lettuce, beetroot and carrots. She cleared the rubble from the ornamental pond.

It was good to feel the soil under her nails, and nurture something again.

18

HAROLD AND THE DECISION

'Good afternoon. I am ringing about a patient called Queenie Hennessy. She sent me a letter just over four weeks ago.'

On the twenty-sixth day, and six miles south of Stroud, Harold decided to stop. He had retraced the five miles to Bath, and kept walking from there for a further four days along the A46, but the mistake he had made about his direction deeply disturbed him, and the going was hard. Hedgerows reduced to ditches, and drystone walls. The land opened out, and stretched to the left and right. Giant pylons marched as far as he could see. He observed these things but felt no interest as to why they occurred. Whichever way he looked at it, the road was something that never stopped, and never yielded its promise. It took every scrap of himself to keep moving when he knew in his heart he could not make it.

Why had he wasted so much time, looking at the sky and the hills, and talking to people, and

205

thinking about life, and remembering, when all along he could have been in a car? Of course he couldn't do it in yachting shoes. Of course Queenie couldn't keep living, just because he'd told her to do so. Every day, the sky hung low and white, lit by a silvery spoke of sunlight. He lowered his head so that he would not see the birds swooping overhead, or the traffic passing in a flash. He felt more lonely and left behind than he would have done up a faraway mountain.

In making his decision, he wasn't only thinking of himself. There was Maureen too. He missed her more and more. He knew he had lost her love, but it was wrong to walk out and leave her to pick up the pieces; already he had caused her too much sorrow. And there was David. In the days since Bath, Harold had felt a painfully long distance from him. He missed them both.

Finally there was the money. The guesthouses had been cheap, but all the same he couldn't afford to keep spending like this. He had checked his account at the bank, and been shocked. If Queenie was still alive, and if she was interested in a visit, he would take the train. He could be in Berwick by the evening.

The woman on the other end of the line said, 'Have you rung before?' He wondered if she was the same nurse with whom he had left his original message. This voice was Scottish, he thought, or was it Irish? He was too tired to know.

'Could I talk to Queenie?'

'I'm very sorry, but I'm afraid you can't.'

It was like hitting a wall he hadn't seen. 'Is she—?' His chest was smarting. 'Is she—?' He couldn't say it.

'Are you the gentleman who was travelling by foot?'

Harold swallowed something sharp. He said that yes, he was. He apologized.

'Mr Fry, Queenie has no family. No friends. When people have no one to stay for, they tend to pass quickly. We have been hoping for your call.'

'I see.' He could barely speak. He could only listen. Even his blood was still and cold.

'After you rang, we all noticed the change in Queenie. It was very marked.'

He saw a body on a stretcher, stiff with not living. He felt what it was to be too late to make a difference. He said with a hoarse whisper, 'Yes.' And then, since she said nothing, he said again, 'Well, of course.' He slumped his forehead against the glass of the booth, followed by his palm, and closed his eyes. If only it was simple to stop feeling.

The woman gave a fluttery noise, like a laugh, but it surely couldn't be. 'We've never seen anything like it. Some days she sits up. She shows us all your postcards.'

Harold shook his head, not understanding. 'I'm sorry?'

'She's waiting, Mr Fry. Like you said she should.'

A cry of joy shot out of him, and took him by surprise. 'She's alive? She's getting better?' He laughed, not meaning to, but it grew bigger, spilling out in waves as tears moistened his cheeks. 'She's waiting for me?' He threw open the door of the kiosk and punched the air.

'When you rang and told us about your walk, I was afraid you'd misunderstood the gravity of things. But, you see, I was wrong. It's a rather unusual kind of healing. I don't know how you came up with it. But maybe it's what the world needs. A little less sense, and a little more faith.'

'Yes. Yes.' He was still laughing. He couldn't stop.

'May I ask how the journey is going?'

'Well. Very well. Yesterday, or maybe the day before, I stayed in Old Sodbury. I also passed Dunkirk. Now I believe I am in Nailsworth.' Even that was funny. The voice was chuckling too.

'One wonders where these names all come from. When should we expect you?'

'Let me think.' Harold blew his nose, and mopped the last of his crying away. He looked at his watch, wondering how quickly he could get a train, and how many different connections it would take. Then once again he pictured the space between himself and Queenie: the hills, the roads, the people, the sky. He saw them as he had done on that first afternoon, but now there was a difference; he placed the image of himself among them. He was a little broken, a little tired, his back to the world, but he wouldn't let Queenie down. 'In about three weeks. Possibly more or indeed less.'

'Goodness.' The voice laughed. 'I'll tell her that.'

'And tell her not to give up. Tell her I will keep walking.' He was laughing again because she was.

'I'll tell her that too.'

'Even when she is afraid, she must wait. She must keep living.'

'I believe she will. God bless you, Mr Fry.'

*   *   *

208

For the rest of the afternoon Harold walked, and into the dusk. The violent doubt he had felt before phoning Queenie was gone. He had escaped a great danger. There were miracles after all. If he had got on a train or in a car, he would be on his way, believing he was right, but all the time it would be wrong. He had nearly given up, but something else had happened and he kept going. He wouldn't try to give up again.

The road led from Nailsworth, past the old mill buildings, and into the outskirts of Stroud. As it dipped towards the centre, he passed a row of redbrick terraced houses, one with scaffolding and ladders and a skip of building rubble parked in the road. A shape caught his eye. On stopping and pushing aside several pieces of plywood, he found a sleeping bag. He gave it a shake to blow off the dust, and although it was ripped and the padding bulged like a soft white tongue from the hole, the tear was only superficial and the zip was still intact. Harold rolled the sleeping bag into a bundle and walked to the house. There were already lights downstairs. When he heard Harold's story, the owner called his wife, and they also offered a fold-up chair, a Teasmade and a yoga mat. Harold assured them the sleeping bag was more than enough.

The wife said, 'I do hope you'll be careful. Only last week, our local petrol station was held up by four men with guns.'

Harold promised he was vigilant; although he had come to trust in the basic goodness of people. The dusk deepened and settled like a layer of fur on the outlines of the roofs and trees.

He watched the squares of buttery light inside the houses, and people going about their business. He thought of how they would settle in their beds and try to sleep through their dreams. It struck him again how much he cared, and how relieved he was that they were somehow safe and warm, while he was free to keep walking. After all it had always been this way; that he was a little apart. The moon drew into focus, full and high, like a silver coin emerging through water.

He tried the door to a shed but it was padlocked. He rooted around in a sports field, but there was no proper shelter, and then a building under construction where the windows were secured with plastic sheeting. He didn't want to go where he was not welcome. Swathes of cloud shone against the sky like a black and silver mackerel. The road and rooftops were bathed in softest blue.

Following a steep hill, he came to a mud track ending in a barn. There were no dogs or cars. The roof was made of corrugated iron, and so were three of its sides, but the fourth had been secured by a sheet of tarpaulin, which was light against the moon. He lifted a lower corner and stooped to step inside. The air smelt both sweet and dry, and the silence was padded.

Hay bales were piled one on top of the other, some low and others reaching as high as the rafters. He climbed up; it was easier to gain a footing in the dark than he had imagined. The hay creaked under his yachting shoes, and was soft beneath his hands. At the top he unrolled his sleeping bag and knelt to unzip the side. He lay very still, although it worried him that later his head and nose might feel the cold. Rooting

210

through the rucksack, he found the soft wool of Queenie's knitted beret. She wouldn't mind his borrowing it. From the opposite side of the valley the house lights trembled.

Harold's mind grew limpid, and his body melted. Rain began to patter on the roof and against the tarpaulin, but it was a gentle sound, full of patience, like Maureen singing David to sleep when he was little. When the sound stopped he missed it, as if it had become part of what he knew. He felt there was no longer anything substantial between himself and the earth and the sky.

Harold woke in the early hours before dawn. He eased himself up on one elbow and watched through the gaps, while the day fought against the night and light seeped into the horizon, so pale it was without colour. Birds burst into song as the distance began to emerge and the day grew more confident; the sky moved through grey, cream, peach, indigo, and into blue. A soft tongue of mist crept the length of the valley floor so that the hilltops and houses seemed to rise out of cloud. Already the moon was a wispy thing.

He had done it. He had spent his first night outside. Harold felt a rush of incredulity that quickly became joy. Stamping his feet and blowing into his cupped hands, he wished he could tell David what he had achieved. The air was drenched with such birdsong and life, it was like standing in rain. He rolled his sleeping bag tightly, and got back to his walking.

He kept going all day, stooping for spring water when he found it, and drinking in palmfuls that tasted cold and clear. From a roadside stall, he stopped to buy coffee and a kebab. When he told the vendor about his walk, the man insisted he should not pay. His mother was in remission from cancer too; it was his pleasure to give Harold a meal. In return Harold offered the bottle of spa water from Bath. There would be more along the way. He passed Slad, where a woman with a kind face looked down from a top-floor window and smiled; and from there to Birdlip. The sun sparkled through the leaves of Cranham Woods and poured on to the beech carpet in a trembling filigree of light. He spent his second night in the open, making an empty woodshed his shelter, and the following day he made his way towards Cheltenham, with the Vale of Gloucester falling to his left like a giant bowl.

Far away the Black Mountains and the Malvern Hills straddled the horizon. He could make out the roofs of factories, and the hazy outline of Gloucester Cathedral, and the tiny shapes that must be people's houses and cars. There was so much out there, so much life, going about its daily business of getting by, of suffering and fighting, and not knowing he was sitting up there, watching. Again he felt in a profound way that he was both inside and outside what he saw; that he was both connected, and passing through. Harold began to understand that this was also the truth about his walk. He was both a part of things, and not.

In order to succeed he must remain true to the feeling that had inspired him in the first place. It didn't matter that other people would do it in a different way; in fact this was inevitable. He would keep to the roads because, despite the odd fast car, he felt safer there. It didn't matter that he had no mobile phone. It didn't matter that he had not planned his route, or brought a road map. He had a different map, and that was the one in his mind, made up of all the people and places he had passed. He would also stick to his yachting shoes because, despite the wear and tear, they were his. He saw that when a person becomes estranged from the things they know, and is a passer-by, strange things take on a new significance. And knowing this, it seemed important to allow himself to be true to the instincts that made him Harold, as opposed to anyone else.

These things made complete sense. Why then was there something remaining that troubled him? He slipped his hands in his pockets and jingled the loose change.

The kindness of the woman with food came back to him, and that of Martina. They had offered him comfort and shelter, even when he was afraid of taking them, and in accepting he had learned something new. It was as much of a gift to receive as it was to give, requiring as it did both courage and humility. He thought of the peace he had found, lying in the sleeping bag in a barn. Harold let these things play in his mind while below him the land melted as far as the sky. Suddenly he knew. He knew what he must do in order to get to Berwick.

* * *

In Cheltenham, Harold donated his washing powder to a student going into a laundrette. Passing a woman from Prestbury who couldn't find her key in her bag, he offered his wind-up torch. The following day, he gave his plasters and

213

antiseptic cream to the mother of a distressed child with a bleeding knee, and also his comb by way of distraction. The guide to Britain he handed to a bewildered German couple who were lost near Cleeve Hill and, since he knew the plant dictionary by heart, he suggested they might like that too. He rewrapped the gifts for Queenie: the pot of honey, the rose quartz, the glittering paperweight, the Roman key ring and the wool hat. He parcelled up the recent souvenirs for Maureen and took them to a post office. The compass and the rucksack he kept, because they were not his to give away.

He would make his way to Broadway, via Winchcombe; from there to Mickleton, Clifford Chambers, and then Stratford-on-Avon.

*   *   *

Two days later, Maureen was coiling her bean plants against stakes when she was called to the gate to receive a parcel. Inside she found a new selection of gifts, as well as Harold's wallet, watch, and a postcard showing a woolly Cotswold sheep.

He had written:

> *Dear Maureen. Please find enclosed my debit card, etc. I am going to walk without so many things. If I keep it simple, I know I can get there. I think of you often. H.*

She climbed the slope to the front door without noticing that she had feet.

Maureen stowed the wallet in his bedside drawer, beneath the photographs of herself and

214

David. The postcard she pinned to Rex's map.

'Oh Harold,' she said softly. And she wondered if, despite the increasing distance between them, he somehow heard.

19

HAROLD AND THE WALK

It had never been such a beautiful May. Every day the sky shone a peerless blue, untouched by cloud. Already, the gardens were crammed with lupins, roses, delphiniums, honeysuckle and lime clouds of lady's mantle. Insects cricked, hovered, bumbled and whizzed. Harold passed fields of buttercups, poppies, ox-eye daisies, clover, vetch and campion. The hedgerows were sweetly scented with bowing heads of elderflower, and wound through with wild clematis, hops and dog roses. The allotments too were burgeoning. There were rows of lettuce, spinach, chard, beetroot, early new potatoes and wigwams of peas. The first of the gooseberries hung like hairy green pods. Gardeners left out boxes of surplus produce for passers-by, with a sign: HELP YOURSELF.

Harold knew that he had found his way. He told the story about Queenie, and the garage girl, and he asked strangers if they would be so good as to help. In return, he listened. He might be offered a sandwich, or a bottle of water, or a fresh set of plasters. He never took more than he needed, and gently refused lifts, or walking equipment, or extra packages of food to keep him going. Snapping a pea pod from a curling stem, he ate it greedily, like sweets. The people he met, the places he passed, were all steps in his journey, and he kept a place inside his heart for each of them.

After the night in the barn, Harold continued to sleep outside. He chose dry places, and was always careful not to upset things. He washed in public lavatories, fountains and streams. He rinsed his clothes where no one was watching. He thought of that half-forgotten world lived in houses and streets and cars, where people ate three times a day, slept by night, and kept each other company. He was glad they were safe, and he was glad too that he was at last outside them.

Harold took the A-roads, B-roads, lanes and tracks. The compass quivered northwards and he followed. He went by day or by night, as the mood took him; mile after mile after mile. If the blisters were bad, he bound them with duct tape. He slept when the need for it came, and then he returned to his feet and walked again. He went under the stars, and the tender light of the moon, when it hung like an eyelash and the tree trunks shone like bones. He walked through wind and weather, and beneath sun-bleached skies. It seemed to Harold that he had been waiting all his life to walk. He no longer knew how far he had come, but only that he was going forward. The pale Cotswold stone became the red brick of Warwickshire, and the land flattened into middle England. Harold reached his hand to his mouth to brush away a fly, and felt a beard growing in thick tufts. Queenie would live. He knew it.

And yet the strangest part in all this was that a driver might overtake him, and briefly observe an old fellow in shirt and tie, perhaps a pair of yachting shoes, and see no more than another man, off down the road. It was so funny, and he was so happy, so much at one with the land beneath his feet, he could laugh and laugh with the simplicity of it.

* * *

From Stratford he made his way to Warwick. South of Coventry, Harold met a convivial young man with soft blue eyes, and sideburns that curled below his cheekbones. He told Harold his name was Mick and bought him a lemonade. Proffering his beer glass, he toasted Harold's courage. 'So you put yourself at the mercy of strangers?' he said.

Harold smiled. 'No. I'm careful. I don't hang about in city centres at night. I avoid trouble. But on the whole the kind of people who stop to listen are the kind of people who are going to help. There have been one or two moments when I was afraid. I thought a man on the A439 was going to mug me, but he was actually about to offer me an embrace. He had lost his wife to cancer. I misjudged him because he was missing his front teeth.' He saw his fingers against the lemonade glass, and how dark they were; the nails chipped and brown.

'And you really believe you will make it to Berwick?'

'I don't push it and I don't hang about. If I just keep putting one foot in front of the other, it stands to reason that I'm going to get there. I've begun to think we sit far more than we're supposed to.' He smiled. 'Why else would we have feet?'

The young man licked his lips, as if he was savouring the taste of something that was not yet in his mouth. 'What you're doing is a pilgrimage for the twenty-first century. It's awesome. Yours is the kind of story people want to hear.'

'Do you think I could trouble you for a packet of salt and vinegar crisps?' said Harold. 'I haven't eaten since lunchtime.'

Before they parted, Mick asked if he might take Harold's photograph on his mobile phone: 'Just to remember you.' Concerned the flash might upset several local men playing darts, he said, 'Could you manage it outside where I can get you on your own?'

He told Harold to stand beneath a sign that pointed north-west towards Wolverhampton. 'It's not where I'm going,' said Harold, but Mick said that the small detail wouldn't show up, what with the dark.

'Look at me as if you're shagged out,' said Mick.

Harold found this came very easily.

Bedworth. Nuneaton. Twycross. Ashby de la Zouch. Through Warwickshire, the western fringes of Leicestershire and into Derbyshire; on he went. There were days when he covered over thirteen miles, and others when the built-up streets confounded him, and he walked fewer than six. The skies turned from blue to black to blue. The soft hills rolled between the industrial cities and towns.

219

It came as a surprise when he reached Ticknall that two hikers stared point-blank. South of Derby, a cab driver passed Harold with his thumbs up, and a busker wearing a purple jester's hat stopped playing his accordion and grinned. In Little Chester, a golden-haired girl offered him a box of fruit juice, and hugged his knees, full of joy. A day later, in Ripley, a group of morris dancers appeared to put down their beers and cheer.

Alfreton. Clay Cross. The silhouette of the crooked spire of Chesterfield announced the start of the Peak District. At a drop-in coffee morning in Dronfield, a man offered Harold his willow cane, and squeezed his shoulder. Seven miles on, a shop assistant in Sheffield pressed her mobile into his hand so that he might ring home. Maureen assured him she was well, although there had been a small problem with a leaking showerhead. After that she asked if he'd seen the news.

'No, Maureen. I haven't seen a paper since the day I set off. What is it?'

He couldn't be sure but he thought she gave a small sob. Then she said, 'Well, you're the news, Harold. You and Queenie Hennessy. You seem to be all over the place.'

220

20

MAUREEN AND THE PUBLICIST

After Harold's story was reported in the *Coventry Telegraph*, there was not a morning in Fossebridge Road that passed without event. It had come on a slack news day. Mentioned on a radio phone-in programme, it was taken up by several local newspapers, including the *South Hams Gazette* where it was given the front three pages. It was then reported in one or two of the nationals, and suddenly no one could get enough. Harold's walk became the theme of *Thought for the Day* on Radio 4, and spawned leading articles about the nature of the modern pilgrimage, quintessential England, and the pluck of the Saga generation. People talked about it in shops, playgrounds, parks, pubs, parties and offices. The story had caught the imagination, just as Mick had promised his editor it would, although as it spread its details began to shift and grow. Some people reported that Harold was in his early seventies, others that he had learning difficulties. Sightings were made of him in Cornwall and Inverness, as well as Kingston upon Thames and the Peak District. There was a handful of journalists waiting on Maureen's crazy paving, and a local-television crew lodged beyond Rex's privet hedge. If you had the wherewithal, you could even follow his journey on Twitter. Maureen hadn't the wherewithal.

What shocked her most when she looked at his photograph in the local paper was how changed he had become. It was just over six weeks since he had set out to post his letter but he looked unfeasibly tall, and at ease with himself. He still wore his waterproof jacket and tie, but his hair was tangled in a mop on top of his head, a mottled beard sprang from his chin, and his skin was so dark she had to keep staring at the photograph to find traces of the man she thought she knew.

THE UNLIKELY PILGRIMAGE OF HAROLD FRY read the caption. The article described how a retired man from Kingsbridge (also home to Miss South Devon), in walking to Berwick without money, phone or maps, was proving himself a hero for the twenty-first century. It ended with a smaller photograph captioned THE FEET THAT WOULD WALK FIVE HUNDRED MILES, and showed a pair of yachting shoes similar to Harold's. Apparently they were enjoying record sales.

The trail of blue thread crept its passage on Rex's map north from Bath, in a route that touched Sheffield. She calculated that if he kept going at this pace, he might reach Berwick within weeks. And yet despite his success, despite also the flourishing of her garden, and the friendship with Rex, not to mention the letters of support that

222

arrived from well-wishers and cancer victims every day in the post, there were times when Maureen felt bereft. It seemed to come at her from nowhere. She could be making a pot of tea, and suddenly the solitariness of her single cup would make her want to scream. She never told Rex, but on those occasions she returned to the bedroom, drew the curtains and, lying under the duvet, she wailed. It would be so easy to stop getting up. To stop washing. To stop eating. Being alone required such constant effort.

Out of the blue, a young woman rang Maureen to offer her services as a PR representative. She said that people wanted to hear her side of the story.

'But I don't have one,' said Maureen.

'What do you think of what your husband is doing?'

'I think it must be very tiring.'

'Is it true there are marital difficulties?'

'I'm sorry, who did you say you are?'

The young woman repeated that she worked in public relations. It was her job to present the general public with the most sympathetic picture, and to protect her clients. Maureen interrupted to ask if she minded holding for a moment. There was a photographer standing on her bean plants, and she needed to tap at the window.

'There are many ways I can help,' said the young lady. She mentioned emotional support, breakfast-television interviews and invitations to B-list parties. 'You only need to name what you want, and I can fix it.'

'That's very kind but I've never been a party animal.' Some days she didn't know which was madder: the world inside her head, or the one you read about in the papers and magazines. She thanked the girl for her generous offer. 'I'm not sure that I need help, though. Unless, of course, you do ironing?'

When she told Rex he laughed. She remembered how the publicity girl hadn't. They were drinking coffee in his front room because Maureen had run out of milk, and there appeared to be a small group of fans waiting outside the garden for news of Harold. They had brought gifts of Dundee cake and hand-knitted socks, but, as she had already explained to several fans, she had no forwarding address.

'One journalist called it the perfect love story,' she said quietly.

'Harold isn't in love with Queenie Hennessy. That's not what his walk is about.'

'The publicist asked if we had problems.'

'You have to have faith in him, Maureen, and in your marriage too. He will be back.'

Maureen studied the hem of her skirt. The stitching had come loose, and a section flapped free. 'But it's so hard to keep believing, Rex. It actually hurts. I don't know if he still loves me. I don't know if he loves Queenie. Some days I think it would be easier if he were dead. At least I'd know where I stood.' She glanced up at Rex, and paled. 'That was an awful thing to say.'

He shrugged. 'It's all right.'

'I know how much you miss Elizabeth.'

'I miss her all the time. I know in my head that she has gone, but I still keep looking. The only difference is that I am getting used to the pain. It's like discovering a great hole in the ground. To begin with, you forget it's there and you keep falling in. After a while, it's still there, but you learn to walk round it.'

Maureen bit her lip and nodded. After all, she had known her share of grief. It struck her again what tumult the human heart continues to feel. To a young person, passing Rex in the street, he would look like a helpless old man. Out of touch with reality, and all spent. Yet, beneath his waxen skin, and inside his portly frame, there was a heart that beat with the same passion as a teenager's.

He said, 'Do you know what I most regret about losing her?'

She shook her head.

'That I didn't fight it.'

'But Elizabeth had a brain tumour, Rex. How could you have fought that?'

'When the doctors told us she was dying I held her hand and gave up. We both did. I know it wouldn't have made any difference in the end but I wish I had let her see how much I wanted to keep her. I should have raged, Maureen.'

He sat bent over his cup of coffee, as if in prayer. He didn't look up. He repeated the words with a quiet intensity she had not seen in him before, so that his cup trembled on its saucer. His knuckles were pure bone. 'I should have raged.'

The conversation stayed with Maureen. She grew low again, and spent hours staring out of windows, remembering the past, but doing very little. She considered the young woman she had been, who was so sure she could be everything for Harold, and then she considered the one she had become. Not even a wife. She retrieved the two photographs she had found in his bedside drawer;

225

the one of herself laughing in the garden after they were married, and the one of David with his first pair of shoes.

Something about the second image made her start. She had to look again. It was the hand. The hand supporting David as he balanced on one leg. A cold shiver slipped the length of her spine. The hand was not hers. It was Harold's.

It was she who had taken the photograph. Of course. She remembered now. Harold had held David's hand while she fetched the camera. How had she blocked that piece of the past from her head? Years she had blamed Harold for never holding their son. For not giving him the love a child needs.

Maureen went to the best room and pulled out the albums that no one looked at. The edges were felted with a layer of dust that she wiped with her skirt. Blotting back tears, she studied every page. They were mostly of herself and David, but tucked among them there were others too. He lay in Harold's lap as a baby, while his father looked down at him, hands in mid-air, as if forbidding himself to touch. There was another of David sitting on his father's shoulders while Harold craned his neck to balance him upright. There was David as a teenager side by side with Harold, the young man in black, and long-haired, the father in jacket and tie, both of them peering over the goldfish pond. She laughed. They had tried for closeness. Not in an obvious way. Not in a way that was everyday. But Harold had wanted it, and even David occasionally. She sat with the album wide open in her lap, and stared into the air, seeing not net curtains but only the past.

226

She found again the day at Bantham, when David had swum out into the current. She watched Harold fiddling over his laces, and she thought of the years she had spent rebuking him. And then she saw the image through a new perspective, as if she had turned the camera and pointed it back on herself. Her stomach jumped. There was a woman at the water's edge, shouting and waving her hands, but not running into the sea. A mother half mad with fright; but doing nothing about it. If David had almost drowned at Bantham, she had been equally to blame.

The days that followed were even worse. The photograph albums lay all over the floor of the best room because she couldn't face putting them back. She put on an early-morning white wash and left it festering all day in the drum of the washing machine. She took to eating cheese and crackers because she couldn't be bothered to heat a pan of water. She was nothing but the remembering.

When Harold managed to ring, she could do no more than listen. 'Goodness,' she would murmur. Or, 'Who'd have thought it?' He told her the places where he had rested, the log bunkers, toolsheds, huts, bus shelters and barns. The words tumbled out of him with such vigour she felt ancient.

'I take care not to upset anything. And I never force a lock,' he'd say. He knew the name of every hedgerow plant, and also its uses. He recited several, but she couldn't keep up. Now, he told her, he was learning about natural navigation. He described the people he had met, and how they had fed him or repaired his shoes; even the addicts, drunks and drop-outs. 'Nobody is so

227

frightening once you stop and listen, Maureen.' He appeared to have time for them all. He was so bewildering to her, this man who walked alone and greeted strangers, that in turn she said mildly high-pitched things she regretted about bunions, or the weather. She never said, 'Harold, I have wronged you.' She never said she had been happy in Eastbourne, or that she wished she had agreed to a dog. She never said, 'Is it really too late?' But she thought these things all the time as she listened.

Left alone, she sat in the cold light of the night sky and cried for what felt like hours, as if she and the solitary moon were the only ones who understood. It wasn't even in her to talk to David.

Maureen stared at the streetlights piercing the dark over Kingsbridge. The safe, sleeping world held no place for her. She couldn't stop thinking of Rex, and how much he still raged for Elizabeth.

21

HAROLD AND THE FOLLOWER

Someone was behind Harold. He could feel it in his spine. He quickened his pace, but the person following him along the hard shoulder did the same, and although they were not yet close enough to become a shadow they would catch up soon. Harold scanned the road ahead for people, but there was no one. Harold turned to look behind him. The ribbon of tarmac stretched towards the horizon between fields of yellow rape, so hot in the afternoon sun it shimmered. Cars appeared to come out of nowhere and vanish as quickly. You couldn't even see the people inside. But there was no one walking. There was no one on the hard shoulder.

However, as he continued he could sense in his skin, all the way up his neck and into his hair, that there was certainly a person behind, and that they were still following. Not wanting to stop again, he found a gap in the traffic and darted into the road, crossing fast at an angle, while also casting an eye to his left. Nobody came into view, and yet minutes later he knew that the person following had also crossed the road. He walked faster, with his breath and heart pounding. A sweat had broken out all over him.

He continued like this for another half-hour, stopping and looking back and seeing no one, but knowing he was not alone. Only once, when he turned, did he notice a low shrub quivering, although there was no wind. For the first time in weeks, he regretted he had no mobile phone. He took refuge that night in an unlocked toolshed, but lay very still in his sleeping bag, listening for the person he knew in his bones was waiting outside.

The following morning, and due north of Barnsley, Harold heard someone shout his name from the opposite side of the A61. A slight young man in reflective shades and a baseball cap dodged between traffic. Gasping for breath, he said he had come to join Harold. He spoke fast. His cheekbones were like pencils. His name was Lf. Harold frowned. 'Ilf,' repeated the boy. And then again: 'Wilf.' He looked undernourished and barely twenty. On his feet he wore trainers with fluorescent-green laces.

'I am going to be a pilgrim, Mr Fry. I'm going to save Queenie Hennessy too.' He lifted a sports bag and held it suspended. It was clearly new, like the trainers. 'I've got my sleeping bag and everything.'

It was like talking to David. Even the young man's hands were shaking.

There was no time to object, because the young man called Wilf had already fallen in beside Harold, and was striding at his pace, chattering

230

nervously. Harold tried to listen but every time he looked at Wilf he found further reminders of his son. The fingernails bitten to the quick. The way he slipped out words as if they weren't really for your hearing. 'I saw your picture in the paper. And then I asked for a sign. I said, "Lord, if I should go to Mr Fry, show me." And guess what He did?'

'I don't know.' A passing van slowed. The driver pointed a mobile phone out of the window and appeared to take Harold's photograph.

'He gave me a dove.'

'A what?' The van drove on.

'Well, maybe a pigeon. But the point is, it was a sign. The Lord is good. Ask the way, Mr Fry, and He will show you.'

There was something about the way the young man used his name that caused Harold further confusion; as if Wilf knew something about him, or had a claim to him, but Harold didn't know it. They continued to walk along the grass verge, although sometimes it narrowed and it was difficult to keep side by side. Wilf's steps were smaller than Harold's so that he cantered at a sideways angle.

'I didn't know you had a dog.'

'I don't.'

The young man pulled a face and glanced over his shoulder. 'Then whose is it?'

He was right. On the other side of the road, a dog had stopped and was studying the sky, panting, with its tongue to one side. It was a small thing, the colour of autumn leaves, with rough fur like a brush. It must have waited all night outside the toolshed.

'That dog is nothing to do with me,' said Harold.

As he started off again, with the young man gambolling to keep up, he could see out of the corner of his eye that the dog had crossed the road and was also trotting behind. Whenever Harold stopped and looked back, the dog shrank into the hedgerow with its head dropped, as if it wasn't there, or was something else. Perhaps a statue of a dog.

'Go away,' called Harold. 'Go home.'

The dog tilted its head as if Harold had just told it something interesting. It trotted up to Harold, and carefully placed a stone beside his shoe.

'Maybe it doesn't have a home,' suggested Wilf.

'Of course it has a home.'

'Well, maybe it doesn't like its home. Maybe it gets beaten or something. That happens. It hasn't got a collar.' The dog picked up its stone and placed it beside Harold's other shoe. It sat on its back legs, looking up at him patiently, not blinking and not moving its head. On the horizon grew the dark moors of the Peak District.

'I can't look after a dog. I don't have food. And I'm walking to Berwick on busy roads. It's too dangerous. Go home, dog.'

They tried to fool it by throwing the stone into a field and hiding behind a hedge, but the dog fetched the stone and sat beside the hedgerow, wagging its tail. 'The trouble is, I reckon it likes you,' whispered Wilf. 'It wants to come too.' They crawled out from the hedge and continued, with the dog now sauntering openly at Harold's side. It wasn't safe to stick with the A61. Harold took a diversion on the quieter B6132, although the going was slow. Wilf had to keep stopping to pull off his trainers and shake them. They covered only a mile.

232

It came as a further surprise to Harold that he was recognized by a woman deadheading roses in her front garden. 'You're the pilgrim, aren't you?' she said. 'I have to say I think what you are doing is absolutely marvellous.' She opened her purse and offered him a twenty-pound note. Wilf wiped his forehead with his cap and whistled.

'I couldn't possibly take it,' said Harold. He felt the young man's eyes boring holes into his side. 'But a round of sandwiches would be kind. And maybe some matches and a candle for tonight. A bit of butter. I don't have any of those things.' He glanced at Wilf's nervous face. 'I think we may need them.'

She urged him to join her for a light supper, and extended her invitation to Wilf, also offering the men bathroom facilities and the use of her telephone.

It gave seven rings before his wife answered. She sounded tense. 'You're not that PR girl again?'

'No, Maureen. It's me.'

'It's gone mad,' she told him. 'Sometimes people ask to come inside the house. Rex found a young man trying to remove a piece of flint from the front wall.'

By the time Harold had showered, it seemed that his hostess had also invited a small number of chums for an impromptu sherry party on the lawn. On greeting him, they raised their glasses and toasted Queenie's health. He had never seen so much backcombed grey-blue hair, or so many corduroy trousers in shades of mustard, gold and russet. Underneath a table, laid out with canapés and cold meats, sat the dog, chewing on something between its paws. Occasionally someone threw the stone, and the dog retrieved it and waited for them to do it again.

The men told stories about their own adventures involving yachts and shooting, and Harold listened patiently. He watched Wilf talking animatedly to their hostess. Her laughter had a shrill quality Harold realized he had almost forgotten. He wondered if anyone would notice if he slipped away.

He was swinging his rucksack up on to his shoulders when Wilf broke free of the woman and caught up. 'I had no idea it was like this,' he said. He crammed a smoked salmon blini into his mouth with all five fingers, as if it were alive. 'Why are we leaving?'

'I need to get on. And it isn't usually like this. I find a place for my sleeping bag and no one notices. I've been living for days on bread rolls and what I find. But you should stay here, if you'd like to. I'm sure you're very welcome.'

Wilf gazed at Harold but he wasn't really listening. He said, 'People keep asking if I'm your son.' Harold smiled, suddenly tender. Turning again to the cocktail guests, he felt he and Wilf were linked in some way, as if, by being outsiders, they shared something bigger than in truth they had. They waved their farewells.

'You're too young to be my son,' said Harold. He patted Wilf's arm. 'We'd better get a move on if we're going to find somewhere to sleep.'

'Good luck!' called the guests. 'Queenie will keep living!'

The dog was already at the gate, and all three walked at an easy pace. Their shadows were pillars against the road and the deepening air smelt sweet with elderflower and privet blossom. Wilf told Harold about his life; how he had tried many things, but been good at none of them. If it wasn't for the Lord, he said, he would be in prison. Sometimes Harold listened, and sometimes he watched for bats, flitting through the dusk. He wondered if the young man would really accompany him all the way to Berwick, and what he would do about the dog. He wondered if David had ever tried God. Far away, the factories belched further cloud into the sky.

After only an hour, Wilf was clearly limping. They had barely covered half a mile.

'Do you need to rest?'

'I'm fine, Mr Fry.' But he was hopping.

Harold searched for a sheltered spot and they stopped early. Wilf copied him, spreading out his sleeping bag beside a storm-felled elm. Plates of dryad's saddle grew out of the dead trunk with mottled markings like feathers. Harold picked the fungi while Wilf jumped from one foot to the other, yelping and calling them gross. Afterwards he searched for fallen leafy branches and velvet pads of moss, which he layered in the earthed hole at the foot of the tree where its roots had ripped through. Harold had not taken such care over his sleeping place in days. As he worked, the dog followed, picking up stones and dropping them at his feet.

'I'm not going to throw them,' he warned, but once or twice he did.

Harold reminded Wilf to check his feet for blisters. It was important to take proper care; later he would show him how to drain the pus. 'And can you light a fire, Wilf?'

235

'Can I shit, Mr Fry. Where's your petrol?'

Harold explained again that he was walking without unnecessary baggage. He sent the boy off to look for more wood, while Harold ripped the fungi into rough slices with his fingernails. They were tougher than he would have liked, but he hoped they might impress. He cooked them over the fire in an old tin he carried in his rucksack especially for the purpose, with the pat of butter, and torn-up leaves of Jack-by-the-hedge. The air smelt of fried garlic.

'Eat,' he told Wilf, offering the tin.

'What with?'

'Your fingers. You can wipe them afterwards on my jacket if you want. Maybe tomorrow we'll find potatoes.'

Wilf refused; he had a laugh that was like a shriek. 'How do I know it's not poisonous?'

'I'm eating it. Look at me. And there's nothing else tonight.'

Wilf posted a small corner between his teeth, and ate with his lips curled back as if he was afraid of being stung.

'Shit,' he kept squealing. 'Shit.' Harold laughed, and the boy ate more.

'It doesn't taste so bad,' said Harold. 'Does it?'

'It tastes of fucking garlic. And mustard.'

'That's the leaves. Most wild food tastes bitter. You'll get used to that. If it tastes of nothing, that's nice. If it tastes good, that's a treat. Maybe we'll spot redcurrants. Or wild strawberries. If you get a really ripe one it's like cheesecake.'

They sat with their knees hunched, watching the flames. Far behind them, Sheffield was a sulphuric glow on the horizon, and there were always cars if

236

you listened hard enough, but he felt they were a long way from other people. Harold told the boy how he had learned to cook over the fire, and how he had taught himself about plant life from a small book he had acquired in Exeter. There were good fungi and bad ones, he said; you had to learn the difference. You had to be sure, for instance, that you didn't pick sulphur tufts instead of branching oysters. Occasionally he leaned over the fire and blew on it, so that the embers bloomed red. Flicks of ash rose into the air, glowing briefly before melting into the dusk. The air was alive with crickets.

'Don't you get scared?' said Wilf.

'When I was a boy, my parents didn't want me. Then, later on in my life, I met my wife and we had a child. That went wrong too. Since I have been out in the open, it seems there's less to be afraid of.' He wished David could hear.

Later, as Harold wiped the cooking tin with a piece of newspaper and returned it to his rucksack, the boy amused himself with throwing a stone into the undergrowth for the dog. It yelped wildly and scurried into the darkness, returning with the stone and posting it at Wilf's feet. It occurred to Harold how much he had grown used to both solitude and silence.

They lay in their sleeping bags, and Wilf asked if they might pray. Harold said, 'I have no objection to other people doing it; but if you don't mind, I won't join in.'

Wilf clenched his hands into a ball, and screwed his eyes closed. With his nails so ragged, the skin at his fingertips looked too tender. He bowed his head, like a child, and whispered words that

237

Harold did not care to overhear. Harold hoped there was someone, or something, apart from himself, listening. There was a trace of light left in the sky as they drifted into sleep. The cloud was low, and the air hung still; he was sure it wouldn't rain.

Despite his prayers, Wilf woke crying out in the night, and shivering. Harold took him in his arms but the boy was covered in sweat. He worried he had been wrong about the fungus, although he hadn't made a mistake so far.

'What's that noise?' Wilf shuddered.

'Just foxes. Maybe dogs. And sheep too. I can definitely hear sheep.'

'We didn't pass any sheep.'

'No. But you hear more of what is around at night. You get used to that quickly. Don't worry. Nothing will hurt you.'

He rubbed his back and coaxed him to sleep, the way Maureen used to do with David when he got the frights after his Lake District holiday. 'It's all right. It's all right,' he repeated, just the way she would. He wished he had found a better place for Wilf's first night; there had been an unlocked glass summerhouse a few evenings back, and Harold had slept in comfort on a wicker sofa. Even underneath a bridge would have been better than this, although there was always the worry of attracting attention.

'It's fucking freaky,' said Wilf. His teeth were knocking. Harold pulled out Queenie's knitted beret and fitted it over the boy's head.

'I used to have bad dreams but they stopped as I walked. It will be the same for you.'

For the first time in weeks, Harold did not

238

sleep that night. He sat watching over the boy, remembering the past, and asking himself why David had made the choices he had; whether Harold should have seen the seeds of them right from the beginning. Would it have been the same, if David had had a different father? It was a long while since such questions had troubled him. The dog lay at his side.

As dawn came, the moon glowed pale yellow in the morning light, surrendering to the sun. They walked through dew with the pink feathery tips of sedge and ribwort brushing wet and cold against their legs. Droplets hung from the stems like gems and spider webs were downy puffs between the blades of grass. The rising sun shone so low and bright that the shapes and colours ahead of them lost their clarity and it was like walking into mist. He showed Wilf the flattened path their feet had made on the verge. 'That's us,' he said.

Wilf's new trainers continued to trouble him and the lack of sleep slowed Harold. In the course of the following two days they made it only as far as Wakefield, but he felt unable to leave the young man behind. The panic attacks, or nightmares, continued. Wilf insisted he had been bad in the past, and that the Lord would save him.

Harold was less sure. The boy was painfully underweight, and prone to mood swings. One minute he was running ahead, racing the dog to find its stone; the next he could barely speak. Harold distracted Wilf by telling him all that he had taught himself about hedgerow plants, and the sky. He pointed out the difference between the low-combed stratus clouds and the tall cirrus clouds that moved high above like boulders. He showed Wilf how, by observing shadows and textures around him, he could deduce his direction. A plant, for instance, that showed a thicker growth on one side was obviously receiving more sunlight there. They could tell from this that the plant was south-facing, and that they must head in the opposite direction. Wilf appeared to learn greedily, although sometimes he would ask a question that suggested he had not been concentrating at all. They sat beneath the poplar and listened to its leaves rattling in the wind.

'The trembling tree,' said Harold. 'You can spot it easily. It shakes so hard that from a distance it looks as if it's covered in little lights.'

He told Wilf about the people he had met at the beginning, and others who had more recently crossed his path. There was a woman living in a straw house, and a couple who drove a goat in their car, and a retired dentist who travelled six miles a day to fetch fresh water from a natural spring. 'He told me about it. He said we all should accept what the earth gives freely. It is an act of grace, he said. Since then I always make a point of stopping to drink from a spring.'

It was only in saying these things that Harold realized how far he had come. He took pleasure in heating water, a little at a time, in a can for Wilf over a candle, and picking the blossom from the lime tree to make tea. He showed him you could eat ox-eye daisies, pineapple weed, toadflax and sweet hop shoots, if you wanted. He felt he was doing everything for David that he hadn't in fact done. There was so much he wanted Wilf to see.

'These are vetch pods. They're sweet, but not good if you have too much. Mind you, nor is vodka.' Wilf held the tiny pod and took one nibbling mouthful, before spitting it out.

'I'd rather have vodka, Mr Fry.'

Harold pretended he hadn't heard. They hunkered down on a bank, waiting for a goose to lay an egg. The boy danced and screamed as it emerged, wet and white and huge against the grass. 'Oh fuck, that's so rank. It came right out of her arse. Shall I throw something?'

'At the goose? No. Throw a stone for the dog.'

'I'd rather hit the goose.'

Harold ushered Wilf away, and pretended he hadn't heard that either.

They talked about Queenie Hennessy, and the small kindnesses she had shown. He described how she could sing backwards, and always liked a riddle. 'I don't think anyone else knew those things about her,' he said. 'We told one another things we probably didn't tell other people. It's easier when you're travelling.' He showed the presents he carried for her in his rucksack. The boy particularly liked the paperweight from Exeter Cathedral that glittered when he tipped it upside down. Sometimes Harold found Wilf had taken it from his rucksack and was playing with it, and had to remind him to take care. In turn, Wilf produced further souvenirs. A piece of flint, a spotted guinea-fowl feather, a stone hooped with rings. Once he produced a small garden gnome with a fishing rod that he promised he had found in a bin. Another time he appeared with three pints of milk, insisting they were going free. Harold warned him not to rush as he drank, but the boy did and was sick after ten minutes.

There were so many offerings, Harold had to

leave them behind when Wilf wasn't looking, taking care to hide them from the dog, who was inclined to retrieve the pebbles at least and return them to Harold's feet. Sometimes the boy turned to shout about something new he had found, and Harold's heart flipped over. It could so easily be David.

22

HAROLD AND THE PILGRIMS

Dear Queenie, There has been a surprising turn of events. So many people ask after you. Best wishes, Harold.
PS. A kind woman at the post office has not charged me for the stamp. She also sends her regards.

On Harold's forty-seventh day of walking, he was joined by a middle-aged woman and a father of two. Kate explained she had recently suffered great pain but wished to leave it behind. She was a small woman, dressed in black, who marched with her chin thrust out and slightly upwards, as if she were struggling to see beyond the brim of a floppy hat. Sweat beaded her hairline, and wet half-moons hung beneath her armpits.

'She's fat,' said Wilf.

'I don't think you should say that.'

'She's still fat.'

243

The man called himself Rich, short for Richard; surname Lion. He had been in finance but had got out of the business in his mid thirties. Since then, he had been 'winging it'. Reading about Harold's journey had filled him with a hope he had not experienced since he was a child. He had packed only a few necessaries and set off. He was a tall man, like Harold, with an assertive voice that had an adenoidal ring. He wore professional boots, camouflage trousers, and a kangaroo-leather bush hat that he had bought online. He carried with him a tent, a sleeping bag and a Swiss Army knife for emergencies.

'To be honest with you,' he confided, 'I made a big mess of my life. I got made redundant, and after that I had a bit of a breakdown. My wife left me, and took the kids.' He struck the ground with the sharp blade of his knife. 'It's the boys, Harold. I miss them so much. I want them to see I can do something. You know? I want them to be proud of me. Have you thought about going cross-country?'

As the newly formed party made their way to Leeds, there were discussions about the route. Rich suggested they should avoid cities and make for the moors. Kate felt they should continue along the A61. What did Harold think, they asked? Uncomfortable with conflict, Harold suggested they were both good ideas, as long as they got to Berwick. He had been alone for so long he found it tiring to be constantly in the company of others. Their questions and their enthusiasm both moved and slowed him. But since they had chosen to walk with him and support Queenie's cause, he also felt responsible for them, as if he had asked them to join, and, as a consequence, must listen to their different needs and secure their safe passage. Wilf sulked at Harold's side, hands dug in his pockets, complaining his trainers were too small. Harold had the feeling he used to have with David, wishing he could be more companionable, and fearing that his insecurity might look like arrogance. It took over an hour to find somewhere everyone agreed they'd be comfortable enough to sleep.

Within two days, Rich had a problem with Kate. It wasn't anything she had said exactly, he told Harold; it was more her manner. She behaved as if she thought she was better simply because she had arrived thirty minutes earlier. 'And you know what?' said Rich. He was beginning to shout. Harold didn't know. He just felt got at. 'She drove here.' On reaching Harrogate, Kate suggested they should visit the Royal Baths to freshen up. Rich sneered but conceded he could do with spare blades for his knife. Not wanting either, Harold sat in the municipal gardens where he was approached by several well-wishers, asking for news of Queenie. Wilf seemed to disappear.

By the time the group reconvened, a young widower whose wife had died of cancer was sitting beside Harold. The man explained he wished to accompany them and that in order to gather further public support for Queenie, he would like to do it in a gorilla suit. Before Harold could dissuade him, Wilf reappeared; although he seemed to have difficulty negotiating his passage along the pavement.

'Jesus wept,' said Rich.

They made their way slowly. Twice Wilf fell. It also transpired that the gorilla man could only be fed through a straw, and was prone to waves of grief accelerated by heat exhaustion. After half a mile, Harold suggested they should stop for the night.

He lit the camp fire and reminded himself it had taken at least a few days to find his own rhythm. It would be unkind to abandon them, when they had sought him out and made such a commitment to Queenie. He even wondered if her chances of survival would be greater, the more people there were who believed in her and kept walking.

From this point, others joined. They came for a day, maybe two. If it was sunny, there could be a crowd. Campaigners, ramblers, families, drop-outs, tourists, musicians. There were banners, camp fires, debates, physical warm-ups and music. People talked movingly about the loved ones they had lost to cancer; and also the things they regretted from their past. The greater the numbers, the slower they became. Not only must they accommodate the less experienced walkers, but they must also feed them. There were roast potatoes, garlic on sticks, beetroot in foil. Rich had a book about natural foraging and insisted on making hogweed fritters. The daily mileage dropped further. Sometimes it was no more than three.

Despite its slowness, the group seemed sure of itself in a way that was new to Harold. They told themselves they were no longer an assortment of torsos and feet and heads and hearts but one single energy, bound by Queenie Hennessy. The walk had been an idea inside himself for so long that when other people pledged their belief in it he was touched. More. He knew it could work. If he had known before, he knew it now in a deeper way.

They put up tents, unrolled sleeping bags and slept beneath the sky. They promised Queenie would live. To their left curved the dark peaks of Keighley Moor.

Within only a few days, however, tensions began to develop. Kate had no time for Rich. He was an egomaniac, she said. In return he called her a bitter cow. Then, during the course of one evening, both the gorilla man and a visiting student slept with the same primary-school teacher, and Rich's attempts to resolve the animosity threatened to end in a punch-up. Wilf could not stop trying to convert fellow walkers to God, or asking for prayers to be said for Queenie, and this led to further aggravation. When an amateur walking group pitched up for the night there were more disagreements: some argued that tents were not in the true spirit of Harold's journey, some wanted to avoid roads altogether and head towards the more challenging Pennine Way. And what about roadkill? asked Rich, sparking off another round. Harold listened with growing unease. He didn't mind where people slept, or how they walked. He didn't mind what they ate. He simply wanted to get to Berwick.

He was in it now with these other people. After all, they had suffered too in different ways. Wilf still got the shakes at night, and Kate often sat by the fire with tears shining on her cheeks. Even Rich, when he spoke of his boys, had to flap open a handkerchief and pretend he had hay fever. No matter how much he regretted their decisions to join him, it was not in Harold's nature to let his companions down. Sometimes he broke free, and washed himself with water, or took lungfuls of air.

He reminded himself there were no rules to his walk. He had been guilty once or twice of believing he understood, only to discover he did not. Maybe it was the same with the pilgrims? Maybe they were the next part of the journey? There were times, he saw, when not knowing was the biggest truth, and you had to stay with that.

News about the pilgrimage continued to gather momentum as if it had acquired an energy of its own. Word had only to get round that they were approaching and everyone with an Aga began to bake. Kate narrowly missed injury from a woman in a Land Rover hell bent on delivering a tray of goat's cheese slices. Rich suggested over the camp fire that Harold should begin each meal with a few words about what it meant to be a pilgrim. When Harold declined, Rich offered to speak instead. He wondered if anyone would care to take notes? The gorilla man obliged, although it was difficult to write with a hairy glove and he had to keep asking Rich to stop.

The press also continued to run testimonies to Harold's goodness. He did not have time to read the papers, but it seemed that Rich was more up to date. A spiritualist in Clitheroe claimed the pilgrim had a golden aura. A young man who'd been on the verge of jumping from the Clifton Suspension Bridge gave a moving account of how Harold had talked him down.

'But I didn't go to Bristol,' Harold said. 'I went to Bath, and from there to Stroud. I remember it clearly because it was the point when I almost gave up. I never met anyone on a bridge. And I am certain I didn't talk them down.'

Rich claimed this was a minor detail. Petty, in

fact. 'Maybe he didn't say he was about to commit suicide. But meeting you gave him hope. I expect you've forgotten.' Again he reminded Harold that he had to look at the bigger picture; no publicity was bad publicity. It occurred to Harold that even though Rich was forty, and therefore about the right age to be his son, he talked as if it was Harold who was the child. He said that Harold was cornering a rich market. You had to strike while the iron was hot. He also mentioned cherry-picking ideas, and singing from the same hymn sheet, but Harold was getting a headache. He had such a congestion of incoherent images in his mind—cherry trees and hymn sheets and steam irons—that he had to keep stopping in order to work out what exactly it was that Rich was talking about. He wished the man would honour the true meaning of words, instead of using them as ammunition.

It was already mid June, and Wilf's estranged father gave a moving interview about the courage of his son ('He's never even met me,' said Wilf). The council of Berwick-upon-Tweed commissioned placards and bunting to welcome the pilgrims' arrival. The owner of a corner shop in Ripon accused them of stealing several items, including whisky.

Rich called a meeting, during which in no uncertain terms he accused Wilf of theft and suggested he should be sent home. For once, Harold stood up and disagreed; but it pained him to be put in a place of confrontation and he saw he could not do it again. Rich listened with his eyes narrowed into slits so that Harold lost words mid-sentence. Rich finally conceded that Wilf should

249

be given another chance, but he avoided Harold for the rest of the afternoon. Then half the group went down with stomach cramps and temperatures, when the boy mistook some mildly poisonous mushrooms for the friendly ones that looked disarmingly similar. Just as they were recovering, the abundance of redcurrants, cherries and raw gooseberries in their diet brought on a compromising spate of diarrhoea. The gorilla man was badly stung while taking notes for Rich when it transpired there was a wasp in his glove. For two days they did not walk at all.

The horizon was a series of blue peaks that Harold longed to climb. The sun hung high in the eastern sky, leaving the moon so pale it looked made of cloud. If only these people would go. Would find something else to believe in. He shook his head, berating himself for his disloyalty.

Rich informed the group that something was needed to distinguish the real pilgrims from their followers. He had the solution. He had been in touch with an old friend in PR, who owed him a favour. The friend in turn had contacted the distributors of a health drink and they would be delighted to provide all official walkers with T-shirts with the word PILGRIM on the front and back. The T-shirts would be available in white and come in three sizes.

'White?' Kate scoffed. 'Where are we going to wash these things?'

'White stands out,' said Rich. 'And its image is pure.'

'There speaks a man; and bollocks,' said Kate.

The company would also provide a limitless supply of healthy fruit drinks. All they wanted in return was for Harold to be seen holding one as often as possible. As soon as the T-shirts arrived, a press call was organized. Harold was to be joined on the A617 by Miss South Devon for the photoshoot.

Harold said, 'I think the others should be in it too. They have made a commitment to the walk as well as me.'

Rich said that clouded the message about faith for the twenty-first century, and also weakened the Queenie love story.

'But I was never trying to make a point about those things,' said Harold. 'And I love my wife.'

Rich handed him a fruit drink and reminded him to hold the bottle with the label facing towards the camera. 'I'm not asking you to finish it. I just want you to hold the thing. And did I say you've been invited to dinner with the mayor?'

'I'm honestly not very hungry.'

'You need to take the dog. His wife is something to do with the Blue Cross.'

*   *   *

It seemed that people were taking offence if the pilgrims did not visit their town. The mayor of a resort in North Devon gave an interview claiming Harold was 'white middle-class elitist', and Harold was so shaken he felt the need to apologize. He even wondered if he would have to walk home, taking in all the places he had failed to pass en route to Berwick. He admitted to Kate the fruit drinks were playing havoc with his digestive system.

'But Rich told you,' she said, 'you don't have to

251

drink them. You can throw it away as soon as the photo's taken.'

He smiled sadly. 'I can't hold the bottle and remove the lid and then not drink it. I'm a postwar child, Kate. We don't talk up our achievements, and we don't throw things away. It's how we were brought up.'

Kate reached up her arms and gave him a damp hug.

He wanted to return it, but he stood rather helpless in her embrace. Maybe that was another symptom of his generation? Certainly he looked at the people around him in their vest tops and their shorts, and wondered if he had become superfluous.

'What's troubling you?' she said. 'You keep wandering off.'

Harold straightened himself. 'I can't help feeling this is wrong. All the noise. All the fuss. I appreciate how much everyone has done but I don't see any more how it's going to help Queenie. We only covered six miles yesterday. And seven the day before that. I wonder if I should go.'

Kate swung round very suddenly, as if she had received some sort of blow to her chin. 'Go?'

'Get back on the road.'

'Without us?' she said. There was panic in her eyes. 'You can't. You can't leave us. Not now.'

Harold nodded.

'Promise me.' She gripped his arm. The gold of her wedding ring caught the sunlight.

'Of course I won't go without you.' They walked on in silence. He wished he had not mentioned his doubts. It was clear she had no room for them.

Yet despite his promise, Harold remained

252

troubled. They had good periods of walking but—with illness and injury and so much public support—it took almost two weeks to cover sixty miles; they were not yet in Darlington. He imagined Maureen seeing pictures of him in the newspapers and he was ashamed. He wondered what she thought when she saw them. If she thought him a fool.

One night, as supporters and well-wishers took out guitars and began to sing by the fire, Harold fetched his rucksack and slipped away. The sky was so clear and black, it throbbed with stars, and the moon was losing its fullness once more. He thought back to the night he had slept in the barn near Stroud. No one knew the real truth about why he was walking to Queenie. They had made assumptions. They thought it was a love story, or a miracle, or an act of beauty, or even bravery, but it was none of those things. The discrepancy between what he knew and what other people believed frightened him. It also made him feel, as he looked back at the camp, that even in the midst of them he was unknown. The fire was a glow of light in the blackness. Voices and laughter came to him, and they were all strangers.

He could keep walking. There was nothing to stop him. Yes, he had made a promise to Kate but his loyalty to Queenie was greater. After all, he had everything he needed. His shoes. The compass. Queenie's gifts. He could take a more indirect route, across the hills perhaps, and avoid people altogether. His pulse quickened as his feet drove forwards. He could walk the nights. The dawns again. He could be in Berwick in weeks.

Then he heard Kate's voice, thin against the

night air, calling his name, and the dog barking at her feet. He heard other voices—some he recognized, some he didn't—all shouting 'Harold' into the darkness. His loyalty to them was not the same as his loyalty to Queenie, but they deserved more than to be abandoned without so much as an explanation. Slowly he returned.

Rich emerged out of the shadows just as Harold hit the circle of soft light from the fire. Spotting the old man, he ran towards him and bundled Harold into his arms.

'We thought you'd gone.'

His voice shook. He had maybe been drinking. There was certainly the smell of it. Rich clung so hard that Harold lost his balance and almost fell.

'Steady on there,' laughed Rich. It was a rare moment of affection, albeit a little stumbling, but locked in this embrace, Harold struggled for breath as if he were being slowly suffocated.

A photograph appeared next day in the papers, with the caption CAN HAROLD FRY MAKE IT? He appeared to be collapsing into Rich's arms.

23

MAUREEN AND HAROLD

Maureen could bear it no longer. She confided in Rex that, against David's advice, she was going to find Harold. She had spoken with her husband on the phone; he hoped the pilgrims would reach Darlington by the following afternoon. She knew it was too late to make amends for the past, but she would have one last stab at persuading him to come home.

As soon as it was light, she fetched the car keys from the hall table and slipped a coral lipstick into her handbag. Locking the front door, she was surprised to hear Rex call her name. He was wearing a sunhat, a pair of shades, and he was clutching a hardback road map of the British Isles.

'I thought you might need someone to navigate,' he said. 'According to the AA, we should be there by late afternoon.'

The miles sped past, but she barely saw them. She said things while knowing that none of them added up; as if she were saying words that were only the tip of the huge mountain of feeling beneath. What if Harold didn't want to see her? What if the other pilgrims were with him?

'Supposing you're wrong, Rex?' she said. 'Supposing he is in love with Queenie after all? Maybe I should write? What do you think? I feel I might say it better in a letter.'

When he said nothing, she turned to Rex and found him looking peaky. 'Are you all right?'

He gave a tight nod, as if he were afraid of moving. 'You have overtaken three articulated lorries and a coach,' he said. 'In single-lane traffic.' He added that he thought he would be fine, if he sat very still and looked out of the window.

*   *   *

It was easy to find Harold, and the pilgrims. Someone had arranged a photo-shoot for the tourist board in the pedestrianized market square and Maureen joined a small crowd. There was a tall man ushering photographers, and also a gorilla who appeared to need a chair, as well as a stout woman eating a sandwich, and a young man looking shifty. Catching sight of Harold as if she were no more than a stranger, Maureen was disarmed. She had seen him on the local news, and she kept the newspaper clippings in her handbag, but none of it had prepared her for seeing him 'in true life', as David used to say. Harold surely couldn't have grown taller or broader, but looking at this weather-beaten pirate of a man, with his skin like dark leather and his curling hair, she felt she had become both one-dimensional and more fragile. It was the pared-down vitality of him that

256

made her tremble; as if he had at last become the man he should have been all along. His pilgrim T-shirt was stained and frayed at the neck. The colour was gone from his yachting shoes, and the shape of his feet was practically through the leather. Harold caught Maureen's eye, and stopped short. He said something to the tall man and broke free.

As Harold walked towards her he laughed so openly she had to look away, unable to meet the fullness of his smile. She didn't know whether to offer him her lips or her cheek, and at the last minute she changed her mind so that he kissed her nose instead and prickled her face with his beard. People were watching.

'Hello, Maureen.' His voice was deep and assured. She felt her knees weaken. 'What brings you all the way to Darlington?'

'Oh,' she shrugged. 'Rex and I fancied a drive.'

He looked round, his face beaming. 'Goodness. Has he come too?'

'He's gone to WH Smith's. He needed paper clips. After that he was keen to visit the railway museum. You can see the *Locomotion*.'

He was standing right over her, gazing into her face and not looking away. It was like being under lights. 'It's a steam train,' she added, because he still didn't seem to be doing anything, just smiling. She couldn't stop staring at his mouth. Despite the beard, his jaw had lost its rigid set. His lips looked soft.

An old fellow shouted into a megaphone to the crowd, 'Shop all you can! This is the word of the Lord! Shopping is what gives our lives purpose! Jesus came on earth to shop!' He had no shoes.

It broke the ice. Harold and Maureen smiled, and she felt there was a conspiracy between them, as if they were the only people in the world who saw it right. 'People.' She shook her head knowingly.

'It takes all sorts,' said Harold.

There was nothing condescending about his remark, nor was there anything reprimanding. It was more generous than anything else, as if the strangeness of other people was a marvellous thing, but it made her feel overwhelmingly parochial. She said, 'Do you have time for a cuppa?' She never normally referred to a pot of Earl Grey as a cuppa. And fancy trying to make up for your plain Englishness by suggesting tea.

'I would love that, Maureen,' said Harold.

*   *   *

They chose a coffee outlet on the ground floor of a department store because she said you could always trust the things you knew. The girl behind the counter stared as if she was trying to place him, and Maureen felt both proud and in the way. She had put on a pair of brand-new trainers at the last minute and they shone on the ends of her legs like beacons.

'So much choice,' said Harold, gazing at the muffins and cakes, each one in its own paper case. 'Are you sure you don't mind paying, Maureen?'

More than anything, she wanted to stare. It was years since she'd seen those blue eyes look so vibrant. He rubbed the curls of his giant beard between his forefinger and thumb so that they stuck out in peaks like royal icing. She wondered if the girl behind the counter realized she was Harold's wife.

'What will you have?' she said. She wanted to add 'darling' but the word was too shy to come out.

He asked if he might have a slice of Mars Bar Tray Bake with a strawberry frappé. Maureen gave a shrill laugh that sounded as if she had just emptied it out of a packet.

'And I'll have tea, please,' she told the girl behind the counter. 'Milk, no sugar.'

Harold shone his benign smile in the direction of the girl, whose name was pinned on her black T-shirt just above her left bosom. To Maureen's amazement, the young woman flushed from her neck upwards and grinned back.

'You're that guy off the news,' she said. 'The pilgrim. My mates think you're awesome. Would you mind signing this?' She held out her arm and a felt-tip pen and Maureen was astonished a second time to witness Harold inscribing his name with indelible ink on the soft flesh above the girl's wrist: *Best wishes, Harold.* He didn't even flinch.

The girl cradled her arm and stared long and hard at it. Then she set the drinks and the Mars Bar cake on a tray, along with one extra scone. 'Have this on me,' she said.

Maureen had never seen anything like it. She let Harold lead the way, and it was as if the room opened and hushed to make space for him. She noticed the other customers staring hard at Harold, and saying things behind cupped hands. At a table in the corner three ladies of her own age were drinking tea. She wondered where their husbands were: if they were playing golf, or dead maybe, or if they had walked out on their wives as

259

well.

'Afternoon,' he said brightly, greeting complete strangers.

He chose a table beside the window so that he could keep an eye on the dog. It lay on the pavement outside, chewing on a stone, as if very interested in the business of waiting. She felt a swell of kinship with the animal.

Maureen and Harold sat opposite each other; not side by side. And even though she had drunk tea with him for forty-seven years, her hands shook as she poured. Harold's cheeks hollowed as his frappé shot up through a straw and entered his mouth with a honk. She waited a polite moment for the drink to go down; only she waited too long, and she opened her mouth to speak at the exact moment he did.

'It's nice to—'

'Lovely to—'

They gave a laugh as if they didn't know one another terribly well.

'No, no—' he said.

'After you,' she said.

It was like another collision, and they each retreated back to their drinks. She added milk to her cup but her hand shook again and the whole lot sloshed out in a rush. 'Do people often recognize you, Harold?' She sounded like a woman interviewing him for the television.

'What gets me, Maureen, is how nice everyone is.'

'Where did you sleep last night?'

'In a field.'

She shook her head in awe but he must have misunderstood because he said in a rush, 'I don't

260

smell, do I?'

'No, no,' she rushed back.

'I washed in a stream, and then again by a drinking fountain. Only I don't have soap.' He had already finished his Mars Bar cake and was slicing open the complimentary scone. He ate food so fast he seemed to inhale it.

She said, 'I could buy you some soap. I'm sure I passed a Body Shop.'

'Thank you. That's really kind. But I don't want to carry too much.'

Maureen felt afresh the shame of not getting it. She longed to show him all her colours, and here she was, a suburban shade of grey. 'Oh,' she said, dipping her head. The pain rose, tightening her throat, making it impossible to speak.

His hand passed her a bundled handkerchief, and Maureen nipped her face into its crumpled warmth. It smelt of him, and long ago. It was no good. The tears came.

'It's just seeing you again,' she said. 'You look so well.'

'You look well too, Maureen.'

'I don't, Harold. I look like someone left behind.'

She wiped her face, but tears were still leaking between her fingers. She was sure the girl at the counter must be looking, and the shoppers, and the ladies without their husbands. Let them. Let them all stare.

'I miss you, Harold. I wish you would come home.' She waited with her blood thumping up and down her veins.

At last Harold rubbed his head, as if he had an ache there or something he needed to dislodge.

'You miss me?'

'Yes.'

'You wish I would come home?'

She nodded. It was too much to repeat it. Harold scratched his head again and then lifted his gaze to hers. She felt her insides pick up and spring over and over.

He said slowly, 'I miss you too. But Maureen, I've spent my life not doing anything. And now at last I am doing something. I have to finish my walk. Queenie is waiting. She believes in me. You see?'

'Well yes,' she said. 'I do see that. Of course I see it.' She took a sip of tea. It was cold. 'I just— I'm sorry, Harold—I don't see where I fit in. I know you're a pilgrim now and everything. But I can't help thinking about myself. I'm not as selfless as you. I'm sorry.'

'I'm no better than anyone else. I'm really not. Anybody can do what I'm doing. But you have to let go. I didn't know that at the beginning but now I do. You have to let go of the things you think you need, like cash cards and phones and maps and things.' He looked at her with his eyes shining, and his steady smile.

She reached again for her tea and remembered as it hit her mouth that it was cold. She wanted to ask if pilgrims travelled without wives as well, but she didn't. She forced another of those jolly faces that seemed to hurt, and then she glanced towards the window where Harold's dog was still waiting.

'He's eating a stone.'

He laughed. 'He does that. You have to be careful not to throw it for him. If you do, he thinks you like throwing stones and he follows you. He doesn't forget.' She smiled again. This one didn't

262

hurt.

'Have you given him a name?'

'Just Dog. It didn't seem right to give him anything else. He's-his-own-animal sort of thing. I felt a name might sound as if I thought I owned him.'

She nodded, all out of words.

'You know,' Harold said suddenly, 'you could walk with us.'

He reached for her fingers and she let him take them. The palms of his hands were so stained and calloused and her own were so pale and slight, she couldn't see how these fingers had ever fitted together. Her hand lay in her husband's, and all the rest of her was numb.

Moments from their marriage passed through her head, like a series of photographs. She saw him creeping out of the bathroom on their wedding night; the nakedness of his chest so beautiful she had gasped out loud, and caused him to dive straight back into his jacket. There was Harold at the hospital, gazing at his new baby son, and stretching out his finger. She saw too all those images in the leather albums that over the years she had cleaned from her memory. They passed through her mind in a flash, recognizable to no one but herself. She sighed.

It was all so far away, and there were so many other things lodged now between them. She saw herself and Harold twenty years ago, side by side in their sunglasses and unable to touch.

His voice parted the blanket of her thoughts. 'What do you think? Do you think you might come, Maureen?'

She eased her hand from Harold's and pushed

263

back her chair. 'It's too late,' she murmured. 'I think not.'

She stood but Harold didn't, so that she felt she was already out of the door. 'There's the garden. And Rex. Besides, I don't have my things.'

'You don't need your—'

'I do,' she said.

He chewed his beard and nodded, but without looking up, as if to say I know.

'I better get back. Rex says hello, by the way. And I brought you some plasters. As well as one of those fruit drinks you like so much.' She slid them into the neutral spot on the table midway between herself and Harold. 'But maybe pilgrims don't use plasters?'

Harold leaned back to slip both her presents into his pocket. His trousers hung loose at his hips. 'Thank you, Maureen. They'll come in very handy.'

'It was selfish of me to ask you to give up your walk. Forgive me, Harold.'

He sunk his head so low she wondered if he had fallen asleep on the table. She could see down his neck to the soft white skin of his back, where the sun hadn't reached. She felt a shiver shoot straight through her, as if she were seeing him naked for the first time. When he lifted his head and met her eye, she blushed.

He spoke so softly, the words were part of the air. 'I'm the one who needs forgiveness.'

*   *   *

Rex was waiting in the passenger seat with coffee in a polystyrene cup, and a doughnut wrapped in a serviette. She sat beside him, and took small gulps of air to stop more weeping. He offered her the drink and the food, but she had no appetite.

'I even said I think not. I can't believe I said that.'

'You have a good cry.'

'Thank you, Rex. But I've cried enough. I'd prefer to stop now.'

She dabbed her eyes and glanced out at the street, where people were going about their business. All around her there seemed to be men and women; old ones, young ones; walking apart, or together. The coupled world looked so busy, so sure of itself. She said, 'Years ago, when Harold and I first met, he called me Maureen. Then it changed to Maw, and that was how it was for years. These days it's Maureen again.' She touched her mouth with her fingers, pressing for silence.

'Would you like to stay?' said Rex's voice. 'Talk to him again?'

She twisted the key in the ignition. 'No. Let's go home.'

And as they pulled away, she saw Harold, this stranger who had been her husband for so many years, with a dog trotting at his side, and a group of followers she didn't know—but she didn't throw a wave, or hoot the horn. Without fanfare or ceremony or even a proper goodbye, she drove away from Harold, and let him walk.

*   *   *

Two days later, Maureen woke to a bright sky full of promise and a light breeze that played at the leaves. The perfect washing day. She fetched the stepladder and took down the net curtains. Light, colour and texture fell over the room as if they had been trapped in the space behind the nets all along. The curtains were white and dry within the day.

Maureen folded them into bags and took them to the charity shop.

24

HAROLD AND RICH

Something happened after Harold walked away from Maureen. It was as if a door closed on a part of him that he wasn't sure he preferred to leave open. He no longer took pleasure in imagining the welcoming party of nurses and patients at the hospice. He could no longer visualize the end of his journey. The going was slow and troubled with so much argument that it took the group almost a week to cover the stretch from Darlington to Newcastle. He lent Wilf the willow cane and never got it back.

Maureen had said she missed him. She wanted him home. He couldn't get that out of his mind. He found excuses to borrow mobile phones and ring.

'I'm fine,' she would say. 'I'm good.' She would tell him about a moving letter that had arrived in the post, or a small gift; or maybe she would describe the progress of her runner beans. 'But you don't want to hear about me,' she'd add. He did, though. He wanted that so much.

'On the phone again?' Rich would ask, with a grin but no empathy.

He accused Wilf of stealing again and privately Harold was afraid he was right. It was painful to keep defending the boy, when he knew in his gut he was as unreliable as David. Wilf didn't even hide his empty bottles. It could take an embarrassingly long time to wake him, and as soon as he was on his feet he complained. Trying to protect him, Harold told the others the old injury on his right leg was playing up. He suggested longer periods of rest. He even suggested they might like to go on ahead. No, no, they chorused; Harold was the walk. They couldn't possibly do it without him.

For the first time, he felt relief on reaching the towns. Wilf seemed to snap alive again. And seeing other people, looking into shop windows, thinking about what he didn't need, offered Harold distraction from his own doubts about what had happened to his journey. He didn't know how he had created something that had grown beyond his ability to keep hold of it.

'A guy offered me a shitload of money for my story,' said Wilf, sprinting up beside him. He had the jitters again and smelt of whisky. 'I said no, Mr Fry. I'm sticking with you.'

The pilgrims set up camp, but Harold no longer sat with them while they cooked or planned the next day's route. Rich had begun hunting for rabbits and birds, which he skinned or plucked and cooked over the flames. The sight of the poor animal, stripped and skewered, made Harold tremble. Besides, there was a hungry wildness in

Rich's eye these days that reminded him of both Napier and his father, and alarmed him. Rich's pilgrim T-shirt was smeared with blood. He had taken to wearing a string of small rodent teeth round his neck. They put Harold off his food.

Tired and increasingly empty, he would stroll through the oncoming night while the crickets creaked and stars pricked the sky. This was the only time he felt free, and connected. He thought of Maureen and Queenie. He remembered the past. Hours could pass and they would seem both like days and no time at all. Returning to the group, some already sleeping, some singing by the camp fire, he would feel a cold wave of panic. What was he doing with these people?

While Harold was out of the way, Rich called a private meeting. He had grave concerns, he said. They were difficult to voice, but someone had to; Queenie couldn't hang on for much longer. In light of this, he suggested that a reconnaissance party, led by himself, should take an alternative, cross-country route. 'I know this is hard for everyone because we love Harold. He's been a father to me. But the guy is slowing down. His leg's bad. He wanders off for half the night. And now this fasting. He's not the man he was—'

'He's not fasting,' objected Kate. 'You make it sound religious. He's just not hungry.'

'Whatever he's doing, he's not up to the journey. You've gotta call a spade a spade. We need to think how we can help.'

Kate sucked something stringy and green from a back tooth. 'You do talk crap,' she said.

Wilf yelped with hysterical laughter and the subject was dropped, but Rich sat very quietly for

269

the rest of the evening, slightly apart from the group, chipping at a stick with his penknife, splintering it and sharpening it to a piercing point.

Harold was woken the following morning by shouts. Rich's knife had gone. After a thorough search of the field, banks and hedgerows, it was clear that Wilf had gone with it. And so, he discovered, had the glittering paperweight for Queenie Hennessy.

The gorilla man reported news that Pilgrim Wilf had set up a Facebook page. It already had over a thousand likes. There were personal anecdotes about his walk, and the people he had saved. There were several prayers. He promised his fans there were more stories to come in the weekend papers.

'I told you he was no good,' said Rich across the camp fire. His eyes pinned Harold through the dark.

*   *   *

Harold was deeply troubled by the boy's disappearance. He walked apart from the group and scanned the shadows for signs. In towns, he stared into pubs and gangs of young men, searching for Wilf's gaunt, sickly face, or listening out for that infuriating yelp of a laugh. He felt he had let the boy down, and that this was how it always was with Harold. Once again, he slept badly at nights, and sometimes he did not sleep at all.

'You look tired,' said Kate. They had moved a little distance from the group and were sitting in a brick tunnel by a stream. The water was still and thick, more like green velvet than fluid. Further along the banks, there was water mint and cress, but Harold knew he'd lost the interest in picking them.

'I feel a long way from where I began. But I also feel a long way from where I am going.' He gave a yawn that seemed to shudder up through his whole body. 'Why do you think Wilf went?'

'He'd had enough. I don't think he was evil or anything like that. He's young. He's flaky.'

Harold felt someone was talking to him at last without frills, as in the early days of his walk, when no one had expectations, including himself. He confided that Wilf had reminded him of his son, and that Harold's betrayal of David sometimes pained him these days even more than his betrayal of Queenie. 'When my son was little, we realized he was clever. He spent all his time in his room, doing schoolwork. If he didn't get top marks, he'd be in tears. But then his intelligence seemed to backfire on him. He was too clever. Too lonely. He got into Cambridge and he started drinking. I was such a no-hoper at school, I was in awe of his intelligence. Failure was about the only thing I was good at.'

Kate laughed and her chin concertina'd into her neck. Despite her brusque manner, he had begun to find comfort in the stalwart bulk of her. She said, 'I never said anything about this to the others, but my wedding ring disappeared a few nights ago too.'

Harold sighed. He knew he had trusted Wilf against the odds, but somehow he had also trusted that there was a basic goodness to be found in everyone, and that this time he could tap into it.

'It doesn't matter about the ring. My ex and I just got divorced. I don't know why I kept on

271

wearing it.' She flexed her naked fingers. 'So maybe Wilf did me a favour.'

'Should I have done more, Kate?'

Kate smiled. 'You can't save everyone.' She paused and then she asked, 'Do you still see your son?'

The question hurt. 'No.'

'I guess you miss him?' she said.

Not since Martina had anyone asked about David; his mouth dried and his heart began to quicken. He wanted to describe what it feels like to find your boy in a pool of vomit and carry him to bed and mop him up and pretend in the morning you have not seen that. He wanted to say what it was like to be a child and find the man who was your father in the same manner. He wanted to say, What happened? Was it me? Am I the link here? But he didn't. He didn't want to burden her with so much. He nodded and said yes; he missed David.

Gripping his knees, he pictured himself lying in his room as a teenager, listening to the silence that did not hold his mother. He remembered hearing that Queenie had left, and sinking to his chair because she had not said goodbye. He saw Maureen, white with hatred, slamming the spare-room door. He relived the last time he had visited his father.

'I am terribly sorry,' the carer had said. She had Harold by his jacket sleeve and was almost tugging him out of range. 'But he seems disturbed. Maybe you had better leave it for today.'

Glancing over his shoulder as he hurried away, his final impression had been of a small man throwing teaspoons and yelling he had no son.

How could he say all this? It amounted to a lifetime. He could try to find the words, but they would never hold the same meaning for her that they did for him. 'My house,' he would say; and the image that would spring to her head would be of her own. There was no saying it.

Kate and Harold sat a while more in silence. He listened to the wind in the leaves of a willow, and watched them flicker. Spikes of rosebay willow herb and evening primrose glowed in the dark. From the camp fire came the sounds of laughter and shouts; Rich was organizing a nocturnal game of tag. 'It's getting late,' said Kate at last. 'You need sleep.'

They returned to the others, but sleep did not come. His head was still full of his mother, and trying to capture a memory of her that might bring comfort. He thought of the cold of his childhood home, and the smell of whisky that was even in his school clothes, and the greatcoat that was his sixteenth-birthday present. For the first time he allowed himself to feel the pain of being a child that is not wanted by mother or father. He ranged for many hours in the dark, under a sky lit with infinitesimal stars. Images passed through his mind of Joan wetting her finger to turn the page of a travel magazine, or rolling her eyes as his father's hands trembled over a bottle, but nowhere could he find her kissing Harold's head, or even telling him he would be all right.

Had she ever asked herself where he was? How he was doing?

He saw the reflection of her face in a compact mirror as she painted on her red lips. She did it with such care, he had felt she was trapping

273

something behind the colour.

A wave of emotion swelled through him as he recalled catching her eye once. She had stopped what she was doing so that her mouth was left half Joan and half mother. With his heart beating so hard it made his voice flutter, he had summoned the courage to speak. 'Please will you tell me? Am I ugly?'

She had burst out laughing. The dimple in her cheek was so deep he could imagine slipping his finger into it.

It wasn't meant to be funny. It was from the heart. But in the absence of all physical affection, her laughter had been the next best thing. He wished he had not torn her only letter to shreds. *Deer son*. It would have been something. It would have been something too to hold David in his arms, and promise him things get better. He felt nothing but anguish for the things that couldn't be undone.

Returning to his sleeping bag before dawn, Harold found a small bundle beneath the zip, containing a heel of bread, an apple and bottled water. He wiped his eyes and ate the food, but still he didn't sleep.

*　　*　　*

As the profile of Newcastle dominated the horizon, tensions rose yet again. Kate wanted to avoid the city altogether. Someone else had bunions and needed a doctor, or at least first aid. Rich had so many thoughts on the nature of the modern pilgrimage that the gorilla man needed a new notebook. Flummoxing them all, Harold asked the group if they might make a detour via Hexham. He produced from his jacket pocket the business card of the man in the hotel where he had spent his first night. It was creased with time, and furry at the edges. But even though those first few days of his walk had almost broken him, he remembered them with envy. They held a simplicity that he felt he was in danger of losing, if he had not lost it already.

'Of course I can't make you come with me,' said Harold, 'but I will stick to my promise.'

A further secret meeting was called by Rich. 'I can't believe I'm the only one who's man enough to say it. But you lot can't see the wood for the trees. The guy's falling apart. We can't go to Hexham. It's over twenty miles in the wrong direction.'

'He made a promise,' said Kate, 'just as he made one to us. He's too polite to renege on that. It's rather English, and very endearing.'

Rich flared. 'In case you've forgotten, Queenie is dying. I vote we form a splinter group and push straight up to Berwick. He's suggested it himself before now. We could be there in a week.'

No one expressed an opinion, but in the morning Kate discovered a lot of campaigning had taken place in the night. Whispered conversations in tents, and over the dying embers of the fire, had confirmed Rich's opinion: they all loved Harold, but it was time to break free. They looked for the old man but he was not to be found. They packed up their sleeping bags and tents, and were gone. Apart from the smouldering embers of a fire, the field was so empty she could almost doubt any of it had happened.

Kate found Harold sitting by a river, throwing stones for the dog. His shoulders were hunched as if a weight pressed down on him. It shocked her, how old he suddenly looked. She told him Rich had persuaded the gorilla man to go ahead, and that they had taken the well-wishers and what was left of the journalists. 'He called a meeting and gave some story about you needing a break. He even squeezed out a few tears. There was nothing I could do. But people won't be fooled for long.'

'I don't mind. To tell the truth, it was getting too much.' The swallows were skimming the water, turning vertically on their wings. He watched them a while.

'What will you do next, Harold? Will you go home?'

He shook his head, but it was a heavy gesture. 'I'll make the trip to Hexham and then I'll head up from there towards Berwick. Not long now. What about you?'

'I'm going home. My ex has been in touch. He wants us to have another go at it.'

Harold's eyes moistened in the morning light. 'That's good,' he said. He reached for her hand and squeezed it. She wondered briefly if he was thinking of his wife.

From there, their arms took the opportunity to catch hold of the other's body. Kate didn't know if it was she who was holding on to Harold or the other way round. He was bone inside his pilgrim T-shirt. They remained in an odd half-embrace, a little off balance, until she broke free and wiped her cheeks.

'Please take care of yourself,' she said. 'I know you are a good man and that seems to give you a

276

way with people. But you look tired. You need to look after yourself, Harold.'

*   *   *

He waited as Kate walked away. She turned several times to wave and he stayed in the same place, letting her go. He had walked too much with other people, and listened to their stories, and followed their routes. It would be a relief to listen again only to himself. All the same, as Kate grew smaller, he felt the wrench of losing her, and it was like a little piece of dying. She reached a break in the trees ahead and he was about to go, when she paused, as if she had lost her way or forgotten something. She began to walk back to him, very fast, almost running, and he felt a shiver of excitement because of all of them, even Wilf, it was Kate he had grown to love. But then she stopped again, and seemed to shake her head. He knew that for her sake he must keep standing and watching her go, a constant in the distance, until she had left him fully behind.

He threw a large wave, two hands beating at the air. She turned her back on him and met the line of trees.

He remained a long time, waiting in case she reappeared, but the air was still and did not bring her.

Harold removed the pilgrim T-shirt and retrieved his shirt and tie from his rucksack. They were screwed up, and very worn now, but it was like being himself again as he put them on. He wondered whether he should take it to Queenie as a further souvenir, but it didn't feel right to carry

277

something that had caused such dispute. Instead he slipped it in a bin when no one was looking. He found he was wearier than he had realized. It took Harold a further three days to reach Hexham.

He rang at the buzzer of the businessman's apartment and waited all afternoon, but there was no sign of his host. A woman from another flat came down and explained that the businessman was on holiday in Ibiza. 'He's always on holiday,' she said. She asked if Harold would like tea, or water for the dog, but he declined both.

*   *   *

A week after the split, reports came of the pilgrims' arrival in Berwick-upon-Tweed. There were photographs in the newspapers of Rich Lion walking hand in hand with his two sons along the quay; and others of a man in a gorilla suit nuzzling the cheek of Miss South Devon. There was a brass band to welcome the party, with a performance by the local cheerleading troupe, and a dinner attended by local councillors and businessmen. Several Sunday papers claimed to have sole access to Rich's diaries. There was talk of a film.

The pilgrims' arrival was also covered on the television news. Courtesy of BBC *Spotlight*, Maureen and Rex watched footage of Rich Lion and several others delivering flowers to the hospice along with a giant basket of muffins, although Queenie was unable to receive them. The reporter added that sadly no one from the hospice was available for comment. She stood with her microphone at the edge of the drive. Behind her there appeared to be a neatly kept garden, with blue hydrangeas, and a man in a boiler suit raking grass clippings.

'Those people didn't even know Queenie,' said Maureen. 'It makes me want to spit. Why couldn't they wait for Harold?'

Rex sipped a cup of Ovaltine. 'I suppose they were impatient to get there.'

'But it was never a race. It was the journey that mattered. And that man didn't walk for Queenie. He walked to prove he was a hero and get his children back.'

'I suppose in the end his was a journey of a kind,' said Rex. 'Just a different one.' He replaced his cup carefully on a coaster, so as not to mark the table.

The reporter made a brief reference to Harold Fry, and an image flashed up in which he was shrinking from the camera. He looked like a shadow: dirty, haggard, afraid. In an exclusive interview, Rich Lion explained from the quayside that the elderly Devon pilgrim was suffering from fatigue and complicated emotional issues; he had been forced to retire from the walk south of Newcastle. 'But Queenie is alive. That's the main thing. It was lucky me and the guys were there to step in.'

Maureen scoffed. 'For heaven's sake, he can't even speak proper English.'

Rich clasped his hands together above his head in a gesture of victory. 'I know Harold would be moved by your support.' The jostling crowd of well-wishers cheered.

The report ended with a shot of the pinkish stones of the quay wall, where several council workers were removing placards that spelt out a slogan. One man worked from the beginning, the other man from the end, picking each letter up and sliding it into their van, so that all that was left was the message WEED WELCOMES HAR. Maureen snapped off the television, and paced the room.

'They're sweeping him under the carpet,' she said. 'They're ashamed of putting their trust in him, and so now they have to make him out to be a fool. It's shocking. He didn't even ask for their attention in the first place.'

Rex pursed his mouth in thought. 'At least people will leave him alone now. At least it's just the walk and Harold.'

Maureen stared out at the sky. She could not speak.

25

HAROLD AND THE DOG

It had come as a relief to Harold to walk alone again. He and Dog took up their own rhythm, and there was no debating, no arguing. From Newcastle to Hexham, they had stopped when they were tired, and taken up when they were refreshed. They began to walk the dawns again, and sometimes the nights, and he was filled with renewed hope. He was happiest like this, watching the lights come on at the windows, and people going about their lives; unobserved, and yet tender for the strangeness of others. He was open once more to the thoughts and memories that played through his head. Maureen, Queenie and David were his companions. He felt whole again.

He thought of Maureen's body against his in the early years of their marriage and the beautiful darkness between her legs. He pictured David staring out of his bedroom window so intently it was as if the outside world had robbed him of something. He remembered driving beside Queenie, while she sucked on mints and sang another song backwards.

Harold and Dog were so close to Berwick they must do nothing but walk. After his experience with the pilgrims, he was anxious to avoid public attention. In talking to strangers, and listening, he feared he had created a need in them to be carried and he hadn't the strength for that any more. If he and Dog came to a built-up area and could not bypass it, they slept in fields on its fringes until dark, and then crossed in the early hours of the morning. They ate what they found in hedgerows, and bins. They picked only from the allotments or trees that looked uncared for. They still stopped to taste spring water wherever it bubbled up, but they troubled no one. Once or twice someone asked for his photograph, and he obliged, though he found it hard to look into the camera. Occasionally a passer-by recognized him and offered food. A man who was possibly a journalist asked if he was Harold Fry. But since he was careful to keep his head low, and since he stuck to the shadows and the wider spaces, people mostly left him alone. He even avoided his reflection.

'I hope you feel better,' said a graceful woman with a greyhound. 'It was such a shame to lose you. My husband and I wept.' Not understanding, Harold thanked her and moved on. The land heaved ahead and formed dark peaks.

Strong winds came from west to north, bringing rain. It was too cold to sleep. He lay rigid within his sleeping bag, watching patches of cloud as they skittered across the moon, and trying to keep warm. The dog lay against him in the sleeping bag.

282

Its ribs were cavernous. He thought of the day David swam out at Bantham, and the fragility of his son against the coastguard's tanned arms. He remembered the nicks in David's skull where he had dug the razor, and how he used to haul David upstairs before he was sick again. All those times David had put his body at risk, as if in defiance of the ordinariness that was his father.

Harold began to shiver. It started as a tremble that caused his teeth to rattle, but seemed to gain momentum. His fingers, toes, arms and legs were shaking so hard they hurt. He looked out, hoping for comfort or distraction, but found no fellowship with the land, as he had before. The moon shone. The wind blew. His need for warmth made no impression. The place was not cruel. It was worse. It didn't notice. Harold was alone, without Maureen or Queenie or David, in a place that did not see, shaking and shaking in a sleeping bag. He tried gritting his teeth and clenching his fists, but that made it worse. Far away foxes were cornering an animal, their anarchic cries cutting through the night air. His wet clothes stung against his skin, and stole the warmth from him. He was cold to the core. The only thing that would stop him shaking would be when his inner organs froze over. He no longer had the wherewithal to resist even the cold.

Harold was sure he would be better once he was back on his feet. But he wasn't. There was no escaping what he had realized as he fought for warmth in the night. With or without him, the moon and the wind would go on, rising and falling. The land would keep stretching ahead until it hit the sea. People would keep dying. It made no difference whether Harold walked, or trembled, or

283

stayed at home.

What began as a flat, subdued feeling grew over the hours into something more violently accusing. The more he dwelt on how little he mattered, the more he believed it. Who was he to go to Queenie? What did it matter if Rich Lion took his place? Every time he paused for breath, or rubbed at his legs to get the blood moving, the dog sat at his feet, watching with concern. It stopped straying from Harold's path. It stopped bringing stones.

Harold thought of his journey so far; the people he had met, the places he had seen, the skies beneath which he had slept. Until now he had held them in his mind like a collection of souvenirs. They had kept him going when the walking was so arduous he had wanted to give up. But now he thought of those people, places and skies and he could no longer see himself among them. The roads he had walked were full of different cars. The people he had passed were passing other people. His footprints, however firm, would be washed away by rain. It was as if he had never been in any of the places he had been, or met the strangers he had met. He looked behind, and already there was no trace, no sign, of him anywhere.

The trees gave up their branches to the wind as fluidly as tentacles in water. He had made a mess of being a husband, father and friend. He had even made a mess of being a son. It wasn't simply that he had betrayed Queenie, and that his parents did not want him. It wasn't simply that he had made a mess of everything with his wife and son. It was rather that he passed through life and left no impression. He meant nothing. Harold went to cross the A696 in the direction of Cambo, and realized the dog was missing.

He felt a shower of panic. He wondered if the dog had been hurt, and he hadn't noticed. He retraced his steps, scouring the road and the gutters, but there was no sign of the animal. He tried to remember when he had last registered its presence. It must be hours since they had shared a sandwich on a bench. Or was that the day before? He couldn't believe he had failed even in this simple task. He was waving down cars, asking drivers if they had seen a dog, a little tufty thing about so high, but they sped away, as if he were dangerous. Catching sight of him, a small child clung to her car seat and sobbed. There was nothing for it but to retrace his steps towards Hexham.

He found Dog sitting in a bus shelter, at the feet of a young girl. She was wearing a school uniform, and had long dark hair that was almost the autumn colour of its fur, and a kind look about her. Stooping to pat its head, she picked up something by her shoe, and stowed it in her pocket.

'Don't throw the stone,' Harold was about to call; but he didn't. The girl's bus drew up beside her and she got on it, followed by the dog. It looked as if it knew where it was heading. He watched the bus drive away, with the girl and the dog on it. They didn't look back or wave.

He reasoned the animal had made its own decision. It had chosen to walk with Harold for a while, and then it had chosen to stop, and walk instead with the young girl. Life was like that. But in losing his last companion, Harold felt a further layer of skin had been ripped from him. He was

285

afraid of what would come next. He knew he hadn't got it in him to take much more.

The hours turned into days and he couldn't remember how one was different from another. He began to make mistakes. He would set off with the first cracks of dawn, compelled to go towards the emerging light, regardless of whether or not it lay in the direction of Berwick. He argued with his compass when it pointed south, convinced it was broken, or worse, that it was deliberately lying. Sometimes he walked ten miles only to discover he had travelled a large looping circle, and was back almost where he had started. He took diversions to follow a shout or a figure, but they led to nothing. Near the crest of a hill, he saw a woman calling for help, but after an hour of climbing he found she was a dead tree trunk. He frequently lost his footing and stumbled. When his glasses snapped a second time, he left them behind.

Deprived of rest and hope, other things began to slip from him. He found he couldn't remember David's face. He could picture his dark eyes, and the way they stared, but when he tried to conjure up the fringe that flopped over them, he could see only Queenie's tight curls. It was like fixing a jigsaw together in his mind, but without all the pieces. How could his head be so cruel? Harold lost all sense of time, and whether or not he had eaten. It wasn't that he had forgotten; he no longer cared. He no longer took any interest in what he saw, or the difference between things, or their names. A tree was no more than another of the things he passed. And sometimes the only words in his head were the ones that asked why he was still walking when it would make no difference. A lone crow passed overhead, its black wings beating the air like a whip, and filled him with such inhuman fear, he went scampering for shelter.

So expansive was the land, and so small was he, that when he glanced back, trying to gauge the distance he had travelled, it seemed as if he had not advanced at all. His feet fell on exactly the same place where he had lifted them. He looked at the peaks on the horizon, the waves of turf, the boulders of rock; the grey houses tucked among them were so small, so temporary, it was a wonder they stayed up. We hang on by so little, he thought, and felt the full despair of knowing that.

Harold walked under the heat of the sun, the pelting of the rain, and the blue cold of the moon, but he no longer knew how far he had come. He sat beneath a hard night sky, alive with stars, and watched as his hands turned purple. He knew he should lift his hands, guide them to his mouth and blow on the knuckles, but the idea of flexing one set of muscles and then another was too much. He couldn't remember which muscles served which limbs. He couldn't remember how it would help. It was easier simply to sit, absorbed in the night and the nothing that was all around him. It was easier to give up than keep moving.

Late one night, Harold rang Maureen from a phone box. He reversed the charges as normal, and when he heard her voice, he said, 'I can't do it. I can't finish.'

She said nothing. He wondered if she had thought better of missing him. Or maybe she had been asleep.

'I can't do it, Maureen,' he repeated.

She gave a gulp down the telephone. 'Harold,

where are you?'

He looked at the outside world. Traffic shot past. There were lights, and people hurrying home. A billboard advertised a television programme, coming this autumn, and showed a giant-sized policewoman smiling. Beyond stood all the darkness that lay between himself and wherever he was going. 'I don't know where I am.'

'Do you know where you've come from?'

'No.'

'The name of a village?'

'I don't know. I think I stopped seeing things quite a while ago.'

'I see,' she said, in a way that sounded as if she saw other things too.

He swallowed hard. 'Wherever I am now might be the Gateway to the Cheviot Hills. Something like that. I maybe noticed a sign. But maybe that was a few days ago. There have been hills. And gorse too. A lot of bracken.' He heard a sharp intake of breath, and then another. He could picture her face; the way her mouth worked open and shut when she was thinking. He said again, 'I want to come home, Maureen. You were right. I can't do it. I don't want to.'

At last her voice came. It sounded slow and careful, as if she were reining in words. 'Harold, I'm going to try and work out where you are and what to do. I want you to give me half an hour. Can you do that?' He pressed his forehead on the glass, savouring the sound of her. 'Can you phone me back?'

He nodded. He forgot she couldn't see.

'Harold?' she called as if he needed reminding who he was. 'Harold, are you there?'

'I'm listening.'

'Give me half an hour. That's all.'

He tried to walk the streets of the town, so that time would pass more quickly. There were people queuing outside a fish and chip shop, and a man being sick in the gutter. The further he strayed from the phone box, the more afraid he became, as if the safe part of himself still remained there, waiting for Maureen. The hills were terrible deep giants impinging on the night sky. A gang of young men were striding into the road, shouting at cars and throwing beer cans. Harold cowered in the shadows, afraid of being seen. He was going home, and he didn't know how he would tell people that he didn't make it, but it didn't matter. It was an insane idea, and he needed to stop. If he wrote another letter, Queenie would understand.

He phoned Maureen and reversed the charges. 'It's me again.'

She didn't reply. She gave a gulping noise. He had to say, 'It's Harold.'

'Yes.' She gulped again.

'Shall I phone later?'

'No.' She paused and then she said slowly, 'Rex is here. We've looked at the map. We made a few calls. He has been on his computer. We even got out your *Motorist's Guide to Great Britain*.' She still sounded not right. Her words came light against his ear, as if she had run a long way and was struggling to settle her breath. Harold had to press the phone against his ear to hear her properly.

'Will you say hello to Rex?'

At this she gave a laugh, a short fluttery one. 'He says hello too.' There followed more strange swallowing noises; like hiccups but smaller. Then:

289

'Rex thinks you must be in Wooler.'

'Wooler?'

'Does that sound right?'

'I don't know. It's all beginning to sound the same.'

'We think you must have taken a wrong turn.' He was about to say he had taken many but it was too much effort. 'There's a hotel called the Black Swan. I think it sounds nice, and so does Rex. I have booked you a room, Harold. They know to expect you.'

'But you're forgetting I have no money. And I must look terrible.'

'I paid over the phone by card. And it doesn't matter how you look.'

'When will you be here? Will Rex come too?' He paused at the end of both questions, but Maureen's voice gave nothing. He even wondered if she had put the phone down. 'You are coming?' he said, his blood warming with panic.

She hadn't gone. He heard her sucking in a long breath, as if she had burnt her hand. Suddenly her voice shot out so loud and fast it hurt his ear. He had to hold the handset slightly away. 'Queenie is still alive, Harold. You asked for her to wait and you see, she is waiting. Rex and I checked the weather forecast and they have slapped happy sun shapes all over the United Kingdom. You'll feel better in the morning.'

'Maureen?' She was his last chance. 'I can't do it. I was wrong.'

She didn't hear, or if she heard she wouldn't allow the gravity of what he was saying. Her voice kept coming at him, rising in pitch: 'Keep walking. It's only sixteen more miles to Berwick. You can do it, Harold. Remember to stay on the B6525.'

He didn't know how to say what he was feeling after that, so he hung up.

*   *   *

As Maureen had told him to, Harold checked into the hotel. He couldn't look at the receptionist or the young porter who insisted on leading him to his room and opening the door on his behalf. The chap drew the curtains over the windows, and showed him how to change the air conditioning, and where he would find the en-suite bathroom, as well as the minibar and Corby trouser press. Harold nodded but he didn't see. The air felt chilled and hard.

'Can I fetch you a drink, sir?' asked the porter.

Harold could not explain about himself and alcohol. He merely turned away. With the porter gone, he lay fully clothed on the bed, and all he could think was that he did not want to keep going. He slept briefly, and woke with a start. Martina's partner's compass. He groped his hand in his trouser pocket, and pulled it out and tried the other. The compass wasn't there. It wasn't in the bed, or on the floor. It wasn't even in the lift. He must have left it in the phone box.

The porter unbolted the main doors, and promised to wait. Harold ran so hard that his breath cut into the cavities of his chest like blows. He swung open the door of the kiosk, but the compass had gone.

Maybe it was the shock of being once more inside a room, and lying on a bed with clean sheets and soft pillows, but that night Harold started to

291

cry. He couldn't believe he had been so foolish as to lose Martina's compass. He tried to tell himself it was only a thing. She would understand. But all he could feel was the loss of its weight from his pocket, so vast its absence amounted to a presence. He feared that in mislaying the compass, he had also lost an essential, steadying part of himself. Even when he briefly slipped into something that was like unconsciousness, his head swarmed with images. He saw the man from Bath in the dress, with his punched eye. He saw the oncologist staring at Queenie's letter, and the woman who loved Jane Austen talking into mid-air. There was the cycling mother with her scarred arms; he asked himself again why a person would do that. He curled into the pillow and dreamed of the silver-haired gentleman, who travelled by train to see the boy with trainers. He saw Martina waiting for the man who was never going to return. And what about the waitress who would never leave South Brent? And Wilf? And Kate too? All those people, searching for happiness. He woke crying, and continued to cry all day as he walked.

*   *   *

Maureen received a postcard with a picture of the Cheviots, bearing no stamp. The message read, *Weather good. H. x.* There was another postcard the following day, showing Hadrian's Wall, but this had no message.

The cards came every day; sometimes there were several. He wrote the briefest messages: *Rain. Not good. Walking. I miss you.* Once he drew a hill shape. Another time a squiggly *w* that was possibly a bird. Often the cards were blank. She asked the postman to look out for them at the sorting office; she would pay the extra charges. The messages were more precious than love letters, she said.

Harold did not ring again. She waited in every night, but to no avail. It tortured her that she had let him go, when he needed her help. She had booked the hotel and spoken to Harold through tears. But she and Rex had talked it over and over; if he gave up when he was so close to arriving, he would regret it for the rest of his life.

Early July had brought winds and heavy rain. Her bamboo stakes tilted at a drunken angle towards the ground, and the tips of her bean plants groped their blind passage into air. Harold's postcards continued to arrive, but they no longer mapped a steady northward path. There was one from Kelso, but by her reckoning that was twenty-three miles west of where he should be. Another came from Eccles, and also Coldstream; again too far west of Berwick. Almost every hour, she resolved to ring the police, only to realize as she lifted the phone that it was not her place to stop Harold when he must surely arrive any day.

She rarely slept a full night. She feared that by giving in to unconsciousness, she surrendered her one contact with her husband, and might lose him altogether. She sat outside on a patio chair beneath the stars, keeping vigil for the man who somewhere very far away was sheltering under that same sky. Now and again, Rex brought her tea in the early morning, and a travel blanket from his car. They watched the night lose its darkness, and the pearl light of dawn, without speaking or moving.

More than anything, Maureen wanted Harold home.

26

HAROLD AND THE CAFÉ

The last stretch was the worst. All Harold could see was road. He had no thoughts. The earlier damage to his right leg had flared up again, and caused him to limp. There was no pleasure to be had; he was in a place where it did not exist. Flies swarmed in a cloud round his head. Sometimes there were bites. Maybe stings. The fields were immense and empty, and the cars were drawn along the roads like toys. Another peak. Another sky. Another mile. It was all the same. It both bored and overwhelmed him to the point of surrender. He often forgot where he was heading.

Without love, nothing had—what? What was the word for it? He couldn't remember. He thought it began with a *v*, and he wanted to say *vulva*, but that surely wasn't right. Nothing could be made to matter very much. The blackness crept from the sky. The rain slashed his skin. The winds blew so hard he struggled to keep his balance. He fell asleep wet, and woke wet. He would never know again what it was to be warm.

The nightmare pictures Harold thought he had left behind were back, and there was no escaping them. Awake or asleep, he relived the past, and felt the fresh horror of it. He saw himself flailing with an axe at the wooden planks of his garden shed, his hands ripped and full of splinters, his head swinging with whisky. He saw his fists sprouting blood over thousands of coloured glass pins. He heard himself praying, eyes screwed up, hands clenched, and the words meaning nothing. Other times, he saw Maureen turn her back on him and disappear into a dazzling ball of light. The twenty years that had passed were shorn away. There was no hiding behind the ordinary or even the cliché. Like the detail in the land, these things no longer existed.

No one could imagine such loneliness. He shouted once but no sound came back. He felt the cold deep inside him, as if even his bones were freezing over. He closed his eyes to sleep, convinced he would not survive, and having no will to fight that. When he woke, and felt the stiffness of his clothes cutting his skin, and his face burnt with the sun, or maybe the cold, he got up and plodded on.

A bulging in his shoes made a rip at the seam and the soles were thin as fabric. His toes would be through the leather at any moment. He bound them with the roll of blue duct tape, round and round and round, crossing underneath the foot and up over towards the ankle, so that the shoe was a part of himself. Or was it the other way round? He was beginning to believe they had a will of their own.

On, on, on. These were the only words. He didn't know whether they were ones he cried out, or words in his mind; or whether someone else was calling them. He thought he might be the only person left in the world. There was no more than the road. He was no more than a body that housed a walk. He was blue-duct-tape feet and Berwick-upon-Tweed.

*　　*　　*

At three thirty on a Tuesday afternoon Harold smelt salt in the wind. An hour later he reached the brow of a hill and saw a town lying before him, fringed by the endless gap that was the sea. He approached the pinkish-grey town walls but no one stopped, or looked twice, or offered him food.

Eighty-seven days after setting out to post a letter, Harold Fry arrived at the gates of St Bernadine's Hospice. Including mistakes and diversions, his journey had amounted to six hundred and twenty-seven miles. The building before him was modern and unassuming, flanked by trembling trees. There was an old-fashioned street lamp close to the main entrance, and a sign pointing to a car park. Several bodies sat in deck chairs on the lawn, like clothes set out to dry. A seagull wheeled and barked overhead.

Harold walked the soft curve of the tarmac drive and lifted his finger to the buzzer. He wished the moment would hold itself, like an image cut out of time, his dark finger against the white button, the sun on his shoulders, the seagull laughing. His journey was over.

Harold's mind fled back over the miles that had brought him to this place. He saw roads, hills, houses, fences, shopping centres, streetlights and post boxes, and there was nothing extraordinary about any of them. They were simply things he had passed; that anyone might have passed. The thought filled him with sudden anguish, and he was afraid at the point where he had least expected to feel anything other than triumph. How did he ever believe that those very commonplace things would add up to something more? His finger remained, suspended over the buzzer but not pressing it. What had it all been about?

He thought of the people who had helped him. He thought of the unwanted, the unloved; he numbered himself among them. And then he considered what must follow from here. He would give his presents to Queenie, and thank her; but then what? He would return to the old life he had almost forgotten, where people staked trinkets between themselves and the outside world. Where he lay in one bedroom, not sleeping, and Maureen lay in another.

Harold replaced his rucksack on his shoulder and turned from the hospice. As he left the gates the figures lying in deck chairs did not look up. No one was expecting him and so no one appeared to notice his arrival or his departure. The most extraordinary moment of Harold's life had come and gone without trace.

In a small café, Harold asked a waitress for a glass of water, and use of the bathroom. He apologized that he had no money. He waited patiently as the waitress's eye took in his tangled hair, his ripped jacket and tie, and travelled down

298

the length of his mud-soaked trousers, to land on his feet that were more blue duct tape than yachting shoe. Her mouth frowned and she glanced over her shoulder towards an older woman in a grey jacket who was talking to customers. This second woman was clearly the more senior. The waitress said, 'You'd better be quick then.' She ushered him towards a door, without touching any part of him.

In the mirror, Harold met a face he only dimly knew. The skin hung in dark folds, as if there was too much of it for the bone behind. He appeared to have several cuts to the forehead and cheekbone. His hair and beard were wilder than he expected, and from his eyebrows and nostrils shot stray long hairs like wires. He was a joke old man. A misfit. He looked nothing like the man who had set off with a letter. He looked nothing like the man who had posed for photographs and worn a pilgrim T-shirt.

The waitress provided water in a disposable cup but did not invite him to sit. He asked if anyone might lend him a razor or a comb, but the manageress in the grey jacket came swiftly over and pointed to the sign at the window: NO BEGGING. She asked him to leave, or she would have to call the police. No one looked up as he moved to the door. He wondered if he smelt bad. He had been outside so long he had forgotten which smells were good and which were not. He knew people were embarrassed on his behalf, and wished to spare them that.

At a table beside the window, a young man and his wife crooned over their baby. There rose such pain inside Harold, he didn't know how he would keep upright.

He turned to the manageress and the teashop people and he met them face on. He said, 'I want my son.'

Speaking the words sent his body shaking; not with a gentle shiver but a spasmic shudder that came from deep inside. His face twisted as grief tore through his chest muscles and swelled its passage up his throat.

'Where is he?' said the manageress.

Harold squeezed his hands to keep himself from falling.

The manageress said, 'Do you see your son here? Is he in Berwick?'

A customer put his hand on Harold's arm. He said more gently, 'Excuse me, sir. Are you the man who was walking?'

Harold gasped. It was the kindness of the man that unpicked him.

'My wife and I read about what you did. We had a friend we had lost touch with. Last weekend we went to visit. We spoke of you.'

Harold let the man talk, and hold his arm, but he couldn't reply or move his face.

'Who is your son? What is his name?' said the man. 'Maybe I could help?'

'His name is—'

Suddenly Harold's heart plummeted, as if he had stepped over a wall and was tumbling through emptiness. 'He's my son. His name is—'

The manageress looked coolly back at him, waiting, waiting, with the customers behind her, and the kind man with his hand on Harold's sleeve. They had no idea. No idea of the horror, the confusion, the remorse raging inside him. He

300

couldn't remember his son's name.

Out on the street, a young woman tried to give him a piece of paper.

'It's salsa dancing classes for the over sixties,' she said. 'You should come. It's never too late.'

But it was. It was far too late. Harold shook his head wildly, and took a few more staggering steps. His legs felt boned.

'Please take the leaflet,' said the girl. 'Take the lot. You can throw them in the bin if you like. I just want to go home.'

Harold stumbled the streets of Berwick with the wodge of leaflets, not knowing where he was going. People swerved to avoid him, but he didn't stop. He could forgive his parents for not wanting him. For not showing him how to love, or even giving him the vocabulary. He could forgive their parents, and their parents before that.

All Harold wanted was his child.

27

HAROLD AND ANOTHER LETTER

Dear Girl in the Garage,
    I owe you the full story. Twenty years ago I buried my son. It is not something a father should have to do. I wanted to know the man he would become. I still do.
    To this day, I don't understand why he did it. He was depressed, and addicted to mixing alcohol with pills. He couldn't get a job. But I wish with all my heart he had spoken to me.
    He hanged himself in my garden shed. He did it with some rope, tied to one of the hooks I used for garden tools. He was so full of the alcohol and pills, the coroner said it must have taken a long time to tie the noose. The verdict was suicide.
    It was me who discovered him. I can barely write this. At the time I prayed, although as I told you at the garage I am

not a religious man. I said, Dear God, please let him be OK. I will do anything. I lifted him down, but there was no life. I was too late.

I wish they hadn't told me about him taking all that time to tie the noose.

My wife took it terribly. She wouldn't leave the house. She put up net curtains because she didn't want the neighbours prying. Gradually those people moved away and no one knew about us, or what had happened. But every time Maureen looked at me, I knew she saw David dead.

She began talking to him. He was with her, she said. She was always waiting for him. Maureen keeps his room exactly as it was the day he died. And sometimes it makes me sad all over again, but it is what my wife wants. She can't let him be dead, and I understand that. It is too much for a mother to bear.

Queenie knew all about David, but she didn't say anything. She looked out for me. She fetched tea with sugar and talked about the weather. Only once she said, Maybe you've had enough now, Mr Fry. Because that was the other thing. I was drinking.

It started off as just one to keep me steady before the coroner's report. But I was keeping the bottles in paper bags under my desk. God knows how I drove home at night. I just wanted to stop feeling.

When I was really out of it one night, I

dismantled the garden shed. But even that wasn't enough. So I broke into the brewery and I did something terrible. Queenie knew it had to be me and she took the blame.

She was fired on the spot and then she disappeared. I heard she had been warned to get out of the South West, if she knew what was good for her. I also overheard a secretary who was friendly with Queenie's landlady saying that she had not left a forwarding address. I let her go. I let her take the blame. But I gave up drinking.

Maureen and I fought for a long time, and then gradually we stopped talking. She moved out of our bedroom. She stopped loving me. There were many times I thought she would leave, but she didn't. I slept badly every night.

People think I am walking because there was a romance between myself and Queenie all those years ago, but it isn't true. I walked because she saved me, and I never said thank you. And this is why I am writing to you. I want you to know how much you helped me all those weeks ago, when you told me about your faith and your aunt, although I fear my courage has never matched yours.

With best wishes and my humble thanks,

Harold (Fry)

PS. I apologize for not knowing your name.

28

MAUREEN AND THE VISITOR

For days Maureen had been preparing the house for Harold's return. She had taken the two photographs he kept in his bedside drawer and measured them up for frames. She had repainted the best room a soft shade of yellow, and hung a pair of pale-blue velvet curtains at the window, which she had picked up at the charity shop, good as new, and shortened. She baked cakes to store in the freezer, as well as a selection of pies, moussaka, lasagne and boeuf bourguignon; all those dishes she had cooked in the days when David was alive. There were jars of her runner bean chutney in the cupboard, along with pickled onions and beetroot. She kept lists in the kitchen and bedroom. There was so much to do. And yet sometimes, when she looked out of the window, or lay awake listening to the gulls crying like children, she felt that despite her activity there was something about it that was inactive, as if she were missing the point.

Supposing Harold returned home and told her he needed to walk again? Supposing he had outgrown her, after all?

A ring at the doorbell in the early morning brought her downstairs. She found a sallow-faced young girl waiting on the threshold, with lank hair, and wearing a black duffel coat although it was already warm.

'Please could I come in, Mrs Fry?'

Over tea and several apricot flapjacks, the girl told her she was the one who had given Harold the burger all those weeks ago. He had sent her many lovely postcards; although due to his sudden rise to fame there had been an inconvenient number of fans and journalists hanging about the garage. In the end her boss had been obliged to ask her to leave for health and safety reasons.

'You lost your job? That's terrible,' said Maureen. 'Harold will be very sorry to hear this.'

'It's all right, Mrs Fry. I didn't like the job anyway. Customers were always shouting, and in too much of a hurry. But what I said to your husband about the power of faith has been bothering me ever since.' She looked fidgety and anxious; she kept tucking the same strand of hair behind her ear, although it wasn't out of place. 'I think I gave him the wrong impression.'

'But Harold was inspired by what you said. It was your faith that gave him the idea to walk.'

The girl sat bunched up in her coat and gnawed at her lip so hard Maureen was afraid she would draw blood. Then she tugged an envelope out of her pocket, and removed several sheets of paper. She held them out, but her hand was trembling.

'Here,' she said.

Maureen's mouth bent into a frown. 'Salsa for the over sixties?'

The girl reached for the papers and flipped them over. 'The writing's on the other side. It's a letter from your husband. It came to the garage. My friend warned me to fetch it before the boss saw.'

Maureen read in silence, weeping over each sentence. The loss that had wrenched them apart twenty years ago was as lacerating and incomprehensible as if it was happening afresh. When she finished, she thanked the girl and folded the letter, running her nail along the crease. Then she posted the letter back inside its envelope. She sat, very still.

'Mrs Fry?'

'There's something I need to explain.'

Maureen wet her lips and let the words come. It was a relief. Moved as she was by Harold's confession, it felt right to share the facts at last about David's suicide, and the grief that had split his parents apart. 'We shouted for a while. I blamed Harold terribly. I said awful things. That he should have been a better father. That the drinking was in Harold's family. And then we seemed to run out of words. It was about that time I began talking to David.'

'You mean he was a ghost?' said the girl. She had clearly seen too many films.

Maureen shook her head. 'Not a ghost, no. More like a presence. A feeling of David. It was my only comfort. I said little things at first. "Where are you?" "I miss you." Things like that. But as time went by, I said more. I said everything that I

307

didn't say to Harold. There were times when I almost wished I hadn't started; but then I worried that if I stopped talking, I would somehow betray David. Supposing he really was there? Supposing he needed me? I told myself that if I waited long enough I might see him. You read about things like that in those magazines at the doctor's, while you're waiting. I wanted to see him so much.' She wiped her eyes. 'But it never happened. I looked and looked but he never came.'

The girl stuffed her face into a tissue, and bawled. 'Oh God, that's too sad.' When she emerged her eyes were so small and her cheeks so red her face looked peeled. Strings of saliva looped from her nose and mouth. 'I'm such a fraud, Mrs Fry.'

Maureen reached out her hand for the girl's. It was small as a child's, but surprisingly warm. She gave it a squeeze.

'You're not a fraud. It was you who began his journey. You inspired him when you talked about your aunt. You mustn't cry.'

The girl let out another sob and plunged her face back into the tissue. Raising her head again, she blinked her poor eyes and took a shuddering deep breath. 'That's just it,' she said at last. 'My aunt's dead. She went years ago.'

Maureen felt something falling away. The room seemed to give a tremendous jolt, as if she'd just missed her step on the stairs. 'She's what?' Words stuck in her mouth. She opened it and swallowed and swallowed again. Then in a rush: 'But what about your faith? I thought it saved her? I thought that was the whole point?'

The girl dug her teeth into the corner of her

upper lip, so that her jaw shot out sideways. 'If cancer's got hold of you, there's nothing that's going to stop it.'

It was like seeing the truth for the first time, and realizing she had known it all along. Of course there was no stopping terminal cancer. Maureen thought of the many people who had come to trust in Harold's walk. She thought of Harold, trudging, even while they spoke. A shiver ran through her. 'I told you I was a fraud,' said the girl.

Maureen pummelled her forehead lightly with her fingertips. She could feel more coming from a long way deep inside, but unlike the truth about David, this caused her racking shame. She said slowly, 'If anyone is the fraud here, I'm afraid it's me.'

The girl shook her head, clearly not understanding.

Maureen began to tell her story, quietly and slowly, not looking at the girl because she had to focus on tugging out each word from the secret place where she had been hiding them for all this time. She told how, twenty years ago, after David's suicide, Queenie Hennessy had come to 13 Fossebridge Road, asking for Harold. She had looked very pale, and she was carrying flowers. There was something extremely ordinary and yet very dignified about her.

'She said, could I give Harold a message. It was about the brewery; there was something she needed him to know. And after she had told me what it was, she gave me the flowers and went away. I suppose I was the last person she saw before she left. I put the flowers in the bin, and I never gave him the message.' She stopped; it was too painful and too shameful to go on.

'What did she tell you, Mrs Fry?' said the girl. Her voice was so gentle it was like a guiding hand in the dark.

Maureen faltered. It had been a difficult time back then, she said. This could not excuse what she had done, or not done, and she wished it had been otherwise.

'But I was angry. David was dead. I was jealous too. Queenie was kind to Harold, when I couldn't be. If I gave him her message, I was afraid he would find comfort. And I couldn't do that. I didn't want him to find comfort when there was none for me.'

Maureen wiped her face, and continued.

'Queenie told me how Harold had broken into Napier's office one night. She had seen him sitting outside the brewery earlier that evening in his car. She hadn't gone over. She thought he might be crying and didn't wish to intrude. It was only when the news went round the following day that she had put two and two together. It was grief, she said; grief made people behave in the strangest ways. In her opinion Harold was on a course of self-destruction. In smashing those Murano glass clowns to smithereens, he was deliberately challenging Napier to do his worst. Their boss was hell bent on revenge.' Maureen paused and dabbed her nose. 'So Queenie took the blame. Being a plain woman, she said, made it easier; Napier was thrown off balance. She told him she had accidentally knocked the clowns while dusting.'

The girl laughed, but she too was crying. 'You mean to say this all happened because your

310

husband smashed some glass clowns? Were they valuable?'

'Not at all. They had belonged to his mother. Napier was a vicious thug. He had three wives, and he gave them all black eyes. One ended up in hospital with broken ribs. But he loved his mother.' She gave a limp smile, which hung on her face a moment, until she shrugged and cleared it away. 'So Queenie stood there and took the blame for what Harold had done; and then she let Napier fire her. She told me all this, and she asked me to tell Harold not to worry. He had been kind to her, she said. It was the least she could do.'

'But you didn't tell him?'

'No. I let him suffer. And then it became another of the things we couldn't say, and drove us further apart.' She opened her eyes wide and let the tears fall. 'You see, he was right to walk out on me.'

The garage girl didn't answer. She took a further flapjack and for several minutes she seemed to be thinking of nothing other than the taste of it. Then she said, 'I don't think it's true that he walked out on you. I don't think you're a fraud either, Mrs Fry. We all make mistakes. But I do know one thing.'

'What? What?' moaned Maureen, rocking her head in her hands. How could she ever mend the mistakes of so long ago? Her marriage was over.

'If I were you, I wouldn't be stuck here, making biscuits and talking to me. I'd be doing something.'

'But I drove all the way to Darlington. It made no difference.'

'That was when things were good. A lot has happened since then.' Her voice was so slow and certain Maureen lifted her head. The girl's face

311

was still pale, but it suddenly shone with disarming clarity. Maureen maybe gave a start, or even cried out, because the garage girl laughed. 'Get yourself to Berwick-upon-Tweed.'

312

29

HAROLD AND QUEENIE

After writing his letter, Harold had persuaded a young man to buy him an envelope and a first-class stamp. It was too late to visit Queenie, so he spent the night in his sleeping bag on a bench in the municipal park. Come the early morning, he visited the public lavatories where he washed and combed his hair with his fingers. Someone had left a plastic razor on the sink, and he pulled it through his beard. It didn't give him a proper shave but the bulk of it was gone, so that it was more like prickles than curls, but the odd tuft remained. The flesh around his mouth looked bleached, and somehow disconnected from the leathery skin that held his nose and eyes. He lifted his rucksack over his shoulder, and made his way to the hospice. His body felt hollowed out, and he wondered if he needed food. He had no appetite. If anything, he felt sick.

The sky was covered with thick white cloud,

although the salt air smelt already warm. Cars of families were arriving with picnics and chairs to set up home on the beach. Far out on the horizon, the metal sea sparkled against the morning light.

Harold knew an end was coming, but had no idea how it would be, or what he would do afterwards.

He turned into the drive of St Bernadine's Hospice, and once more walked the length of the tarmac. It had been recently laid; his feet fell softly. He pressed the buzzer, without hesitating, and while he waited he closed his eyes and groped for the wall. He wondered if the nurse who would greet him might be the same woman he had spoken with on the telephone. He hoped he wouldn't have too much to explain. He hadn't the energy for words. The door opened.

Before him stood a woman whose hair was covered, and who wore a long, cream high-collared robe, with a belted black over-garment. His skin shivered all over.

'I'm Harold Fry,' he said. 'I have walked an awfully long way to save Queenie Hennessy.' He was suddenly desperate for water. His legs trembled. He needed a chair.

The nun smiled. Her skin was soft and smooth; what he could see of her hair was grey at the roots. She reached out her hands and took Harold's between her own. They were warm, and rough; strong hands. He was afraid he would cry. 'Welcome, Harold,' she said. She introduced herself as Sister Philomena and urged him to enter.

He wiped his feet, and then he did it again.

'Don't worry,' she said, but he couldn't stop. He

314

was pounding his shoes on the threshold. He lifted them to check there was nothing on them, and he was right, but still he kept scraping his soles against the stiff mat; the way he used to have to do for his aunts before they would allow him into the house.

He stooped to unpeel the duct tape but it took a while and kept attaching itself to his fingers. The longer he took, the more he wished he wasn't doing it.

'I think I should leave my yachting shoes at the door.' The air inside was cool and still. There was a smell of disinfectant that reminded him of Maureen, and another that was hot food, possibly potato. He used the toe of one shoe to ram his other foot free, and then he repeated the process. Standing in his socks, he felt both naked and small.

The nun smiled. 'I'm sure you're longing to see Queenie.' She asked if he was ready to follow and he nodded.

Their feet marked the passage along the blue carpet in silence. There was no applause. There were no laughing nurses; no cheering patients. There was simply Harold, following the loose silhouette of a nun down a clean and empty corridor. He wondered if he could hear singing in the air, but listening again, he thought he was probably imagining it. Maybe it was the wind trapped in the Velux windows ahead, or someone calling. He realized he had forgotten to bring flowers.

'Are you all right?' she said.

Again he nodded.

As they reached them, Harold noticed the windows to his left opened out over a garden. He looked with longing at the closely cropped lawn,

315

and imagined his bare feet sinking into its softness. There were benches set out, and a sprinkler, whipping the air with bowing curves of water that caught the light from time to time. Ahead there stretched a series of closed doors. He was sure Queenie must be behind one of them. He fixed his gaze towards the garden and felt a powerful surge of dread.

'How long did you say you had been walking?'

'Oh,' he said. The significance of his journey was reducing to nothing even as he followed her. 'A long time.'

She said, 'I'm afraid we didn't invite those other pilgrims inside. We watched them on the television. We found them altogether rather noisy.' She turned and he thought she gave a wink; though that was surely not possible.

They passed a half-open door. He wouldn't look inside.

'Sister Philomena!' called a voice, frail as a whisper.

She stopped, looking into another room, her arms stretched out between the doorframe. 'I'll only be a moment,' she said to whoever was inside. The nun stood, with one foot slightly lifted and pointed behind her, as if she were a dancer, but wearing trainers. Turning back to Harold, she gave a warm smile, and said they were nearly there. He was cold, or tired, or something that seemed to squeeze the life out of him.

The nun walked a few more paces and stopped to knock gently at a door. She listened a moment, with her knuckles resting on the wood and her ear flat against it, and then she opened the door a crack and peered inside.

'We have a visitor,' she said to the room he could not yet see.

Pushing the door to the wall, she flattened herself against it as he passed. 'How exciting,' she said. He took a deep breath that seemed to come from his feet, and lifted his gaze to the room ahead.

There was no more than a window, with thin curtains partially drawn, and beyond that a sky that appeared far away. There was a simple bed set under a wooden cross, with a pan beneath it and an empty chair at its side.

'But she's not here.' He felt a giddying wave of unexpected relief.

Sister Philomena laughed. 'Of course she's here.' She nodded in the direction of the bed, and looking at it again he found a slight form beneath the ice-white sheets. Something stretched at its side, like a long white claw, and then as Harold peered again it occurred to him that this was Queenie's arm. He felt the blood rush to his head.

'Harold,' came the nun's voice. Her face was close to his, the skin a web of fine wrinkles. 'Queenie is confused, and in some pain. But she has waited. As you said she should.' She withdrew to let him pass.

He took a few steps closer, and then a few more, with his heart throbbing. And as Harold Fry finally arrived at the side of the woman for whom he had travelled so many miles, his legs almost gave way. She lay, not moving, only a few feet from his touch, her face towards the light at the window. He wondered if she was sleeping, or maybe drugged, or waiting for something that wasn't him. It was intensely private; the way she did not move, or notice his arrival. Her body made almost no shape against the sheets. She had the smallness of a child.

Harold pulled the rucksack from his shoulder and held it flat against his stomach, as if to keep the image in front of him at bay. He ventured one step closer. Two.

What was left of Queenie's hair was thin and white like a seedhead in a hedgerow; puffed over her scalp, and pulled sideways, as if she'd been caught in a violent wind. He could see the papery thin skin of her skull. Her neck was bandaged.

Queenie Hennessy looked like someone else. Like someone he had never met. A ghost. A shell. He glanced behind him for Sister Philomena, but the doorway was empty. She had gone.

He could drop the presents and go. Maybe with a card. The idea of writing seemed by far the best idea; he could say something comforting. A burst of energy shot through him. He was about to retreat when Queenie's head began a slow and steady journey from the window, and he was struck still again, watching. First came the left eye, then the nose, then the right side of her cheek, until she was facing him, and they met for the first time in twenty years. Harold's breath stopped.

Her head was all wrong. It was two heads in one, the second growing out of the first. It began somewhere above her cheekbone and protruded over the jaw. It was so big, this growth, this second face without features, it looked as if it would erupt through her skin at any moment. It had forced the right eye to close and was tugging it towards her ear. The lower half of her mouth was jammed sideways and sliding towards her jaw. It was inhuman. She lifted her claw fingers, as if to hide,

318

but there was no not seeing. Harold groaned.

The noise was out of him before he was aware of making it. Her hand groped for something she didn't find.

He wished he could pretend it wasn't horrible to look at. But he couldn't. His mouth opened and two words shuffled out. 'Hello, Queenie.' Over six hundred miles, and that was all he could come up with.

She said nothing.

'It's Harold,' he said. 'Harold Fry.' He was aware he was nodding, and shaping the words with exaggeration, and directing them not at her disfigured face but at her claw hand. 'We worked together a long time ago. Do you remember?'

He snatched one more glance at the gargantuan tumour. It was a shining bulbous mass of thread-like veins and bruising, as if it hurt the skin to contain it. Queenie's one open eye blinked at him. From the other slid a trail of something wet towards her pillow.

'Did you get my letter?'

The look was naked, like an animal trapped inside a box.

'My postcards?'

Am I dying? said her marble eye. Will it hurt?

He couldn't look. Pulling open the rucksack, he rooted through its contents, although it was dark inside the bag and his fingers were trembling, and he was so aware of Queenie watching him he kept forgetting what he was looking for. 'I have some small souvenirs. I picked them up as I walked. There's a hanging quartz that will look nice at your window. I just have to find it. And some honey somewhere.' It dawned on him that with a growth

319

that size she probably couldn't eat. 'You may not like honey, of course. But the pot is nice. For putting pens in, maybe. It's from Buckfast Abbey.'

He pulled out the paper bag containing the rose pendant, and offered it to her. She didn't move. He laid it a little way from her clawed hand. He patted it twice. When he looked up, his skin froze. Queenie Hennessy was slipping down the pillow, as if the weight of her terrible face was dragging her earthwards.

He didn't know what to do. He knew he should help, but he didn't know how. He was afraid that underneath her bandaged neck there would be more. More butchery. More brutal evidence of her human frailty. He couldn't bear that. Harold called for help. He tried to do it quietly at first, so as not to alarm her. But then he called again, getting louder and louder.

'Hello, Queenie,' called the nun entering the room; only it seemed this was not the same one as before. Her voice was younger, her body fuller and her manner more bold. 'Let's get some light. It's like a morgue in here.' She walked to the curtains and tugged them back with a yank so that the rings screamed on the metal pole. 'How nice to have a visitor.' Everything about her struck Harold as too alive for the room, and for Queenie's fragile condition. It made him angry they had let her look after someone so delicate as Queenie, although he was relieved she was able to take over.

'She's—' He couldn't finish the sentence. He pointed.

'Not again,' said the nun, all bright, as if Queenie was a child and had spilt food down her blouse.

320

From the other side of the bed, she adjusted Queenie's pillows and pulled her upright, hooking under the armpits and lifting. Queenie submitted like a rag doll, and that was how Harold thought he would always remember her; enduring and enduring, while someone hoicked her against a pillow and made funny comments that he hated.

'Apparently Henry has walked. All the way from— Where are you from, Henry?'

Harold opened his mouth to explain that he wasn't Henry, and that he lived in Kingsbridge, but the will to say either disappeared. It didn't seem worth the effort of correcting her. At that moment it didn't even seem worth being himself.

'Dorset, did you say?' said the sister.

'Yes. That's right,' said Harold, adopting the same tone, so that it sounded for a moment as if they were both shouting over the sea wind. 'Down south.'

'Shall we offer him tea?' she asked Queenie, without looking at her. 'You sit yourself down, Henry, and catch up while I make us all a cuppa. It's been pretty busy for us, hasn't it? There have been so many letters and cards. Last week a lady even wrote from Perth.' She turned to Harold as she left. 'She can hear you,' she said. He thought that if Queenie could really hear, it wasn't considerate to go talking about it. But he didn't say that. They were down to basics now.

Harold took the chair at Queenie's bedside. He scraped it back a few inches, so as not to be in the way. He slotted his hands between his knees.

'Hello,' he said again, as if they were meeting for the first time. 'I must say, you're doing very well. My wife—do you remember Maureen?—my

321

wife sends her best regards.' It felt safer now that he had conjured Maureen into the conversation. He wished Queenie would say something to break the ice, but she didn't.

'Yes, you're doing well.' And then: 'Really, really well.' He looked behind to see if the nun was on her way with the tea, but they were still alone. He gave a long yawn, although he felt wide awake. 'I walked a long time,' he said weakly. 'Shall I hang up your quartz? In the shop, they had it at the window. I think you'll like it. It's supposed to have healing powers.' Her opened eye met his. 'But I don't know about that.'

He wondered how much longer he was going to have to go through this. He got up, with the quartz swinging on its thread between his fingers, and pretended to look for a suitable place to hang it. The sky beyond the window was so white he couldn't tell if it was cloud or bright sun. Down in the garden, a nun in a straw hat pushed a patient in a wheelchair across the grass, talking gently. He wondered if she was praying. He envied her certainty.

Harold felt the stir of old emotions and images from the past, buried for all this time, because living with them every day was more than a human being could bear. He gripped the windowsill, taking deep breaths, but the air was hot too and brought no relief.

He lived again the afternoon he had driven Maureen to the funeral director's to see David one last time in the coffin. She had packed a few things: a red rose, a teddy bear, and a pillow to go beneath his head. In the car, she had asked Harold what he was going to give, knowing he had nothing.

322

The sun had shone very low, torching his eye as he drove. They both wore sunglasses. Even at home, she didn't take them off.

At the funeral director's she had surprised him by saying she wanted to say goodbye to David alone. He had sat outside with his head in his hands, waiting his turn, until a passer-by had stopped to offer a cigarette and Harold had taken it, although he had not smoked since the days on the buses. He tried to imagine what a father said to his dead son. His fingers shook so hard on the cigarette the passer-by used three matches to light it.

The thick nicotine caught in his throat and wound through his insides, causing them to tip upwards. As he stood and bent over a rubbish bin, he was met with the bitter stench of decay. Then, from behind him, the air was pierced with a harsh, deep sobbing cry, so animal in its intensity he was struck still, braced over the contents of the bin.

'No!' Maureen screamed from inside the funeral parlour. 'No! No! No!' The words seemed to reverberate through him and beat against the metal sky.

Harold had heaved a white spume of foam into the bin.

When she came out, she caught his eye once, and then her hand shot to her sunshades. She had been crying so hard her whole being seemed liquid. He realized with shock how thin she'd grown; her shoulders were like a hanger inside her black dress. He wanted to walk to her, to hold her, and be held, but he smelt of the cigarette and his vomit. He hovered beside the bin, pretending he had not seen her, and she walked straight past him to the car.

The space that set them apart shone against the sun like glass. He wiped his face and his hands, and eventually he went after her.

As they drove home in silence, Harold knew that something had passed between them which could never be undone. He had not said goodbye to his son. Maureen had; but Harold had not. There would always be this difference. There followed a small cremation, but she wanted no mourners. She hung up net curtains to stop people prying, although sometimes he felt it was more to stop herself from seeing out. For a while she railed, and blamed Harold, and then even that stopped. They passed one another on the stairs and were no more than strangers.

Harold thought of the day when she came out of the funeral director's and looked at him before snapping down her sunglasses, and he felt that in that one glance they had made a pact that would oblige them for the rest of their lives to say only what they did not mean, and to wrench apart what they most loved.

Remembering all this in the hospice where Queenie lay dying, Harold trembled with pain.

He had believed that when he saw her he could say thank you and even goodbye. That there would be a meeting of a kind, and that somehow it would absolve the terrible mistakes of the past. But there could not be a meeting, or even a goodbye, because the woman he had once known had already left. Harold thought he should stay, leaning on the windowsill, until he could accept this. He wondered if he should sit again; if being in the chair would make a difference. But even before he sat, he knew it wouldn't. Sitting or standing, he knew that it would take a long while before he could sew into the fabric of his life the knowledge that Queenie was reduced to this. David was dead too; there was no bringing him back. Harold tied the quartz to a curtain ring with a quick knot. It hung against the light, and twisted, so slight it was barely noticeable.

He remembered fiddling with his laces the day David almost drowned. He remembered driving from the funeral parlour with Maureen, knowing everything was over. There was more. He saw himself as a boy, after his mother had left, prostrate on his bed, and wondering if the stiller you kept, the greater the chances might be of dying. And yet here, years later, was a woman he had known briefly, but tenderly, fighting to keep the small amount of life that was left. It was not enough. It was not enough to stay on the sidelines.

In silence, he walked to Queenie's bedside. And as her head turned, and her eye found his, he sat in the space beside her. He reached for her hand. Her fingers were fragile, barely flesh at all. They curled imperceptibly and touched his. He smiled.

'It seems a long time since I found you in the stationery cupboard,' he said. At least he wanted to say that; but maybe it was only a thought. The air remained still and empty for a long time, until her hand slipped out of his, and her breathing grew slow.

A rattle of china caused him to start. 'Are you all right, Henry?' asked the young sister, jollying into the room with a tray.

Harold looked again at Queenie. She was dozing.

'Do you mind if I leave the tea?' he said. 'I have

to go now.'
    And Harold did.

326

30

MAUREEN AND HAROLD

Alone, a broken figure sat on a bench, hunched against the wind, and looking out towards the water's edge as if he had been there all his life. The sky was so grey and heavy, and the sea so grey and heavy, that it was impossible to tell where one began and the other ended.

Maureen paused. Her heart hammered inside her ribs. She walked towards Harold, and then she stopped again, standing right beside him, although he didn't look up or speak. His hair touched the collar of his waterproof jacket in soft curls that she ached to reach out and stroke.

'Hello, stranger,' she said. 'Do you mind if I sit with you?'

He didn't answer, but he tucked his jacket close to his hips and shunted along the bench to make space. Waves came at the beach and broke in white fringes of foam, flinging forward small stones and broken pieces of shell, and then leaving them behind. The tide was coming in.

She took her place beside him but a little way apart. 'How far do you think those waves have travelled?' she said.

He shrugged and shook his head, as if to say, That is a very good question, and I really don't know. His profile was so hollow it looked eaten away, and shadows hung beneath his eyes, dark as bruises. He was a different man yet again. He seemed to have aged years. What was left of his beard was pitiful.

'How was it?' she said. 'Did you visit Queenie?'

Harold kept his hands slotted between his knees. He nodded. He didn't speak.

She said, 'Did she have any idea you were arriving today? Was she pleased?'

He gave a sigh like something cracking.

'You did—see her?'

He nodded, but the nod kept moving up and down, as if he had omitted to send his brain the message to stop.

'So did you talk? What did you say? Did Queenie laugh?'

'Laugh?' he repeated.

'Yes. Was she pleased?'

'No.' His voice was weak. 'She didn't say anything.'

'Nothing? Are you sure?'

Another series of nods. His reticence was like a disease. It seemed to creep over Maureen too. She tugged her collar closer to her chin. She had expected him to be sad and exhausted; but that, she had assumed, would come from finishing his journey. This was a sort of apathy that sucked the life out of you.

328

She said, 'What about her presents? Did she like them?'

'I left the rucksack with the nuns. I thought that was best.' He spoke quietly and carefully, balancing on the words, but suggesting he was in danger at any moment of falling off into the crater of feeling beneath. 'I should never have done it. I should have sent a letter. A letter would have been enough. If I had simply stuck with the letter, I could have—' She waited but he stared out at the horizon. He seemed to have forgotten that he was talking.

'Still,' she said, 'I'm surprised—after everything you did—that Queenie said nothing.'

At last he turned and met her eye. His face, like his voice, was drained of life. 'She can't. She has no tongue.'

'I beg your pardon?' Maureen's gasp walloped the air.

'I believe they've cut it out. Along with half her throat, and some of her spine. It was a last-ditch attempt to save her, but it hasn't worked. The cancer's inoperable because there are no operable bits of her left. Now she has a tumour growing out of her face.'

He looked away, back towards the sky, with his eyes half closed, as if he was blocking out the external world in order to see more clearly the truth that was taking shape inside his head. 'That's why she could never talk to me on the telephone. She can't speak.'

Maureen turned once more to the sea, trying to understand. Far out the waves were flat, and metal-coloured. She wondered if they knew the end of their journey lay ahead.

Harold's voice came again. 'I didn't stop because there were no words for me to say. There weren't when I first read her letter. Maureen, I'm the kind of man who thanks the talking clock. What difference was I ever going to make? How did I ever think I could stop a woman from dying?'

A violent surge of grief seemed to force its way through him. His eyes crumpled shut, and his mouth opened, and he sat tall as his mouth emitted a series of soundless sobs. 'She was such a good woman. She wanted to help. Every time I drove her, she brought something nice for the journey home. She asked about David, and Cambridge—' He couldn't finish. His body was shaking with it. His face twisted as fierce tears screwed up his eyes and his cheeks. 'You should see. You should see her, Maw. It's not fair.'

'I know.' She reached her left hand around Harold's and held it tight. She looked at the darkness of his fingers on his lap; the blue ridges of his veins. Despite the strangeness of the last weeks, she knew this hand so well. Even without looking she knew it. She kept hold as he wept. He grew calmer; a quiet flow of tears.

He said, 'As I walked, I have been remembering so much. Things I didn't know I'd forgotten. Things about David, and you and me. I have even remembered my mother. Some of the memories have been hard. But most of them have been beautiful. And I'm frightened. I'm frightened that one day, maybe soon, I will lose them again, and this time it will be for ever.' His voice wavered. Taking a new, brave breath, he began to tell her all he had remembered; the moments from David's life that had opened up for him like the most

330

precious scrapbook. 'I don't want to forget his head when he was a baby. Or the way he slept when you sang. I want to keep all those things.'

'Of course you will,' she said. She tried to laugh, not wanting to continue with this conversation, although she could tell from the way he kept on looking at her that he wanted more.

'I couldn't remember David's name. How could I have forgotten that? I can't bear the thought that I might look at your face one day, and not even know you.'

She felt pain pricking at her eyelids and shook her head. 'You're not losing your memory, Harold. You're just very, very tired.'

When she met his gaze, it was naked. He held her eye, and she held his, and the years fell away. Maureen saw again the wild young man who had danced like a demon all those years ago, and filled every vein of her with the chaos of love. She blinked hard, and wiped her eyes. The waves kept throwing themselves further and further up the shoreline. All that energy, all that power, crossing oceans, carrying ships and liners, and ending just a short distance from her feet, in a last flume of spray.

She considered all the things that must happen from here. There would be regular visits to the GP. There might be colds that turned to pneumonia. There would be blood tests, hearing tests, eye tests. Maybe, God help them, there would be operations, and periods of convalescence. And then, of course, there must also follow a day when one of them was alone for good. She shivered. Harold was right; it was too much to bear. To have come all this way and discovered what it was you wanted, only to know that you must lose it again. She wondered if they should drive home via the Cotswolds, and stop a few days; or maybe take a detour and go to Norfolk. She'd love to return to Holt. But maybe they wouldn't. It was all too big to contemplate, and she didn't know. The waves fell over, and over, and over.

'One day at a time,' she murmured. She moved close to Harold and lifted her arms.

'Oh Maw,' he cried quietly.

Maureen held him tight until the grief passed. He was tall, and stiff, and her own. 'You dear man.' She groped for his face with her mouth and kissed his salty wet cheeks. 'You got up, and you did something. And if trying to find a way when you don't even know you can get there isn't a small miracle, then I don't know what is.'

Her mouth trembled. She cupped his face in her palms; they were so close now that his features lost distinction and all she could see was the feeling she had for him.

'I love you, Harold Fry,' she whispered. 'That is what you did.'

31

QUEENIE AND THE PRESENT

Queenie stared at the blurred world and found something she had not seen before. She narrowed her eye, willing it into focus. A pink shining light that somehow hung in the air, twisting, and every now and then sent a myriad of colour across the wall. It was beautiful for a while and then to keep hunting for it was too tiring and she let it go.

She was almost nothing. Blink a moment, and she'd be gone.

Someone had come, and now they had gone. Someone she liked. It wasn't the nuns, although they were all kind. It wasn't her father, but it was another good man. He had said something about walking, and that was right, she remembered; he had walked. But she couldn't remember how far he had come. Maybe it was from the car park. She had a pain in her head, and she wanted to call for water, and she would do that, in a moment, but just

333

for now she would stay here, lying very still and easy at last. She would sleep.

Harold Fry. She remembered now. He had come to say goodbye.

Once she had been a woman called Queenie Hennessy. She did sums, and wrote with an impeccable hand. She had loved a few times, and she had lost, and that was all as it should be. She had touched life, played with it a little, but it is a slippery bugger, and finally we must close the door, and leave it behind. A frightening thought for all these years. But now? Not frightening. Not anything. She was so tired. She dropped her face against her pillow, and felt something opening like a flower in her head, as it grew heavy.

There came a memory long forgotten. It was so close Queenie could almost taste it. She was running down the stairs of her childhood home, in her red leather shoes, and her father was calling her, or was it the good man, Harold Fry? She was rushing, and laughing because it was so funny. 'Queenie?' he was calling. 'Are you there?' She could see the shape of him, tall against the light, but he kept calling her and casting his eyes everywhere except where she stood. The breath caught with a knot in her chest. 'Queenie!' She longed for him to find her at last. 'Where are you? Where is that girl? Are you ready?'

'Yes,' she said. The light was very bright. Even behind her eyelids, it was silvery. 'Yes,' she called, a little louder so that he would hear. 'Here I am.' Something twisted at the window and showered the room with stars.

Queenie parted her lips, hunting for the next intake of air. And when it didn't come, but something else did, it was as easy as breathing.

32

HAROLD AND MAUREEN AND QUEENIE

Maureen took the news quietly. She had booked a double room, close to the seafront. They had eaten a light meal, and afterwards she had run Harold a bath and washed his hair. She had shaved his chin carefully and moisturized the skin. As she trimmed his nails and rubbed his feet, she told him all the things she had done in the past which she so regretted. He said it was the same for him. He seemed to be coming down with a cold.

After she had taken the call from the hospice, she reached for Harold's hand. She told him exactly what Sister Philomena had said; that Queenie looked peaceful at the end. Almost childlike. One of the younger nuns believed she had heard Queenie call something just before she died, as if she were reaching for a person she knew. 'But Sister Lucy is young,' said Sister Philomena.

Maureen asked Harold if he would like to be alone, but he shook his head.

'We'll do this together,' she said.

Already the body had been moved to a room beside the chapel. They walked behind the young nun, without speaking, because words at that moment felt too hard and too brittle. Maureen could hear the sounds of the hospice, the hushed voices, a brief peal of laughter, the slushing of water in pipes. From outside she briefly caught birdsong, or was it singing? She felt she had been swallowed by an inside world. At a closed door, they stopped and again Maureen asked Harold if he would like to be alone. Again he shook his head.

'I'm frightened,' he said, his blue eyes searching hers.

She saw the panic in them, the anguish and the reluctance. And then it dawned on her, very suddenly. The only dead body he had ever seen was David's, in the shed. 'I know. But it's all right. I'm here too. It will be all right this time, Harold.'

'It was a gentle end,' the sister said. She was a plump girl with a rosy bloom to her cheeks. Maureen was comforted that such a young, vibrant woman could care for the dying, and remain so full of life herself. 'Just before she went, she gave a smile. As if she'd found something.'

Maureen glanced at Harold and his face was so white he looked bled. 'I'm glad,' she said. 'We're glad it was peaceful.'

The nun stepped away and then turned back, as if she had remembered more. 'Sister Philomena asked if you would like to join us for evening prayer?'

Maureen gave a polite smile. It was too late to become believers now. 'Thank you, but Harold is

337

very tired. I think what he most needs is rest.'

Unperturbed, the young woman nodded. 'Of course. We only wanted you to know that you are welcome.' She reached for the handle and opened the door.

*   *   *

Maureen recognized the smell of the air as soon as she stepped inside. It held an iced-over stillness, imbued with incense. Beneath a small wooden cross, the body that had once been Queenie Hennessy lay with her white hair brushed over the pillow. Her arms were stretched over the sheet alongside her body, and her hands were open, palms uplifted, as if she had willingly let something go. Her face had been tilted discreetly towards the pillow, so that the tumour was mostly hidden. Maureen and Harold stood beside her in silence, coming to terms once more with how utterly the life vanishes.

She thought of David in his coffin, all those years ago, and how she had lifted his vacant head, and kissed him over and over, not believing that her wanting him alive wasn't enough to bring him back. Harold stood beside her, with his fists clenched into balls.

'She was a good woman,' said Maureen at last. 'She was a true friend.'

She felt something warm against the tip of her fingers, and then she felt the pressure of his hand gripping her own.

'There was nothing more you could have done,' she said. And she was thinking now not only of Queenie, but David too. Though it had cleft them

338

apart and plunged them into separate darkness, their son had after all done what he wanted. 'I was wrong. I was very wrong to blame you.' Her fingers squeezed on his.

She grew aware of light, spilling under and above the door, and the sounds of the hospice, filling the emptiness like water. The room in which they stood had grown so dark that the details lost definition; even the shape of Queenie was dimming. She thought of those waves again, and how a life was not complete without meeting its closure. She would stand at Harold's side as long as he wanted. When he moved, she followed.

Mass was already under way as they closed the door on Queenie. They paused, uncertain whether to give their thanks or slip away. It was Harold who asked to stop a moment. The nuns' voices rose, woven in song, and for one splendid, fleeting moment the beauty of it crammed her with something that felt like joy. If we can't be open, Maureen thought, if we can't accept what we don't know, there really is no hope.

'I'm ready to go now,' said Harold.

*   *   *

They walked along the seafront in the dark. The families had packed up their picnics and their chairs; only a few dog walkers were left, and some joggers in fluorescent jackets. They talked about small things: the last of the peonies, the day David started school, the weather forecast. Small things. The moon shone high, and cast a trembling copy of itself over the deep water. Far out, a ship travelled the horizon, its lights twinkling, and yet so slow its passage was not visible. It was full of life and activity that was nothing to do with Harold and Maureen.

'So many stories. So many people we don't know,' she said.

Harold watched too, but his mind was full of other things. He couldn't say how he knew it, or whether the knowledge made him happy or sad, but he was sure that Queenie would remain with him, and David too. There would be Napier, and Joan, and Harold's father with those aunts; but there would be no more fighting them, and no more anguish for the past. They were part of the air he walked through, just as all the travellers he had met were part of it. He saw that people would make the decisions they wished to make, and some of them would hurt both themselves and those who loved them, and some would pass unnoticed, while others would bring joy. He did not know what would follow from Berwick-upon-Tweed, and he was ready for that.

A memory came of the night all those years ago, when Harold had danced and spotted Maureen watching him across the crowd. He remembered how it felt to fling his arms and legs, as if shaking off all that had come before, while witnessed by such a beautiful young woman. Emboldened, he had danced more, even more crazily, feet kicking the air, hands like slippery eels. He had stopped and checked again. She was still watching. This time she had caught his eye and laughed. She was so full of it, her shoulders shaking, her hair slipping over her face, that for the first occasion in his life he had not been able to resist the temptation to stride through a crowd and touch a stranger. Beneath her velvet hair, the cushion of skin was pale and soft. She had not flinched.

'Hello, you,' he had said. His childhood was shorn away and there was nothing but himself and her. He knew that whatever happened next, their paths were linked. He would do anything for her. Remembering, Harold was filled with lightness, as if he were warm again, somewhere deep inside.

*　　　*　　　*

Maureen pulled her collar up to her ears against the night. The town lights shone in the background. 'Shall we turn back?' she said. 'Are you ready?'

In answer, Harold sneezed. She turned, wanting to offer a handkerchief, but was met with a short gasp that was almost without sound. He smacked his hand to his face. The noise came again. It wasn't a sneeze or a gasp. It was a snort. A snicker.

'Are you all right?' said Maureen. He seemed to be trying very hard to hold something inside his mouth. She tugged at his sleeve. 'Harold?'

He shook his head. The hand was still plastered against his mouth. Out shot another snort.

'Harold?' she said again.

He held his hands either side of his mouth, as if attempting to straighten it. He said, 'I shouldn't be laughing. I don't want to. It's just—' He let out a full-blown guffaw.

She didn't understand, but a smile was tugging on the corners of her mouth too. 'Maybe we need to laugh,' she said. 'What is it that's funny?'

Harold took a deep breath to steady himself. He turned to her with those beautiful eyes of his and

341

they seemed to shine through the dark. 'I've no idea why I'm remembering this. But that night at the dance?'

'When we first met?' Her smile was beginning to make a noise.

'And we laughed like kids?'

'Oh, what was it you said, Harold?'

A roar of laughter bowled out of him with such force he had to grip his stomach. She watched, her smile all bubbly now, ready to erupt; so nearly with him but not quite there yet. He had to bend over with it. He actually looked in pain.

In between splutters, he said, 'It wasn't me. It wasn't what I said. It was you.'

'Me?'

'Yes. I said hello and then you looked up at me. And you said—'

She got it. She remembered. The laughter kicked up from her stomach and filled her like helium. She slapped her hand to her mouth. 'Of course.'

'You said—'

'That's right. I—'

They couldn't say it. They couldn't get it out. They tried, but each time they opened their mouths it was so hilarious they were hit by a fresh wave of helpless laughter. They had to grip hands to steady themselves.

'Oh God,' she spluttered, 'oh God. It wasn't even very witty.' She was laughing and trying not to, so that it came in sobs and squeals. Then another laugh whooshed up behind her like a huge wave, catching her unawares, and erupting into a violent hiccup. That made it even worse. They hung on to one another's arms, and bent over, shaking with how funny it was. Their eyes were streaming; their faces ached. 'People will think we're having a joint heart attack,' she roared.

'You're right. It wasn't even funny,' said Harold, wiping his eyes with his handkerchief. For a moment, he looked sensible again. 'That was the thing, love. It was ordinary. It must have been funny because we were happy.'

They caught hands again, and walked towards the water's edge, two small figures against the black waves. Only halfway there, one of them must have remembered again and it passed like a fresh current of joy between them. They stood at the water's edge, not letting go, and rocked with laughter.

ACKNOWLEDGEMENTS

There are a number of people who have been part of Harold's journey. Anton Rogers, Anna Massey, Niamh Cusack, Tracey Neale, Jeremy Mortimer and Jeremy Howe began with him as an afternoon play for BBC Radio 4. Niamh has also read many pages of the book and encouraged me, as have Paul Venables, Myra Joyce, Anna Parker, Christabelle Dilks, Heather Mulkey and Sarah Lingard. Clare Conville, Jake Smith-Bosanquet and all at Conville & Walsh, Susanna Wadeson and the team at Transworld, Kendra Harpster, Abi Pritchard, Frances Arnold, Richard Skinner, the Faber group of 2010, and Matthew the Stroud Forager have all played an integral part.

And finally Hope, Kezia, Jo and Nell, who have taken to spotting Harold at the roadside.